The yellowbacks… classics of popular fiction

The yellowbacks... classics of popular fiction

The yellowjackets or yellowbacks were a great series of bestselling adventure and crime thrillers that had its origins in the mid to late 19th century following on from the 'penny dreadfuls'. They virtually began the mass market revolution of the early 20th century with a clear standard format and imprint/series livery (what would today be called branding). Hodder & Stoughton published the yellowjackets in two main series with series run dates of: 1923-1939 and later 1949-1957.

As the tagline ('where thrillers really began') on the back cover implies, the imprint and series focused on thrillers that were the bestsellers of their time. This current reissue or retro revival if you will, brings back many of these masterpieces, now classics in their own way and extends it further by including key titles from that period that were either great crime or thriller or even general commercial fiction (including sub-genres of noir, horror, gothic, romance, westerns, etc.) influences of their time. There are some perennial favourites and many rarities either lost or not easily available being revived in the current series. Writers and characters ranged from adventure heroes like Bulldog Drummond, Allan Quatermain, Richard Hannay or the Saint through thriller grandmasters Edgar Wallace and E. Phillips Oppenheim, crime and mystery maestros like Patricia Wentworth, GK Chesterton, Agatha Christie and the Detection club, to western and swashbucklers like Zane Grey, Max Brand, Captain Blood and even romance or general fiction classics like Hermina Black, Denise Robins, Marie Corelli or Stella Morton. These were books that had storytelling at their heart and always entertained.

The yellowbacks had both hardback (with varying design elements) and paperback (which built the series look) versions with the latter still carrying the imprint 'yellowjacket'. The current reissues pay tribute to both and use an amalgam of elements from both editions while retaining the complete yellow (or 'mustard-plaster') livery with the author's name in blue beveled type with a 'simulated emboss' effect and a white outer 'outline', and the book title in black. These reissues retain the distinctive size of the original mass market paperback and follow the three main category variations—the thrillers (crime, westerns, mystery, adventure) had blue lettering for the author's name, while Romance and softer general fiction had red; and other categories like humour had green.

For more detail and a full list of titles visit https://www.hachetteindia.com/home/yellowbacks

ARSÈNE LUPIN

ARSÈNE LUPIN

Edgar Alfred Jepson was an English writer, principally of mainstream adventure and detective fiction, but also of some supernatural and fantasy stories that are better remembered. He was editor for a short period ofVanity Fair magazine and was also well known as a translator, particularly of Leblanc's works.

Maurice Marie Émile Leblanc was a French novelist and writer of short stories, known primarily as the creator of the gentleman burglar, adventurer and detective Arsène Lupin, often described as a French counterpart to Arthur Conan Doyle's Sherlock Holmes and E.W. Hornung's Raffles.

Refusing the career that his father had set up for him at a card factory, Leblanc instead went to Paris in 1888, to pursue writing as a journalist. But he soon turned novelist and storyteller. His first novel, *Une femme (A Woman)*, published in 1893 was a success and was followed by other works, such as *Des couples (The Couples), Voici des ailes (Here are Wings)* and a play La pitié, released in 1902, which was a flop. In 1905, Pierre Lafitte, the director of the monthly Je sais tout, commissioned a short story from Leblanc, with the brief that he was to combine the appeal of A.J Raffles by Ernest William Hornung and Sherlock Holmes. The result was 'L'Arrestation d'Arsène Lupin' ('The Arrest of Arsène Lupin') which was a huge success. Two years later, *Arsène Lupin, Gentleman Burglar* was released, and the rest was history – with one of the most successful series being born.

ARSÈNE LUPIN

Edgar Jepson
and Maurice Leblanc

From the Play by Maurice Leblanc
and Francis de Croisset

Frontispiece by H. Richard Boehm

hachette

Arsène Lupin
First published in 1909 by Curtis Brown & Massie in the United States

This Hodder Yellowback edition © Hachette India 2023
(Registered Name: Hachette Book Publishing India Pvt. Ltd.)
An Hachette UK Company www.hachetteindia.com

1

The texts in these editions in most cases have been reprinted as is, with minimal editorial changes and by and large no bowdlerizing for political correctness; though in some editions, a few words and phrases considered archaic, or those considered offensive now, along with archaic punctuation may have been modified in places to make the text more accessible to today's readers. The narratives, language, beliefs, social mores and/or cultural depictions, in these volumes are a reflection of their times and must be viewed as such. They may also contain certain cultural, racial and gender prejudices and stereotypes that may be outdated or clearly wrong then and wrong today; but their removal would be tantamount to claiming these prejudices never existed. The Publisher does not endorse or support those depictions or stereotypes; and these books have been made available for a discerning audience that will read it for entertainment value and a chronicle/record of popular fiction of past times.

Cover design by Priya Singh adapted from the original classic yellowjacket by Hodder & Stoughton.

Cover illustration by Ishan Trivedi.

Series note: Some of the books in the series (unless otherwise credited) may have cover or inside illustrations from the original yellowbacks or early editions, and while full restoration has been attempted, some images may be grainy or faded due to the condition of the original material. The end notes or bonus material or blurb details may have been sourced from the public domain or free use publications such as Wikipedia and attribution is hereby made also allowing similar free use reproduction from here. Sources requiring further specific attribution may write in and further detailing and/or corrections shall be made in subsequent printings/editions.

Reprint specifications may be subject to change including but not limited to finishes, paper, colour sections.

ISBN: 978-93-5731-226-4

Hachette Book Publishing India Pvt. Ltd.
4th & 5th Floors, Corporate Centre,
Plot No. 94, Sector 44, Gurugram - 122 003, India

Typeset in Electra LT STD 10/12.5 pt by Manipal Technologies Limited, Manipal

Printed and bound in India by Manipal Technologies Limited, Manipal

MIX
Paper from responsible sources
FSC™ C043100

CONTENTS

1. The Millionaire's Daughter 1
2. The Coming of The Charolais 13
3. Lupin's Way 21
4. The Duke Intervenes 34
5. A Letter from Lupin 42
6. Again the Charolais 53
7. The Theft of the Motor-Cars 61
8. The Duke Arrives 71
9. M. Formery Opens the Inquiry 81
10. Guerchard Assists 93
11. The Family Arrives 106
12. The Theft of the Pendant 114
13. Lupin Wires 125
14. Guerchard Picks up the True Scent 133
15. The Examination of Sonia 142
16. Victoire's Slip 150
17. Sonia's Escape 159
18. The Duke Stays 170
19. The Duke Goes 183
20. Lupin Comes Home 197
21. The Cutting of the Telephone Wires 207
22. The Bargain 219
23. The End of the Duel 232

"'If it's for me, plenty of tea, very little cream, and three lumps of sugar,' he cried in a gay, ringing voice"

1

THE MILLIONAIRE'S DAUGHTER

The rays of the September sun flooded the great halls of the old chateau of the Dukes of Charmerace, lighting up with their mellow glow the spoils of so many ages and many lands, jumbled together with the execrable taste which so often afflicts those whose only standard of value is money. The golden light warmed the panelled walls and old furniture to a dull lustre, and gave back to the fading gilt of the First Empire chairs and couches something of its old brightness. It illumined the long line of pictures on the walls, pictures of dead and gone Charmeraces, the stern or debonair faces of the men, soldiers, statesmen, dandies, the gentle or imperious faces of beautiful women. It flashed back from armour of brightly polished steel, and drew dull gleams from armour of bronze. The hues of rare porcelain, of the rich inlays of Oriental or Renaissance cabinets, mingled with the hues of the pictures, the tapestry, the Persian rugs about the polished floor to fill the hall with a rich glow of colour.

But of all the beautiful and precious things which the sun-rays warmed to a clearer beauty, the face of the girl who sat writing at a table in front of the long windows, which opened on to the centuries-old turf of the broad terrace, was the most beautiful and the most precious.

It was a delicate, almost frail, beauty. Her skin was clear with the transparent lustre of old porcelain, and her pale cheeks were only tinted with the pink of the faintest roses. Her straight nose was delicately cut, her rounded chin admirably moulded. A lover of beauty would have been at a loss whether more to admire her clear, germander eyes, so melting and so adorable, or the sensitive mouth, with its rather full lips, inviting all the kisses. But assuredly he would have been grieved by the perpetual air of sadness which rested on the beautiful face—the wistful melancholy of the Slav, deepened by something of personal misfortune and suffering.

Her face was framed by a mass of soft fair hair, shot with strands of gold where the sunlight fell on it; and little curls, rebellious to the comb, strayed over her white forehead, tiny feathers of gold.

She was addressing envelopes, and a long list of names lay on her left hand. When she had addressed an envelope, she slipped into it a wedding-card. On each was printed:

> "M. Gournay-Martin has the honour to inform you of the marriage of his daughter Germaine to the Duke of Charmerace."

She wrote steadily on, adding envelope after envelope to the pile ready for the post, which rose in front of her. But now and again, when the flushed and laughing girls who were playing lawn-tennis on the terrace, raised their voices higher than usual as they called the score, and distracted her attention from her work, her gaze strayed through the open window and lingered on them wistfully; and as her eyes came back to her task she sighed with so faint a wistfulness that she hardly knew she sighed. Then a voice from the terrace cried, "Sonia! Sonia!"

"Yes. Mlle. Germaine?" answered the writing girl.

"Tea! Order tea, will you?" cried the voice, a petulant voice, rather harsh to the ear.

"Very well, Mlle. Germaine," said Sonia; and having finished addressing the envelope under her pen, she laid it on the pile ready to be posted, and, crossing the room to the old, wide fireplace, she rang the bell.

She stood by the fireplace a moment, restoring to its place a rose which had fallen from a vase on the mantelpiece; and her attitude, as with arms upraised she arranged the flowers, displayed the delightful line of a slender figure. As she let fall her arms to her side, a footman entered the room.

"Will you please bring the tea, Alfred," she said in a charming voice of that pure, bell-like tone which has been Nature's most precious gift to but a few of the greatest actresses.

"For how many, miss?" said Alfred.

"For four—unless your master has come back."

"Oh, no; he's not back yet, miss. He went in the car to Rennes to lunch; and it's a good many miles away. He won't be back for another hour."

"And the Duke—he's not back from his ride yet, is he?"

"Not yet, miss," said Alfred, turning to go.

"One moment," said Sonia. "Have all of you got your things packed for the journey to Paris? You will have to start soon, you know. Are all the maids ready?"

"Well, all the men are ready, I know, miss. But about the maids, miss, I can't say. They've been bustling about all day; but it takes them longer than it does us."

"Tell them to hurry up; and be as quick as you can with the tea, please," said Sonia.

Alfred went out of the room; Sonia went back to the writing-table. She did not take up her pen; she took up one of the wedding-cards; and her lips moved slowly as she read it in a pondering depression.

The petulant, imperious voice broke in upon her musing.

"Whatever are you doing, Sonia? Aren't you getting on with those letters?" it cried angrily; and Germaine Gournay-Martin came through the long window into the hall.

The heiress to the Gournay-Martin millions carried her tennis racquet in her hand; and her rosy cheeks were flushed redder than ever by the game. She was a pretty girl in a striking, high-coloured, rather obvious way—the very foil to Sonia's delicate beauty. Her lips were a little too thin, her eyes too shallow; and together they gave her a rather hard air, in strongest contrast to the gentle, sympathetic face of Sonia.

The two friends with whom Germaine had been playing tennis followed her into the hall: Jeanne Gautier, tall, sallow, dark, with a somewhat malicious air; Marie Bullier, short, round, commonplace, and sentimental.

They came to the table at which Sonia was at work; and pointing to the pile of envelopes, Marie said, "Are these all wedding-cards?"

"Yes; and we've only got to the letter V," said Germaine, frowning at Sonia.

"Princesse de Vernan—Duchesse de Vauvieuse—Marquess—Marchioness? You've invited the whole Faubourg Saint-Germain," said Marie, shuffling the pile of envelopes with an envious air.

"You'll know very few people at your wedding," said Jeanne, with a spiteful little giggle.

"I beg your pardon, my dear," said Germaine boastfully. "Madame de Relzieres, my fiance's cousin, gave an At Home the other day in my honour. At it she introduced half of Paris to me—the Paris I'm destined to know, the Paris you'll see in my drawing-rooms."

"But we shall no longer be fit friends for you when you're the Duchess of Charmerace," said Jeanne.

"Why?" said Germaine; and then she added quickly, "Above everything, Sonia, don't forget Veauleglise, 33, University Street—33, University Street."

"Veauleglise—33, University Street," said Sonia, taking a fresh envelope, and beginning to address it.

"Wait—wait! Don't close the envelope. I'm wondering whether Veauleglise ought to have a cross, a double cross, or a triple cross," said Germaine, with an air of extreme importance.

"What's that?" cried Marie and Jeanne together.

"A single cross means an invitation to the church, a double cross an invitation to the marriage and the wedding-breakfast, and the triple cross means an invitation to the marriage, the breakfast, and the signing of the marriage-contract. What do you think the Duchess of Veauleglise ought to have?"

"Don't ask me. I haven't the honour of knowing that great lady," cried Jeanne.

"Nor I," said Marie.

"Nor I," said Germaine. "But I have here the visiting-list of the late Duchess of Charmerace, Jacques' mother. The two duchesses were on excellent terms. Besides the Duchess of Veauleglise is rather worn-out, but greatly admired for her piety. She goes to early service three times a week."

"Then put three crosses," said Jeanne.

"I shouldn't," said Marie quickly. "In your place, my dear, I shouldn't risk a slip. I should ask my fiance's advice. He knows this world."

"Oh, goodness—my fiance! He doesn't care a rap about this kind of thing. He has changed so in the last seven years. Seven years ago he took nothing seriously. Why, he set off on an expedition to the South Pole—just to show off. Oh, in those days he was truly a duke."

"And to-day?" said Jeanne.

"Oh, to-day he's a regular slow-coach. Society gets on his nerves. He's as sober as a judge," said Germaine.

"He's as gay as a lark," said Sonia, in sudden protest.

Germaine pouted at her, and said: "Oh, he's gay enough when he's making fun of people. But apart from that he's as sober as a judge."

"Your father must be delighted with the change," said Jeanne.

"Naturally he's delighted. Why, he's lunching at Rennes today with the Minister, with the sole object of getting Jacques decorated."

"Well; the Legion of Honour is a fine thing to have," said Marie.

"My dear! The Legion of Honour is all very well for middle-class people, but it's quite out of place for a duke!" cried Germaine.

Alfred came in, bearing the tea-tray, and set it on a little table near that at which Sonia was sitting.

Germaine, who was feeling too important to sit still, was walking up and down the room. Suddenly she stopped short, and pointing to a silver statuette which stood on the piano, she said, "What's this? Why is this statuette here?"

"Why, when we came in, it was on the cabinet, in its usual place," said Sonia in some astonishment.

"Did you come into the hall while we were out in the garden, Alfred?" said Germaine to the footman.

"No, miss," said Alfred.

"But some one must have come into it," Germaine persisted.

"I've not heard any one. I was in my pantry," said Alfred.

"It's very odd," said Germaine.

"It is odd," said Sonia. "Statuettes don't move about of themselves."

All of them stared at the statuette as if they expected it to move again forthwith, under their very eyes. Then Alfred put it back in its usual place on one of the cabinets, and went out of the room.

Sonia poured out the tea; and over it they babbled about the coming marriage, the frocks they would wear at it, and the presents Germaine had already received. That reminded her to ask Sonia if any one had yet telephoned from her father's house in Paris; and Sonia said that no one had.

"That's very annoying," said Germaine. "It shows that nobody has sent me a present to-day."

Pouting, she shrugged her shoulders with an air of a spoiled child, which sat but poorly on a well-developed young woman of twenty-three.

"It's Sunday. The shops don't deliver things on Sunday," said Sonia gently.

But Germaine still pouted like a spoiled child.

"Isn't your beautiful Duke coming to have tea with us?" said Jeanne a little anxiously.

"Oh, yes; I'm expecting him at half-past four. He had to go for a ride with the two Du Buits. They're coming to tea here, too," said Germaine.

"Gone for a ride with the two Du Buits? But when?" cried Marie quickly.

"This afternoon."

"He can't be," said Marie. "My brother went to the Du Buits' house after lunch, to see Andre and Georges. They went for a drive this morning, and won't be back till late to-night."

"Well, but—but why did the Duke tell me so?" said Germaine, knitting her brow with a puzzled air.

"If I were you, I should inquire into this thoroughly. Dukes—well, we know what dukes are—it will be just as well to keep an eye on him," said Jeanne maliciously.

Germaine flushed quickly; and her eyes flashed. "Thank you. I have every confidence in Jacques. I am absolutely sure of him," she said angrily.

"Oh, well—if you're sure, it's all right," said Jeanne.

The ringing of the telephone-bell made a fortunate diversion.

Germaine rushed to it, clapped the receiver to her ear, and cried: "Hello, is that you, Pierre? ... Oh, it's Victoire, is it? ... Ah, some presents have come, have they? ... Well, well, what are they? ... What! A paper-knife—another paper-knife! ... Another Louis XVI. inkstand—oh, bother! ... Who are they from? ... Oh, from the Countess Rudolph and the Baron de Valery." Her voice rose high, thrilling with pride.

Then she turned her face to her friends, with the receiver still at her ear, and cried: "Oh, girls, a pearl necklace too! A large one! The pearls are big ones!"

"How jolly!" said Marie.

"Who sent it?" said Germaine, turning to the telephone again. "Oh, a friend of papa's," she added in a tone of disappointment. "Never mind, after all it's a pearl necklace. You'll be sure and lock the doors carefully, Victoire, won't you? And lock up the necklace in the secret cupboard... Yes; thanks very much, Victoire. I shall see you to-morrow."

She hung up the receiver, and came away from the telephone frowning.

"It's preposterous!" she said pettishly. "Papa's friends and relations give me marvellous presents, and all the swells send me paper-knives. It's all Jacques' fault. He's above all this kind of thing. The Faubourg Saint-Germain hardly knows that we're engaged."

"He doesn't go about advertising it," said Jeanne, smiling.

"You're joking, but all the same what you say is true," said Germaine. "That's exactly what his cousin Madame de Relzieres said to me the other day at the At Home she gave in my honour—wasn't it, Sonia?" And she walked to the window, and, turning her back on them, stared out of it.

"She HAS got her mouth full of that At Home," said Jeanne to Marie in a low voice.

There was an awkward silence. Marie broke it:

"Speaking of Madame de Relzieres, do you know that she is on pins and needles with anxiety? Her son is fighting a duel to-day," she said.

"With whom?" said Sonia.

"No one knows. She got hold of a letter from the seconds," said Marie.

"My mind is quite at rest about Relzieres," said Germaine. "He's a first-class swordsman. No one could beat him."

Sonia did not seem to share her freedom from anxiety. Her forehead was puckered in little lines of perplexity, as if she were puzzling out some problem; and there was a look of something very like fear in her gentle eyes.

"Wasn't Relzieres a great friend of your fiance at one time?" said Jeanne.

"A great friend? I should think he was," said Germaine. "Why, it was through Relzieres that we got to know Jacques."

"Where was that?" said Marie.

"Here—in this very chateau," said Germaine.

"Actually in his own house?" said Marie, in some surprise.

"Yes; actually here. Isn't life funny?" said Germaine. "If, a few months after his father's death, Jacques had not found himself hard-up, and obliged to dispose of this chateau, to raise the money for his expedition to the South Pole; and if papa and I had not wanted an historic chateau; and lastly, if papa had not suffered from rheumatism, I should not be calling myself in a month from now the Duchess of Charmerace."

"Now what on earth has your father's rheumatism got to do with your being Duchess of Charmerace?" cried Jeanne.

"Everything," said Germaine. "Papa was afraid that this chateau was damp. To prove to papa that he had nothing to fear, Jacques, en grand seigneur, offered him his hospitality, here, at Charmerace, for three weeks."

"That was truly ducal," said Marie.

"But he is always like that," said Sonia.

"Oh, he's all right in that way, little as he cares about society," said Germaine. "Well, by a miracle my father got cured of his rheumatism here. Jacques fell in love with me; papa made up his mind to buy the chateau; and I demanded the hand of Jacques in marriage."

"You did? But you were only sixteen then," said Marie, with some surprise.

"Yes; but even at sixteen a girl ought to know that a duke is a duke. I did," said Germaine. "Then since Jacques was setting out for the South Pole, and papa considered me much too young to get married, I promised Jacques to wait for his return."

"Why, it was everything that's romantic!" cried Marie.

"Romantic? Oh, yes," said Germaine; and she pouted. "But between ourselves, if I'd known that he was going to stay all that time at the South Pole—"

"That's true," broke in Marie. "To go away for three years and stay away seven—at the end of the world."

"All Germaine's beautiful youth," said Jeanne, with her malicious smile.

"Thanks!" said Germaine tartly.

"Well, you ARE twenty-three. It's the flower of one's age," said Jeanne.

"Not quite twenty-three," said Germaine hastily. "And look at the wretched luck I've had. The Duke falls ill and is treated at Montevideo. As soon as he recovers, since he's the most obstinate person in the world, he resolves to go on with the expedition. He sets out; and for an age, without a word of warning, there's no more news of him—no news of any kind. For six months, you know, we believed him dead."

"Dead? Oh, how unhappy you must have been!" said Sonia.

"Oh, don't speak of it! For six months I daren't put on a light frock," said Germaine, turning to her.

"A lot she must have cared for him," whispered Jeanne to Marie.

"Fortunately, one fine day, the letters began again. Three months ago a telegram informed us that he was coming back;

and at last the Duke returned," said Germaine, with a theatrical air.

"The Duke returned," cried Jeanne, mimicking her.

"Never mind. Fancy waiting nearly seven years for one's fiance. That was constancy," said Sonia.

"Oh, you're a sentimentalist, Mlle. Kritchnoff," said Jeanne, in a tone of mockery. "It was the influence of the castle."

"What do you mean?" said Germaine.

"Oh, to own the castle of Charmerace and call oneself Mlle. Gournay-Martin—it's not worth doing. One MUST become a duchess," said Jeanne.

"Yes, yes; and for all this wonderful constancy, seven years of it, Germaine was on the point of becoming engaged to another man," said Marie, smiling.

"And he a mere baron," said Jeanne, laughing.

"What? Is that true?" said Sonia.

"Didn't you know, Mlle. Kritchnoff? She nearly became engaged to the Duke's cousin, the Baron de Relzieres. It was not nearly so grand."

"Oh, it's all very well to laugh at me; but being the cousin and heir of the Duke, Relzieres would have assumed the title, and I should have been Duchess just the same," said Germaine triumphantly.

"Evidently that was all that mattered," said Jeanne. "Well, dear, I must be off. We've promised to run in to see the Comtesse de Grosjean. You know the Comtesse de Grosjean?"

She spoke with an air of careless pride, and rose to go.

"Only by name. Papa used to know her husband on the Stock Exchange when he was still called simply M. Grosjean. For his part, papa preferred to keep his name intact," said Germaine, with quiet pride.

"Intact? That's one way of looking at it. Well, then, I'll see you in Paris. You still intend to start to-morrow?" said Jeanne.

"Yes; to-morrow morning," said Germaine.

Jeanne and Marie slipped on their dust-coats to the accompaniment of chattering and kissing, and went out of the room.

As she closed the door on them, Germaine turned to Sonia, and said: "I do hate those two girls! They're such horrible snobs."

"Oh, they're good-natured enough," said Sonia.

"Good-natured? Why, you idiot, they're just bursting with envy of me—bursting!" said Germaine. "Well, they've every reason to be," she added confidently, surveying herself in a Venetian mirror with a petted child's self-content.

2

THE COMING OF THE CHAROLAIS

Sonia went back to her table, and once more began putting wedding-cards in their envelopes and addressing them. Germaine moved restlessly about the room, fidgeting with the bric-a-brac on the cabinets, shifting the pieces about, interrupting Sonia to ask whether she preferred this arrangement or that, throwing herself into a chair to read a magazine, getting up in a couple of minutes to straighten a picture on the wall, throwing out all the while idle questions not worth answering. Ninety-nine human beings would have been irritated to exasperation by her fidgeting; Sonia endured it with a perfect patience. Five times Germaine asked her whether she should wear her heliotrope or her pink gown at a forthcoming dinner at Madame de Relzieres'. Five times Sonia said, without the slightest variation in her tone, "I think you look better in the pink." And all the while the pile of addressed envelopes rose steadily.

Presently the door opened, and Alfred stood on the threshold.

"Two gentlemen have called to see you, miss," he said.

"Ah, the two Du Buits," cried Germaine.

"They didn't give their names, miss."

"A gentleman in the prime of life and a younger one?" said Germaine.

"Yes, miss."

"I thought so. Show them in."

"Yes, miss. And have you any orders for me to give Victoire when we get to Paris?" said Alfred.

"No. Are you starting soon?"

"Yes, miss. We're all going by the seven o'clock train. It's a long way from here to Paris; we shall only reach it at nine in the morning. That will give us just time to get the house ready for you by the time you get there to-morrow evening," said Alfred.

"Is everything packed?"

"Yes, miss—everything. The cart has already taken the heavy luggage to the station. All you'll have to do is to see after your bags."

"That's all right. Show M. du Buit and his brother in," said Germaine.

She moved to a chair near the window, and disposed herself in an attitude of studied, and obviously studied, grace.

As she leant her head at a charming angle back against the tall back of the chair, her eyes fell on the window, and they opened wide.

"Why, whatever's this?" she cried, pointing to it.

"Whatever's what?" said Sonia, without raising her eyes from the envelope she was addressing.

"Why, the window. Look! One of the panes has been taken out. It looks as if it had been cut."

"So it has—just at the level of the fastening," said Sonia. And the two girls stared at the gap.

"Haven't you noticed it before?" said Germaine.

"No; the broken glass must have fallen outside," said Sonia.

The noise of the opening of the door drew their attention from the window. Two figures were advancing towards them—a short, round, tubby man of fifty-five, red-faced, bald, with bright grey eyes, which seemed to be continually dancing away from meeting the eyes of any other human being. Behind him came a slim young man, dark and grave. For all the difference in their colouring, it was clear that they were father and son: their eyes were set so close together. The son seemed to have inherited, along with her black eyes, his mother's nose, thin and aquiline; the nose of the father started thin from the brow, but ended in a scarlet bulb eloquent of an exhaustive acquaintance with the vintages of the world.

Germaine rose, looking at them with an air of some surprise and uncertainty: these were not her friends, the Du Buits.

The elder man, advancing with a smiling bonhomie, bowed, and said in an adenoid voice, ingratiating of tone: "I'm M. Charolais, young ladies—M. Charolais—retired brewer—chevalier of the Legion of Honour—landowner at Rennes. Let me introduce my son." The young man bowed awkwardly. "We came from Rennes this morning, and we lunched at Kerlor's farm."

"Shall I order tea for them?" whispered Sonia.

"Gracious, no!" said Germaine sharply under her breath; then, louder, she said to M. Charolais, "And what is your object in calling?"

"We asked to see your father," said M. Charolais, smiling with broad amiability, while his eyes danced across her face, avoiding any meeting with hers. "The footman told us that M. Gournay-Martin was out, but that his daughter was at home. And we were unable, quite unable, to deny ourselves the pleasure of meeting you." With that he sat down; and his son followed his example.

Sonia and Germaine, taken aback, looked at one another in some perplexity.

"What a fine chateau, papa!" said the young man.

"Yes, my boy; it's a very fine chateau," said M. Charolais, looking round the hall with appreciative but greedy eyes.

There was a pause.

"It's a very fine chateau, young ladies," said M. Charolais.

"Yes; but excuse me, what is it you have called about?" said Germaine.

M. Charolais crossed his legs, leant back in his chair, thrust his thumbs into the arm-holes of his waistcoat, and said: "Well, we've come about the advertisement we saw in the RENNES ADVERTISER, that M. Gournay-Martin wanted to get rid of a motor-car; and my son is always saying to me, 'I should like a motor-car which rushes the hills, papa.' He means a sixty horse-power."

"We've got a sixty horse-power; but it's not for sale. My father is even using it himself to-day," said Germaine.

"Perhaps it's the car we saw in the stable-yard," said M. Charolais.

"No; that's a thirty to forty horse-power. It belongs to me. But if your son really loves rushing hills, as you say, we have a hundred horse-power car which my father wants to get rid of. Wait; where's the photograph of it, Sonia? It ought to be here somewhere."

The two girls rose, went to a table set against the wall beyond the window, and began turning over the papers with which it was loaded in the search for the photograph. They had barely turned their backs, when the hand of young Charolais shot out as swiftly as the tongue of a lizard catching a fly, closed round the silver statuette on the top of the cabinet beside him, and flashed it into his jacket pocket.

Charolais was watching the two girls; one would have said that he had eyes for nothing else, yet, without moving a muscle of his face, set in its perpetual beaming smile, he hissed in an angry whisper, "Drop it, you idiot! Put it back!"

The young man scowled askance at him.

"Curse you! Put it back!" hissed Charolais.

The young man's arm shot out with the same quickness, and the statuette stood in its place.

There was just the faintest sigh of relief from Charolais, as Germaine turned and came to him with the photograph in her hand. She gave it to him.

"Ah, here we are," he said, putting on a pair of gold-rimmed pince-nez. "A hundred horse-power car. Well, well, this is something to talk over. What's the least you'll take for it?"

"I have nothing to do with this kind of thing," cried Germaine. "You must see my father. He will be back from Rennes soon. Then you can settle the matter with him."

M. Charolais rose, and said: "Very good. We will go now, and come back presently. I'm sorry to have intruded on you, young ladies—taking up your time like this—"

"Not at all—not at all," murmured Germaine politely.

"Good-bye—good-bye," said M. Charolais; and he and his son went to the door, and bowed themselves out.

"What creatures!" said Germaine, going to the window, as the door closed behind the two visitors. "All the same, if they do buy the hundred horse-power, papa will be awfully pleased. It is odd about that pane. I wonder how it happened. It's odd too that Jacques hasn't come back yet. He told me that he would be here between half-past four and five."

"And the Du Buits have not come either," said Sonia. "But it's hardly five yet."

"Yes; that's so. The Du Buits have not come either. What on earth are you wasting your time for?" she added sharply, raising her voice. "Just finish addressing those letters while you're waiting."

"They're nearly finished," said Sonia.

"Nearly isn't quite. Get on with them, can't you!" snapped Germaine.

Sonia went back to the writing-table; just the slightest deepening of the faint pink roses in her cheeks marked her sense of Germaine's rudeness. After three years as companion to

Germaine Gournay-Martin, she was well inured to millionaire manners; they had almost lost the power to move her.

Germaine dropped into a chair for twenty seconds; then flung out of it.

"Ten minutes to five!" she cried. "Jacques is late. It's the first time I've ever known him late."

She went to the window, and looked across the wide stretch of meadow-land and woodland on which the chateau, set on the very crown of the ridge, looked down. The road, running with the irritating straightness of so many of the roads of France, was visible for a full three miles. It was empty.

"Perhaps the Duke went to the Chateau de Relzieres to see his cousin—though I fancy that at bottom the Duke does not care very much for the Baron de Relzieres. They always look as though they detested one another," said Sonia, without raising her eyes from the letter she was addressing.

"You've noticed that, have you?" said Germaine. "Now, as far as Jacques is concerned—he's—he's so indifferent. None the less, when we were at the Relzieres on Thursday, I caught him quarrelling with Paul de Relzieres."

"Quarrelling?" said Sonia sharply, with a sudden uneasiness in air and eyes and voice.

"Yes; quarrelling. And they said good-bye to one another in the oddest way."

"But surely they shook hands?" said Sonia.

"Not a bit of it. They bowed as if each of them had swallowed a poker."

"Why—then—then—" said Sonia, starting up with a frightened air; and her voice stuck in her throat.

"Then what?" said Germaine, a little startled by her panic-stricken face.

"The duel! Monsieur de Relzieres' duel!" cried Sonia.

"What? You don't think it was with Jacques?"

"I don't know—but this quarrel—the Duke's manner this morning—the Du Buits' drive—" said Sonia.

"Of course—of course! It's quite possible—in fact it's certain!" cried Germaine.

"It's horrible!" gasped Sonia. "Consider—just consider! Suppose something happened to him. Suppose the Duke—"

"It's me the Duke's fighting about!" cried Germaine proudly, with a little skipping jump of triumphant joy.

Sonia stared through her without seeing her. Her face was a dead white—fear had chilled the lustre from her skin; her breath panted through her parted lips; and her dilated eyes seemed to look on some dreadful picture.

Germaine pirouetted about the hall at the very height of triumph. To have a Duke fighting a duel about her was far beyond the wildest dreams of snobbishness. She chuckled again and again, and once she clapped her hands and laughed aloud.

"He's fighting a swordsman of the first class—an invincible swordsman—you said so yourself," Sonia muttered in a tone of anguish. "And there's nothing to be done—nothing."

She pressed her hands to her eyes as if to shut out a hideous vision.

Germaine did not hear her; she was staring at herself in a mirror, and bridling to her own image.

Sonia tottered to the window and stared down at the road along which must come the tidings of weal or irremediable woe. She kept passing her hand over her eyes as if to clear their vision.

Suddenly she started, and bent forward, rigid, all her being concentrated in the effort to see.

Then she cried: "Mademoiselle Germaine! Look! Look!"

"What is it?" said Germaine, coming to her side.

"A horseman! Look! There!" said Sonia, waving a hand towards the road.

"Yes; and isn't he galloping!" said Germaine.

"It's he! It's the Duke!" cried Sonia.

"Do you think so?" said Germaine doubtfully.

"I'm sure of it—sure!"

"Well, he gets here just in time for tea," said Germaine in a tone of extreme satisfaction. "He knows that I hate to be kept waiting. He said to me, 'I shall be back by five at the latest.' And here he is."

"It's impossible," said Sonia. "He has to go all the way round the park. There's no direct road; the brook is between us."

"All the same, he's coming in a straight line," said Germaine.

It was true. The horseman had left the road and was galloping across the meadows straight for the brook. In twenty seconds he reached its treacherous bank, and as he set his horse at it, Sonia covered her eyes.

"He's over!" said Germaine. "My father gave three hundred guineas for that horse."

3

LUPIN'S WAY

Sonia, in a sudden revulsion of feeling, in a reaction from her fears, slipped back and sat down at the tea-table, panting quickly, struggling to keep back the tears of relief. She did not see the Duke gallop up the slope, dismount, and hand over his horse to the groom who came running to him. There was still a mist in her eyes to blur his figure as he came through the window.

"If it's for me, plenty of tea, very little cream, and three lumps of sugar," he cried in a gay, ringing voice, and pulled out his watch. "Five to the minute—that's all right." And he bent down, took Germaine's hand, and kissed it with an air of gallant devotion.

If he had indeed just fought a duel, there were no signs of it in his bearing. His air, his voice, were entirely careless. He was a man whose whole thought at the moment was fixed on his tea and his punctuality.

He drew a chair near the tea-table for Germaine; sat down himself; and Sonia handed him a cup of tea with so shaky a hand that the spoon clinked in the saucer.

"You've been fighting a duel?" said Germaine.

"What! You've heard already?" said the Duke in some surprise.

"I've heard," said Germaine. "Why did you fight it?"

"You're not wounded, your Grace?" said Sonia anxiously.

"Not a scratch," said the Duke, smiling at her.

"Will you be so good as to get on with those wedding-cards, Sonia," said Germaine sharply; and Sonia went back to the writing-table.

Turning to the Duke, Germaine said, "Did you fight on my account?"

"Would you be pleased to know that I had fought on your account?" said the Duke; and there was a faint mocking light in his eyes, far too faint for the self-satisfied Germaine to perceive.

"Yes. But it isn't true. You've been fighting about some woman," said Germaine petulantly.

"If I had been fighting about a woman, it could only be you," said the Duke.

"Yes, that is so. Of course. It could hardly be about Sonia, or my maid," said Germaine. "But what was the reason of the duel?"

"Oh, the reason of it was entirely childish," said the Duke. "I was in a bad temper; and De Relzieres said something that annoyed me."

"Then it wasn't about me; and if it wasn't about me, it wasn't really worth while fighting," said Germaine in a tone of acute disappointment.

The mocking light deepened a little in the Duke's eyes.

"Yes. But if I had been killed, everybody would have said, 'The Duke of Charmerace has been killed in a duel about Mademoiselle Gournay-Martin.' That would have sounded very fine indeed," said the Duke; and a touch of mockery had crept into his voice.

"Now, don't begin trying to annoy me again," said Germaine pettishly.

"The last thing I should dream of, my dear girl," said the Duke, smiling.

"And De Relzieres? Is he wounded?" said Germaine.

"Poor dear De Relzieres: he won't be out of bed for the next six months," said the Duke; and he laughed lightly and gaily.

"Good gracious!" cried Germaine.

"It will do poor dear De Relzieres a world of good. He has a touch of enteritis; and for enteritis there is nothing like rest," said the Duke.

Sonia was not getting on very quickly with the wedding-cards. Germaine was sitting with her back to her; and over her shoulder Sonia could watch the face of the Duke—an extraordinarily mobile face, changing with every passing mood. Sometimes his eyes met hers; and hers fell before them. But as soon as they turned away from her she was watching him again, almost greedily, as if she could not see enough of his face in which strength of will and purpose was mingled with a faint, ironic scepticism, and tempered by a fine air of race.

He finished his tea; then he took a morocco case from his pocket, and said to Germaine, "It must be quite three days since I gave you anything."

He opened the case, disclosed a pearl pendant, and handed it to her.

"Oh, how nice!" she cried, taking it.

She took it from the case, saying that it was a beauty. She showed it to Sonia; then she put it on and stood before a mirror admiring the effect. To tell the truth, the effect was not entirely desirable. The pearls did not improve the look of her rather coarse brown skin; and her skin added nothing to the beauty of the pearls. Sonia saw this, and so did the Duke. He looked at Sonia's white throat. She met his eyes and blushed. She knew that the same thought was in both their minds; the pearls would have looked infinitely better there.

Germaine finished admiring herself; she was incapable even of suspecting that so expensive a pendant could not suit her perfectly.

The Duke said idly: "Goodness! Are all those invitations to the wedding?"

"That's only down to the letter V," said Germaine proudly.

"And there are twenty-five letters in the alphabet! You must be inviting the whole world. You'll have to have the Madeleine enlarged. It won't hold them all. There isn't a church in Paris that will," said the Duke.

"Won't it be a splendid marriage!" said Germaine. "There'll be something like a crush. There are sure to be accidents."

"If I were you, I should have careful arrangements made," said the Duke.

"Oh, let people look after themselves. They'll remember it better if they're crushed a little," said Germaine.

There was a flicker of contemptuous wonder in the Duke's eyes. But he only shrugged his shoulders, and turning to Sonia, said, "Will you be an angel and play me a little Grieg, Mademoiselle Kritchnoff? I heard you playing yesterday. No one plays Grieg like you."

"Excuse me, Jacques, but Mademoiselle Kritchnoff has her work to do," said Germaine tartly.

"Five minutes' interval—just a morsel of Grieg, I beg," said the Duke, with an irresistible smile.

"All right," said Germaine grudgingly. "But I've something important to talk to you about."

"By Jove! So have I. I was forgetting. I've the last photograph I took of you and Mademoiselle Sonia." Germaine frowned and shrugged her shoulders. "With your light frocks in the open air, you look like two big flowers," said the Duke.

"You call that important!" cried Germaine.

"It's very important—like all trifles," said the Duke, smiling. "Look! Isn't it nice?" And he took a photograph from his pocket, and held it out to her.

"Nice? It's shocking! We're making the most appalling faces," said Germaine, looking at the photograph in his hand.

"Well, perhaps you ARE making faces," said the Duke seriously, considering the photograph with grave earnestness. "But they're not appalling faces—not by any means. You shall be judge, Mademoiselle Sonia. The faces—well, we won't talk about the faces—but the outlines. Look at the movement of your scarf." And he handed the photograph to Sonia.

"Jacques!" said Germaine impatiently.

"Oh, yes, you've something important to tell me. What is it?" said the Duke, with an air of resignation; and he took the photograph from Sonia and put it carefully back in his pocket.

"Victoire has telephoned from Paris to say that we've had a paper-knife and a Louis Seize inkstand given us," said Germaine.

"Hurrah!" cried the Duke in a sudden shout that made them both jump.

"And a pearl necklace," said Germaine.

"Hurrah!" cried the Duke.

"You're perfectly childish," said Germaine pettishly. "I tell you we've been given a paper-knife, and you shout 'hurrah!' I say we've been given a pearl necklace, and you shout 'hurrah!' You can't have the slightest sense of values."

"I beg your pardon. This pearl necklace is from one of your father's friends, isn't it?" said the Duke.

"Yes; why?" said Germaine.

"But the inkstand and the paper-knife must be from the Faubourg Saint-Germain, and well on the shabby side?" said the Duke.

"Yes; well?"

"Well then, my dear girl, what are you complaining about? They balance; the equilibrium is restored. You can't have everything," said the Duke; and he laughed mischievously.

Germaine flushed, and bit her lip; her eyes sparkled.

"You don't care a rap about me," she said stormily.

"But I find you adorable," said the Duke.

"You keep annoying me," said Germaine pettishly. "And you do it on purpose. I think it's in very bad taste. I shall end by taking a dislike to you—I know I shall."

"Wait till we're married for that, my dear girl," said the Duke; and he laughed again, with a blithe, boyish cheerfulness, which deepened the angry flush in Germaine's cheeks.

"Can't you be serious about anything?" she cried.

"I am the most serious man in Europe," said the Duke.

Germaine went to the window and stared out of it sulkily.

The Duke walked up and down the hall, looking at the pictures of some of his ancestors—somewhat grotesque persons—with humorous appreciation. Between addressing the envelopes Sonia kept glancing at him. Once he caught her eye, and smiled at her. Germaine's back was eloquent of her displeasure. The Duke stopped at a gap in the line of pictures in which there hung a strip of old tapestry.

"I can never understand why you have left all these ancestors of mine staring from the walls and have taken away the quite admirable and interesting portrait of myself," he said carelessly.

Germaine turned sharply from the window; Sonia stopped in the middle of addressing an envelope; and both the girls stared at him in astonishment.

"There certainly was a portrait of me where that tapestry hangs. What have you done with it?" said the Duke.

"You're making fun of us again," said Germaine.

"Surely your Grace knows what happened," said Sonia.

"We wrote all the details to you and sent you all the papers three years ago. Didn't you get them?" said Germaine.

"Not a detail or a newspaper. Three years ago I was in the neighbourhood of the South Pole, and lost at that," said the Duke.

"But it was most dramatic, my dear Jacques. All Paris was talking of it," said Germaine. "Your portrait was stolen."

"Stolen? Who stole it?" said the Duke.

Germaine crossed the hall quickly to the gap in the line of pictures.

"I'll show you," she said.

She drew aside the piece of tapestry, and in the middle of the panel over which the portrait of the Duke had hung he saw written in chalk the words:

ARSÈNE LUPIN

"What do you think of that autograph?" said Germaine.

"'Arsène Lupin?'" said the Duke in a tone of some bewilderment.

"He left his signature. It seems that he always does so," said Sonia in an explanatory tone.

"But who is he?" said the Duke.

"Arsène Lupin? Surely you know who Arsène Lupin is?" said Germaine impatiently.

"I haven't the slightest notion," said the Duke.

"Oh, come! No one is as South-Pole as all that!" cried Germaine. "You don't know who Lupin is? The most whimsical, the most audacious, and the most genial thief in France. For the last ten years he has kept the police at bay. He has baffled Ganimard, Holmlock Shears, the great English detective, and even Guerchard, whom everybody says is the greatest detective we've had in France since Vidocq. In fact, he's our national robber. Do you mean to say you don't know him?"

"Not even enough to ask him to lunch at a restaurant," said the Duke flippantly. "What's he like?"

"Like? Nobody has the slightest idea. He has a thousand disguises. He has dined two evenings running at the English Embassy."

"But if nobody knows him, how did they learn that?" said the Duke, with a puzzled air.

"Because the second evening, about ten o'clock, they noticed that one of the guests had disappeared, and with him all the jewels of the ambassadress."

"All of them?" said the Duke.

"Yes; and Lupin left his card behind him with these words scribbled on it:

"'This is not a robbery; it is a restitution. You took the Wallace collection from us.'"

"But it was a hoax, wasn't it?" said the Duke.

"No, your Grace; and he has done better than that. You remember the affair of the Daray Bank—the savings bank for poor people?" said Sonia, her gentle face glowing with a sudden enthusiastic animation.

"Let's see," said the Duke. "Wasn't that the financier who doubled his fortune at the expense of a heap of poor wretches and ruined two thousand people?"

"Yes; that's the man," said Sonia. "And Lupin stripped Daray's house and took from him everything he had in his strong-box. He didn't leave him a sou of the money. And then, when he'd taken it from him, he distributed it among all the poor wretches whom Daray had ruined."

"But this isn't a thief you're talking about—it's a philanthropist," said the Duke.

"A fine sort of philanthropist!" broke in Germaine in a peevish tone. "There was a lot of philanthropy about his robbing papa, wasn't there?"

"Well," said the Duke, with an air of profound reflection, "if you come to think of it, that robbery was not worthy of this national hero. My portrait, if you except the charm and beauty of the face itself, is not worth much."

"If you think he was satisfied with your portrait, you're very much mistaken. All my father's collections were robbed," said Germaine.

"Your father's collections?" said the Duke. "But they're better guarded than the Bank of France. Your father is as careful of them as the apple of his eye."

"That's exactly it—he was too careful of them. That's why Lupin succeeded."

"This is very interesting," said the Duke; and he sat down on a couch before the gap in the pictures, to go into the matter more at his ease. "I suppose he had accomplices in the house itself?"

"Yes, one accomplice," said Germaine.

"Who was that?" asked the Duke.

"Papa!" said Germaine.

"Oh, come! What on earth do you mean?" said the Duke. "You're getting quite incomprehensible, my dear girl."

"Well, I'll make it clear to you. One morning papa received a letter—but wait. Sonia, get me the Lupin papers out of the bureau."

Sonia rose from the writing-table, and went to a bureau, an admirable example of the work of the great English maker, Chippendale. It stood on the other side of the hall between an Oriental cabinet and a sixteenth-century Italian cabinet—for all the world as if it were standing in a crowded curiosity shop—with the natural effect that the three pieces, by their mere incongruity, took something each from the beauty of the other. Sonia raised the flap of the bureau, and taking from one of the drawers a small portfolio, turned over the papers in it and handed a letter to the Duke.

"This is the envelope," she said. "It's addressed to M. Gournay-Martin, Collector, at the Chateau de Charmerace, Ile-et-Vilaine."

The Duke opened the envelope and took out a letter.

"It's an odd handwriting," he said.

"Read it—carefully," said Germaine.

It was an uncommon handwriting. The letters of it were small, but perfectly formed. It looked the handwriting of a man who knew exactly what he wanted to say, and liked to say it with extreme precision. The letter ran:

"DEAR SIR,"

"Please forgive my writing to you without our having been introduced to one another; but I flatter myself that you know me, at any rate, by name."

"There is in the drawing-room next to your hall a Gainsborough of admirable quality which affords me infinite pleasure. Your Goyas in the same drawing-room are also to my liking, as well as your Van Dyck. In the further drawing-room I note the Renaissance cabinets—a marvellous pair—the Flemish tapestry, the Fragonard, the clock signed Boulle, and various other objects of less importance. But above all I have set my heart on that coronet which you bought at the sale of the Marquise de Ferronaye, and which was formerly worn by the unfortunate Princesse de Lamballe. I take the greatest interest in this coronet: in the first place, on account of the charming and tragic memories which it calls up in the mind of a poet passionately fond of history, and in the second place—though it is hardly worth while talking about that kind of thing—on account of its intrinsic value. I reckon indeed that the stones in your coronet are, at the very lowest, worth half a million francs."

"I beg you, my dear sir, to have these different objects properly packed up, and to forward them, addressed to me, carriage paid, to the Batignolles Station. Failing this, I shall Proceed to remove them myself on the night of Thursday, August 7th."

"Please pardon the slight trouble to which I am putting you, and believe me,"

"Yours very sincerely,"

"ARSÈNE LUPIN."

"P.S.—It occurs to me that the pictures have not glass before them. It would be as well to repair this omission before forwarding them to me, and I am sure that you will take this extra trouble cheerfully. I am aware, of course, that some of the best judges declare that a picture loses some of its quality when seen through glass. But it preserves them, and we should always be ready and willing to sacrifice a portion of our own pleasure for the benefit of posterity. France demands it of us.—A. L."

The Duke laughed, and said, "Really, this is extraordinarily funny. It must have made your father laugh."

"Laugh?" said Germaine. "You should have seen his face. He took it seriously enough, I can tell you."

"Not to the point of forwarding the things to Batignolles, I hope," said the Duke.

"No, but to the point of being driven wild," said Germaine. "And since the police had always been baffled by Lupin, he had the brilliant idea of trying what soldiers could do. The Commandant at Rennes is a great friend of papa's; and papa went to him, and told him about Lupin's letter and what he feared. The colonel laughed at him; but he offered him a corporal and six soldiers to guard his collection, on the night of the seventh. It was arranged that they should come from Rennes by the last train so that the burglars should have no warning of their coming. Well, they came, seven picked men—men who had seen service in Tonquin. We gave them supper; and then the corporal posted them in the hall and the two drawing-rooms where the pictures and things were. At eleven we all went to bed, after promising the corporal that, in the event of any fight with the burglars, we would not stir from our rooms. I can tell you I felt awfully nervous. I couldn't get to sleep for ages and ages. Then, when I did, I did not wake till morning. The night had passed absolutely quietly. Nothing out of the common had happened. There had not been the slightest noise. I awoke Sonia and my father. We dressed as quickly as we could, and rushed down to the drawing-room."

She paused dramatically.

"Well?" said the Duke.

"Well, it was done."

"What was done?" said the Duke.

"Everything," said Germaine. "Pictures had gone, tapestries had gone, cabinets had gone, and the clock had gone."

"And the coronet too?" said the Duke.

"Oh, no. That was at the Bank of France. And it was doubtless to make up for not getting it that Lupin stole your portrait. At any rate he didn't say that he was going to steal it in his letter."

"But, come! This is incredible. Had he hypnotized the corporal and the six soldiers? Or had he murdered them all?" said the Duke.

"Corporal? There wasn't any corporal, and there weren't any soldiers. The corporal was Lupin, and the soldiers were part of his gang," said Germaine.

"I don't understand," said the Duke. "The colonel promised your father a corporal and six men. Didn't they come?"

"They came to the railway station all right," said Germaine. "But you know the little inn half-way between the railway station and the chateau? They stopped to drink there, and at eleven o'clock next morning one of the villagers found all seven of them, along with the footman who was guiding them to the chateau, sleeping like logs in the little wood half a mile from the inn. Of course the innkeeper could not explain when their wine was drugged. He could only tell us that a motorist, who had stopped at the inn to get some supper, had called the soldiers in and insisted on standing them drinks. They had seemed a little fuddled before they left the inn, and the motorist had insisted on driving them to the chateau in his car. When the drug took effect he simply carried them out of it one by one, and laid them in the wood to sleep it off."

"Lupin seems to have made a thorough job of it, anyhow," said the Duke.

"I should think so," said Germaine. "Guerchard was sent down from Paris; but he could not find a single clue. It was not for want of trying, for he hates Lupin. It's a regular fight between them, and so far Lupin has scored every point."

"He must be as clever as they make 'em," said the Duke.

"He is," said Germaine. "And do you know, I shouldn't be at all surprised if he's in the neighbourhood now."

"What on earth do you mean?" said the Duke.

"I'm not joking," said Germaine. "Odd things are happening. Someone has been changing the place of things. That silver statuette now—it was on the cabinet, and we found it moved to the piano. Yet nobody had touched it. And look at this window. Some one has broken a pane in it just at the height of the fastening."

"The deuce they have!" said the Duke.

4

THE DUKE INTERVENES

The Duke rose, came to the window, and looked at the broken pane. He stepped out on to the terrace and looked at the turf; then he came back into the room.

"This looks serious," he said. "That pane has not been broken at all. If it had been broken, the pieces of glass would be lying on the turf. It has been cut out. We must warn your father to look to his treasures."

"I told you so," said Germaine. "I said that Arsène Lupin was in the neighbourhood."

"Arsène Lupin is a very capable man," said the Duke, smiling. "But there's no reason to suppose that he's the only burglar in France or even in Ile-et-Vilaine."

"I'm sure that he's in the neighbourhood. I have a feeling that he is," said Germaine stubbornly.

The Duke shrugged his shoulders, and said with a smile: "Far be it from me to contradict you. A woman's intuition is always—well, it's always a woman's intuition."

He came back into the hall, and as he did so the door opened and a shock-headed man in the dress of a gamekeeper stood on the threshold.

"There are visitors to see you, Mademoiselle Germaine," he said, in a very deep bass voice.

"What! Are you answering the door, Firmin?" said Germaine.

"Yes, Mademoiselle Germaine: there's only me to do it. All the servants have started for the station, and my wife and I are going to see after the family to-night and to-morrow morning. Shall I show these gentlemen in?"

"Who are they?" said Germaine.

"Two gentlemen who say they have an appointment."

"What are their names?" said Germaine.

"They are two gentlemen. I don't know what their names are. I've no memory for names."

"That's an advantage to any one who answers doors," said the Duke, smiling at the stolid Firmin.

"Well, it can't be the two Charolais again. It's not time for them to come back. I told them papa would not be back yet," said Germaine.

"No, it can't be them, Mademoiselle Germaine," said Firmin, with decision.

"Very well; show them in," she said.

Firmin went out, leaving the door open behind him; and they heard his hob-nailed boots clatter and squeak on the stone floor of the outer hall.

"Charolais?" said the Duke idly. "I don't know the name. Who are they?"

"A little while ago Alfred announced two gentlemen. I thought they were Georges and Andre du Buit, for they promised to come to tea. I told Alfred to show them in, and to my surprise there appeared two horrible provincials. I never—Oh!"

She stopped short, for there, coming through the door, were the two Charolais, father and son.

M. Charolais pressed his motor-cap to his bosom, and bowed low. "Once more I salute you, mademoiselle," he said.

His son bowed, and revealed behind him another young man.

"My second son. He has a chemist's shop," said M. Charolais, waving a large red hand at the young man.

The young man, also blessed with the family eyes, set close together, entered the hall and bowed to the two girls. The Duke raised his eyebrows ever so slightly.

"I'm very sorry, gentlemen," said Germaine, "but my father has not yet returned."

"Please don't apologize. There is not the slightest need," said M. Charolais; and he and his two sons settled themselves down on three chairs, with the air of people who had come to make a considerable stay.

For a moment, Germaine, taken aback by their coolness, was speechless; then she said hastily: "Very likely he won't be back for another hour. I shouldn't like you to waste your time."

"Oh, it doesn't matter," said M. Charolais, with an indulgent air; and turning to the Duke, he added, "However, while we're waiting, if you're a member of the family, sir, we might perhaps discuss the least you will take for the motor-car."

"I'm sorry," said the Duke, "but I have nothing to do with it."

Before M. Charolais could reply the door opened, and Firmin's deep voice said:

"Will you please come in here, sir?"

A third young man came into the hall.

"What, you here, Bernard?" said M. Charolais. "I told you to wait at the park gates."

"I wanted to see the car too," said Bernard.

"My third son. He is destined for the Bar," said M. Charolais, with a great air of paternal pride.

"But how many are there?" said Germaine faintly.

Before M. Charolais could answer, Firmin once more appeared on the threshold.

"The master's just come back, miss," he said.

"Thank goodness for that!" said Germaine; and turning to M. Charolais, she added, "If you will come with me, gentlemen,

I will take you to my father, and you can discuss the price of the car at once."

As she spoke she moved towards the door. M. Charolais and his sons rose and made way for her. The father and the two eldest sons made haste to follow her out of the room. But Bernard lingered behind, apparently to admire the bric-a-brac on the cabinets. With infinite quickness he grabbed two objects off the nearest, and followed his brothers. The Duke sprang across the hall in three strides, caught him by the arm on the very threshold, jerked him back into the hall, and shut the door.

"No you don't, my young friend," he said sharply.

"Don't what?" said Bernard, trying to shake off his grip.

"You've taken a cigarette-case," said the Duke.

"No, no, I haven't—nothing of the kind!" stammered Bernard.

The Duke grasped the young man's left wrist, plunged his hand into the motor-cap which he was carrying, drew out of it a silver cigarette-case, and held it before his eyes.

Bernard turned pale to the lips. His frightened eyes seemed about to leap from their sockets.

"It—it—was a m-m-m-mistake," he stammered.

The Duke shifted his grip to his collar, and thrust his hand into the breast-pocket of his coat. Bernard, helpless in his grip, and utterly taken aback by his quickness, made no resistance.

The Duke drew out a morocco case, and said: "Is this a mistake too?"

"Heavens! The pendant!" cried Sonia, who was watching the scene with parted lips and amazed eyes.

Bernard dropped on his knees and clasped his hands.

"Forgive me!" he cried, in a choking voice. "Forgive me! Don't tell any one! For God's sake, don't tell any one!"

And the tears came streaming from his eyes.

"You young rogue!" said the Duke quietly.

"I'll never do it again—never! Oh, have pity on me! If my father knew! Oh, let me off!" cried Bernard.

The Duke hesitated, and looked down on him, frowning and pulling at his moustache. Then, more quickly than one would have expected from so careless a trifler, his mind was made up.

"All right," he said slowly. "Just for this once ... be off with you." And he jerked him to his feet and almost threw him into the outer hall.

"Thanks! ... Oh, thanks!" said Bernard.

The Duke shut the door and looked at Sonia, breathing quickly.

"Well? Did you ever see anything like that? That young fellow will go a long way. The cheek of the thing! Right under our very eyes! And this pendant, too: it would have been a pity to lose it. Upon my word, I ought to have handed him over to the police."

"No, no!" cried Sonia. "You did quite right to let him off—quite right."

The Duke set the pendant on the ledge of the bureau, and came down the hall to Sonia.

"What's the matter?" he said gently. "You're quite pale."

"It has upset me ... that unfortunate boy," said Sonia; and her eyes were swimming with tears.

"Do you pity the young rogue?" said the Duke.

"Yes; it's dreadful. His eyes were so terrified, and so boyish. And, to be caught like that ... stealing ... in the act. Oh, it's hateful!"

"Come, come, how sensitive you are!" said the Duke, in a soothing, almost caressing tone. His eyes, resting on her charming, troubled face, were glowing with a warm admiration.

"Yes; it's silly," said Sonia; "but you noticed his eyes—the hunted look in them? You pitied him, didn't you? For you are kind at bottom."

"Why at bottom?" said the Duke.

"Oh, I said at bottom because you look sarcastic, and at first sight you're so cold. But often that's only the mask of those who have suffered the most... They are the most indulgent," said Sonia slowly, hesitating, picking her words.

"Yes, I suppose they are," said the Duke thoughtfully.

"It's because when one has suffered one understands... Yes: one understands," said Sonia.

There was a pause. The Duke's eyes still rested on her face. The admiration in them was mingled with compassion.

"You're very unhappy here, aren't you?" he said gently.

"Me? Why?" said Sonia quickly.

"Your smile is so sad, and your eyes so timid," said the Duke slowly. "You're just like a little child one longs to protect. Are you quite alone in the world?"

His eyes and tones were full of pity; and a faint flush mantled Sonia's cheeks.

"Yes, I'm alone," she said.

"But have you no relations—no friends?" said the Duke.

"No," said Sonia.

"I don't mean here in France, but in your own country... Surely you have some in Russia?"

"No, not a soul. You see, my father was a Revolutionist. He died in Siberia when I was a baby. And my mother, she died too—in Paris. She had fled from Russia. I was two years old when she died."

"It must be hard to be alone like that," said the Duke.

"No," said Sonia, with a faint smile, "I don't mind having no relations. I grew used to that so young ... so very young. But what is hard—but you'll laugh at me—"

"Heaven forbid!" said the Duke gravely.

"Well, what is hard is, never to get a letter ... an envelope that one opens ... from someone who thinks about one—"

She paused, and then added gravely: "But I tell myself that it's nonsense. I have a certain amount of philosophy."

She smiled at him—an adorable child's smile.

The Duke smiled too. "A certain amount of philosophy," he said softly. "You look like a philosopher!"

As they stood looking at one another with serious eyes, almost with eyes that probed one another's souls, the drawing-room door flung open, and Germaine's harsh voice broke on their ears.

"You're getting quite impossible, Sonia!" she cried. "It's absolutely useless telling you anything. I told you particularly to pack my leather writing-case in my bag with your own hand. I happen to open a drawer, and what do I see? My leather writing-case."

"I'm sorry," said Sonia. "I was going—"

"Oh, there's no need to bother about it. I'll see after it myself," said Germaine. "But upon my word, you might be one of our guests, seeing how easily you take things. You're negligence personified."

"Come, Germaine ... a mere oversight," said the Duke, in a coaxing tone.

"Now, excuse me, Jacques; but you've got an unfortunate habit of interfering in household matters. You did it only the other day. I can no longer say a word to a servant—"

"Germaine!" said the Duke, in sharp protest.

Germaine turned from him to Sonia, and pointed to a packet of envelopes and some letters, which Bernard Charolais had knocked off the table, and said, "Pick up those envelopes and letters, and bring everything to my room, and be quick about it!"

She flung out of the room, and slammed the door behind her.

Sonia seemed entirely unmoved by the outburst: no flush of mortification stained her cheeks, her lips did not quiver. She stooped to pick up the fallen papers.

"No, no; let me, I beg you," said the Duke, in a tone of distress. And dropping on one knee, he began to gather together the fallen papers. He set them on the table, and then he said: "You mustn't mind what Germaine says. She's—she's—she's all right at heart. It's her manner. She's always been happy, and had everything she wanted. She's been spoiled, don't you know. Those kind of people never have any consideration for any one else. You mustn't let her outburst hurt you."

"Oh, but I don't. I don't really," protested Sonia.

"I'm glad of that," said the Duke. "It isn't really worth noticing."

He drew the envelopes and unused cards into a packet, and handed them to her.

"There!" he said, with a smile. "That won't be too heavy for you."

"Thank you," said Sonia, taking it from him.

"Shall I carry them for you?" said the Duke.

"No, thank you, your Grace," said Sonia.

With a quick, careless, almost irresponsible movement, he caught her hand, bent down, and kissed it. A great wave of rosy colour flowed over her face, flooding its whiteness to her hair and throat. She stood for a moment turned to stone; she put her hand to her heart. Then on hasty, faltering feet she went to the door, opened it, paused on the threshold, turned and looked back at him, and vanished.

5

A LETTER FROM LUPIN

The Duke stood for a while staring thoughtfully at the door through which Sonia had passed, a faint smile playing round his lips. He crossed the hall to the Chippendale bureau, took a cigarette from a box which stood on the ledge of it, beside the morocco case which held the pendant, lighted it, and went slowly out on to the terrace. He crossed it slowly, paused for a moment on the edge of it, and looked across the stretch of country with musing eyes, which saw nothing of its beauty. Then he turned to the right, went down a flight of steps to the lower terrace, crossed the lawn, and took a narrow path which led into the heart of a shrubbery of tall deodoras. In the middle of it he came to one of those old stone benches, moss-covered and weather-stained, which adorn the gardens of so many French chateaux. It faced a marble basin from which rose the slender column of a pattering fountain. The figure of a Cupid danced joyously on a tall pedestal to the right of the basin. The Duke sat down on the bench, and was still, with that rare stillness which only comes of nerves in perfect harmony, his brow knitted in careful thought. Now and again the frown cleared from his face, and his intent features relaxed into a faint smile, a smile of pleasant memory. Once he rose, walked round the fountain frowning, came back to the bench, and sat down again. The early September dusk was upon him when at last he rose and with quick steps took his way through the shrubbery, with the air of a man whose mind, for good or ill, was at last made up.

When he came on to the upper terrace his eyes fell on a group which stood at the further corner, near the entrance of the chateau, and he sauntered slowly up to it.

In the middle of it stood M. Gournay-Martin, a big, round, flabby hulk of a man. He was nearly as red in the face as M. Charolais; and he looked a great deal redder owing to the extreme whiteness of the whiskers which stuck out on either side of his vast expanse of cheek. As he came up, it struck the Duke as rather odd that he should have the Charolais eyes, set close together; any one who did not know that they were strangers to one another might have thought it a family likeness.

The millionaire was waving his hands and roaring after the manner of a man who has cultivated the art of brow-beating those with whom he does business; and as the Duke neared the group, he caught the words:

"No; that's the lowest I'll take. Take it or leave it. You can say Yes, or you can say Good-bye; and I don't care a hang which."

"It's very dear," said M. Charolais, in a mournful tone.

"Dear!" roared M. Gournay-Martin. "I should like to see any one else sell a hundred horse-power car for eight hundred pounds. Why, my good sir, you're having me!"

"No, no," protested M. Charolais feebly.

"I tell you you're having me," roared M. Gournay-Martin. "I'm letting you have a magnificent car for which I paid thirteen hundred pounds for eight hundred! It's scandalous the way you've beaten me down!"

"No, no," protested M. Charolais.

He seemed frightened out of his life by the vehemence of the big man.

"You wait till you've seen how it goes," said M. Gournay-Martin.

"Eight hundred is very dear," said M. Charolais.

"Come, come! You're too sharp, that's what you are. But don't say any more till you've tried the car."

He turned to his chauffeur, who stood by watching the struggle with an appreciative grin on his brown face, and said: "Now, Jean, take these gentlemen to the garage, and run them down to the station. Show them what the car can do. Do whatever they ask you—everything."

He winked at Jean, turned again to M. Charolais, and said: "You know, M. Charolais, you're too good a man of business for me. You're hot stuff, that's what you are—hot stuff. You go along and try the car. Good-bye—good-bye."

The four Charolais murmured good-bye in deep depression, and went off with Jean, wearing something of the air of whipped dogs. When they had gone round the corner the millionaire turned to the Duke and said, with a chuckle: "He'll buy the car all right—had him fine!"

"No business success of yours could surprise me," said the Duke blandly, with a faint, ironical smile.

M. Gournay-Martin's little pig's eyes danced and sparkled; and the smiles flowed over the distended skin of his face like little ripples over a stagnant pool, reluctantly. It seemed to be too tightly stretched for smiles.

"The car's four years old," he said joyfully. "He'll give me eight hundred for it, and it's not worth a pipe of tobacco. And eight hundred pounds is just the price of a little Watteau I've had my eye on for some time—a first-class investment."

They strolled down the terrace, and through one of the windows into the hall. Firmin had lighted the lamps, two of them. They made but a small oasis of light in a desert of dim hall. The millionaire let himself down very gingerly into an

Empire chair, as if he feared, with excellent reason, that it might collapse under his weight.

"Well, my dear Duke," he said, "you don't ask me the result of my official lunch or what the minister said."

"Is there any news?" said the Duke carelessly.

"Yes. The decree will be signed to-morrow. You can consider yourself decorated. I hope you feel a happy man," said the millionaire, rubbing his fat hands together with prodigious satisfaction.

"Oh, charmed—charmed," said the Duke, with entire indifference.

"As for me, I'm delighted—delighted," said the millionaire. "I was extremely keen on your being decorated. After that, and after a volume or two of travels, and after you've published your grandfather's letters with a good introduction, you can begin to think of the Academy."

"The Academy!" said the Duke, startled from his usual coolness. "But I've no title to become an Academician."

"How, no title?" said the millionaire solemnly; and his little eyes opened wide. "You're a duke."

"There's no doubt about that," said the Duke, watching him with admiring curiosity.

"I mean to marry my daughter to a worker—a worker, my dear Duke," said the millionaire, slapping his big left hand with his bigger right. "I've no prejudices—not I. I wish to have for son-in-law a duke who wears the Order of the Legion of Honour, and belongs to the Academie Francaise, because that is personal merit. I'm no snob."

A gentle, irrepressible laugh broke from the Duke.

"What are you laughing at?" said the millionaire, and a sudden lowering gloom overspread his beaming face.

"Nothing—nothing," said the Duke quietly. "Only you're so full of surprises."

"I've startled you, have I? I thought I should. It's true that I'm full of surprises. It's my knowledge. I understand so much. I understand business, and I love art, pictures, a good bargain, bric-a-brac, fine tapestry. They're first-class investments. Yes, certainly I do love the beautiful. And I don't want to boast, but I understand it. I have taste, and I've something better than taste; I have a flair, the dealer's flair."

"Yes, your collections, especially your collection in Paris, prove it," said the Duke, stifling a yawn.

"And yet you haven't seen the finest thing I have—the coronet of the Princesse de Lamballe. It's worth half a million francs."

"So I've heard," said the Duke, a little wearily. "I don't wonder that Arsène Lupin envied you it."

The Empire chair creaked as the millionaire jumped.

"Don't speak of the swine!" he roared. "Don't mention his name before me."

"Germaine showed me his letter," said the Duke. "It is amusing."

"His letter! The blackguard! I just missed a fit of apoplexy from it," roared the millionaire. "I was in this very hall where we are now, chatting quietly, when all at once in comes Firmin, and hands me a letter."

He was interrupted by the opening of the door. Firmin came clumping down the room, and said in his deep voice, "A letter for you, sir."

"Thank you," said the millionaire, taking the letter, and, as he fitted his eye-glass into his eye, he went on, "Yes, Firmin brought me a letter of which the handwriting,"—he raised the envelope he was holding to his eyes, and bellowed, "Good heavens!"

"What's the matter?" said the Duke, jumping in his chair at the sudden, startling burst of sound.

"The handwriting!—the handwriting!—it's THE SAME HANDWRITING!" gasped the millionaire. And he let himself fall heavily backwards against the back of his chair.

There was a crash. The Duke had a vision of huge arms and legs waving in the air as the chair-back gave. There was another crash. The chair collapsed. The huge bulk banged to the floor.

The laughter of the Duke rang out uncontrollably. He caught one of the waving arms, and jerked the flabby giant to his feet with an ease which seemed to show that his muscles were of steel.

"Come," he said, laughing still. "This is nonsense! What do you mean by the same handwriting? It can't be."

"It is the same handwriting. Am I likely to make a mistake about it?" spluttered the millionaire. And he tore open the envelope with an air of frenzy.

He ran his eyes over it, and they grew larger and larger—they grew almost of an average size.

"Listen," he said "listen:

> "DEAR SIR,"
>
> "My collection of pictures, which I had the pleasure of starting three years ago with some of your own, only contains, as far as Old Masters go, one Velasquez, one Rembrandt, and three paltry Rubens. You have a great many more. Since it is a shame such masterpieces should be in your hands, I propose to appropriate them; and I shall set about a respectful acquisition of them in your Paris house tomorrow morning."
>
> "Yours very sincerely,"
>
> "ARSÈNE LUPIN."

"He's humbugging," said the Duke.

"Wait! Wait!" gasped the millionaire. "There's a postscript. Listen:

> "P.S.—You must understand that since you have been keeping the coronet of the Princesse de Lamballe during these three years, I shall avail myself of the same

occasion to compel you to restore that piece of jewellery to me.—A. L."

"The thief! The scoundrel! I'm choking!" gasped the millionaire, clutching at his collar.

To judge from the blackness of his face, and the way he staggered and dropped on to a couch, which was fortunately stronger than the chair, he was speaking the truth.

"Firmin! Firmin!" shouted the Duke. "A glass of water! Quick! Your master's ill."

He rushed to the side of the millionaire, who gasped: "Telephone! Telephone to the Prefecture of Police! Be quick!"

The Duke loosened his collar with deft fingers; tore a Van Loo fan from its case hanging on the wall, and fanned him furiously. Firmin came clumping into the room with a glass of water in his hand.

The drawing-room door opened, and Germaine and Sonia, alarmed by the Duke's shout, hurried in.

"Quick! Your smelling-salts!" said the Duke.

Sonia ran across the hall, opened one of the drawers in the Oriental cabinet, and ran to the millionaire with a large bottle of smelling-salts in her hand. The Duke took it from her, and applied it to the millionaire's nose. The millionaire sneezed thrice with terrific violence. The Duke snatched the glass from Firmin and dashed the water into his host's purple face. The millionaire gasped and spluttered.

Germaine stood staring helplessly at her gasping sire.

"Whatever's the matter?" she said.

"It's this letter," said the Duke. "A letter from Lupin."

"I told you so—I said that Lupin was in the neighbourhood," cried Germaine triumphantly.

"Firmin—where's Firmin?" said the millionaire, dragging himself upright. He seemed to have recovered a great deal of his voice. "Oh, there you are!"

He jumped up, caught the gamekeeper by the shoulder, and shook him furiously.

"This letter. Where did it come from? Who brought it?" he roared.

"It was in the letter-box—the letter-box of the lodge at the bottom of the park. My wife found it there," said Firmin, and he twisted out of the millionaire's grasp.

"Just as it was three years ago," roared the millionaire, with an air of desperation. "It's exactly the same coup. Oh, what a catastrophe! What a catastrophe!"

He made as if to tear out his hair; then, remembering its scantiness, refrained.

"Now, come, it's no use losing your head," said the Duke, with quiet firmness. "If this letter isn't a hoax—"

"Hoax?" bellowed the millionaire. "Was it a hoax three years ago?"

"Very good," said the Duke. "But if this robbery with which you're threatened is genuine, it's just childish."

"How?" said the millionaire.

"Look at the date of the letter—Sunday, September the third. This letter was written to-day."

"Yes. Well, what of it?" said the millionaire.

"Look at the letter: 'I shall set about a respectful acquisition of them in your Paris house to-morrow morning'—to-morrow morning."

"Yes, yes; 'to-morrow morning'—what of it?" said the millionaire.

"One of two things," said the Duke. "Either it's a hoax, and we needn't bother about it; or the threat is genuine, and we have the time to stop the robbery."

"Of course we have. Whatever was I thinking of?" said the millionaire. And his anguish cleared from his face.

"For once in a way our dear Lupin's fondness for warning people will have given him a painful jar," said the Duke.

"Come on! Let me get at the telephone," cried the millionaire.

"But the telephone's no good," said Sonia quickly.

"No good! Why?" roared the millionaire, dashing heavily across the room to it.

"Look at the time," said Sonia; "the telephone doesn't work as late as this. It's Sunday."

The millionaire stopped dead.

"It's true. It's appalling," he groaned.

"But that doesn't matter. You can always telegraph," said Germaine.

"But you can't. It's impossible," said Sonia. "You can't get a message through. It's Sunday; and the telegraph offices shut at twelve o'clock."

"Oh, what a Government!" groaned the millionaire. And he sank down gently on a chair beside the telephone, and mopped the beads of anguish from his brow. They looked at him, and they looked at one another, cudgelling their brains for yet another way of communicating with the Paris police.

"Hang it all!" said the Duke. "There must be some way out of the difficulty."

"What way?" said the millionaire.

The Duke did not answer. He put his hands in his pockets and walked impatiently up and down the hall. Germaine sat down on a chair. Sonia put her hands on the back of a couch, and leaned forward, watching him. Firmin stood by the door, whither he had retired to be out of the reach of his excited master, with a look of perplexity on his stolid face. They all watched the Duke with the air of people waiting for an oracle to deliver its message. The millionaire kept mopping the beads of anguish from his brow. The more he thought of his impending loss, the more freely he perspired. Germaine's maid, Irma, came to the door leading into the outer hall, which Firmin, according to his usual custom, had left open, and peered in wonder at the silent group.

"I have it!" cried the Duke at last. "There is a way out."

"What is it?" said the millionaire, rising and coming to the middle of the hall.

"What time is it?" said the Duke, pulling out his watch.

The millionaire pulled out his watch. Germaine pulled out hers. Firmin, after a struggle, produced from some pocket difficult of access an object not unlike a silver turnip. There was a brisk dispute between Germaine and the millionaire about which of their watches was right. Firmin, whose watch apparently did not agree with the watch of either of them, made his deep voice heard above theirs. The Duke came to the conclusion that it must be a few minutes past seven.

"It's seven or a few minutes past," he said sharply. "Well, I'm going to take a car and hurry off to Paris. I ought to get there, bar accidents, between two and three in the morning, just in time to inform the police and catch the burglars in the very midst of their burglary. I'll just get a few things together."

So saying, he rushed out of the hall.

"Excellent! Excellent!" said the millionaire. "Your young man is a man of resource, Germaine. It seems almost a pity that he's a duke. He'd do wonders in the building trade. But I'm going to Paris too, and you're coming with me. I couldn't wait idly here, to save my life. And I can't leave you here, either. This scoundrel may be going to make a simultaneous attempt on the chateau—not that there's much here that I really value. There's that statuette that moved, and the pane cut out of the window. I can't leave you two girls with burglars in the house. After all, there's the sixty horse-power and the thirty horse-power car—there'll be lots of room for all of us."

"Oh, but it's nonsense, papa; we shall get there before the servants," said Germaine pettishly. "Think of arriving at an empty house in the dead of night."

"Nonsense!" said the millionaire. "Hurry off and get ready. Your bag ought to be packed. Where are my keys? Sonia, where are my keys—the keys of the Paris house?"

"They're in the bureau," said Sonia.

"Well, see that I don't go without them. Now hurry up. Firmin, go and tell Jean that we shall want both cars. I will drive one, the Duke the other. Jean must stay with you and help guard the chateau."

So saying he bustled out of the hall, driving the two girls before him.

6

AGAIN THE CHAROLAIS

Hardly had the door closed behind the millionaire when the head of M. Charolais appeared at one of the windows opening on to the terrace. He looked round the empty hall, whistled softly, and stepped inside. Inside of ten seconds his three sons came in through the windows, and with them came Jean, the millionaire's chauffeur.

"Take the door into the outer hall, Jean," said M. Charolais, in a low voice. "Bernard, take that door into the drawing-room. Pierre and Louis, help me go through the drawers. The whole family is going to Paris, and if we're not quick we shan't get the cars."

"That comes of this silly fondness for warning people of a coup," growled Jean, as he hurried to the door of the outer hall. "It would have been so simple to rob the Paris house without sending that infernal letter. It was sure to knock them all silly."

"What harm can the letter do, you fool?" said M. Charolais. "It's Sunday. We want them knocked silly for to-morrow, to get hold of the coronet. Oh, to get hold of that coronet! It must be in Paris. I've been ransacking this chateau for hours."

Jean opened the door of the outer hall half an inch, and glued his eyes to it. Bernard had done the same with the door opening into the drawing-room. M. Charolais, Pierre, and

Louis were opening drawers, ransacking them, and shutting them with infinite quickness and noiselessly.

"Bureau! Which is the bureau? The place is stuffed with bureaux!" growled M. Charolais. "I must have those keys."

"That plain thing with the brass handles in the middle on the left—that's a bureau," said Bernard softly.

"Why didn't you say so?" growled M. Charolais.

He dashed to it, and tried it. It was locked.

"Locked, of course! Just my luck! Come and get it open, Pierre. Be smart!"

The son he had described as an engineer came quickly to the bureau, fitting together as he came the two halves of a small jemmy. He fitted it into the top of the flap. There was a crunch, and the old lock gave. He opened the flap, and he and M. Charolais pulled open drawer after drawer.

"Quick! Here's that fat old fool!" said Jean, in a hoarse, hissing whisper.

He moved down the hall, blowing out one of the lamps as he passed it. In the seventh drawer lay a bunch of keys. M. Charolais snatched it up, glanced at it, took a bunch of keys from his own pocket, put it in the drawer, closed it, closed the flap, and rushed to the window. Jean and his sons were already out on the terrace.

M. Charolais was still a yard from the window when the door into the outer hall opened and in came M. Gournay-Martin.

He caught a glimpse of a back vanishing through the window, and bellowed: "Hi! A man! A burglar! Firmin! Firmin!"

He ran blundering down the hall, tangled his feet in the fragments of the broken chair, and came sprawling a thundering cropper, which knocked every breath of wind out of his capacious body. He lay flat on his face for a couple of minutes, his broad back wriggling convulsively—a pathetic sight!—in the painful effort to get his breath back. Then he sat up, and with perfect frankness burst into tears. He sobbed and blubbered, like a small child that has hurt itself, for three or four minutes. Then, having recovered his magnificent voice, he bellowed furiously: "Firmin! Firmin! Charmerace! Charmerace!"

Then he rose painfully to his feet, and stood staring at the open windows.

Presently he roared again: "Firmin! Firmin! Charmerace! Charmerace!"

He kept looking at the window with terrified eyes, as though he expected somebody to step in and cut his throat from ear to ear.

"Firmin! Firmin! Charmerace! Charmerace!" he bellowed again.

The Duke came quietly into the hall, dressed in a heavy motor-coat, his motor-cap on his head, and carrying a kit-bag in his hand.

"Did I hear you call?" he said.

"Call?" said the millionaire. "I shouted. The burglars are here already. I've just seen one of them. He was bolting through the middle window."

The Duke raised his eyebrows.

"Nerves," he said gently—"nerves."

"Nerves be hanged!" said the millionaire. "I tell you I saw him as plainly as I see you."

"Well, you can't see me at all, seeing that you're lighting an acre and a half of hall with a single lamp," said the Duke, still in a tone of utter incredulity.

"It's that fool Firmin! He ought to have lighted six. Firmin! Firmin!" bellowed the millionaire.

They listened for the sonorous clumping of the promoted gamekeeper's boots, but they did not hear it. Evidently Firmin was still giving his master's instructions about the cars to Jean.

"Well, we may as well shut the windows, anyhow," said the Duke, proceeding to do so. "If you think Firmin would be any good, you might post him in this hall with a gun to-night. There could be no harm in putting a charge of small shot into the legs of these ruffians. He has only to get one of them, and the others will go for their lives. Yet I don't like leaving you and Germaine in this big house with only Firmin to look after you."

"I shouldn't like it myself, and I'm not going to chance it," growled the millionaire. "We're going to motor to Paris along with you, and leave Jean to help Firmin fight these burglars. Firmin's all right—he's an old soldier. He fought in '70. Not that I've much belief in soldiers against this cursed Lupin, after the way he dealt with that corporal and his men three years ago."

"I'm glad you're coming to Paris," said the Duke. "It'll be a weight off my mind. I'd better drive the limousine, and you take the landaulet."

"That won't do," said the millionaire. "Germaine won't go in the limousine. You know she has taken a dislike to it."

"Nevertheless, I'd better bucket on to Paris, and let you follow slowly with Germaine. The sooner I get to Paris the better for your collection. I'll take Mademoiselle Kritchnoff with me, and, if you like, Irma, though the lighter I travel the sooner I shall get there."

"No, I'll take Irma and Germaine," said the millionaire. "Germaine would prefer to have Irma with her, in case you had an accident. She wouldn't like to get to Paris and have to find a fresh maid."

The drawing-room door opened, and in came Germaine, followed by Sonia and Irma. They wore motor-cloaks and hoods and veils. Sonia and Irma were carrying hand-bags.

"I think it's extremely tiresome your dragging us off to Paris like this in the middle of the night," said Germaine pettishly.

"Do you?" said the millionaire. "Well, then, you'll be interested to hear that I've just seen a burglar here in this very room. I frightened him, and he bolted through the window on to the terrace."

"He was greenish-pink, slightly tinged with yellow," said the Duke softly.

"Greenish-pink? Oh, do stop your jesting, Jacques! Is this a time for idiocy?" cried Germaine, in a tone of acute exasperation.

"It was the dim light which made your father see him in those colours. In a bright light, I think he would have been an Alsatian blue," said the Duke suavely.

"You'll have to break yourself of this silly habit of trifling, my dear Duke, if ever you expect to be a member of the Academie Francaise," said the millionaire with some acrimony. "I tell you I did see a burglar."

"Yes, yes. I admitted it frankly. It was his colour I was talking about," said the Duke, with an ironical smile.

"Oh, stop your idiotic jokes! We're all sick to death of them!" said Germaine, with something of the fine fury which so often distinguished her father.

"There are times for all things," said the millionaire solemnly. "And I must say that, with the fate of my collection and of the coronet trembling in the balance, this does not seem to me a season for idle jests."

"I stand reproved," said the Duke; and he smiled at Sonia.

"My keys, Sonia—the keys of the Paris house," said the millionaire.

Sonia took her own keys from her pocket and went to the bureau. She slipped a key into the lock and tried to turn it. It would not turn; and she bent down to look at it.

"Why—why, someone's been tampering with the lock! It's broken!" she cried.

"I told you I'd seen a burglar!" cried the millionaire triumphantly. "He was after the keys."

Sonia drew back the flap of the bureau and hastily pulled open the drawer in which the keys had been.

"They're here!" she cried, taking them out of the drawer and holding them up.

"Then I was just in time," said the millionaire. "I startled him in the very act of stealing the keys."

"I withdraw! I withdraw!" said the Duke. "You did see a burglar, evidently. But still I believe he was greenish-pink. They often are. However, you'd better give me those keys, Mademoiselle Sonia, since I'm to get to Paris first. I should look rather silly if, when I got there, I had to break into the house to catch the burglars."

Sonia handed the keys to the Duke. He contrived to take her little hand, keys and all, into his own, as he received them, and squeezed it. The light was too dim for the others to see the flush which flamed in her face. She went back and stood beside the bureau.

"Now, papa, are you going to motor to Paris in a thin coat and linen waistcoat? If we're going, we'd better go. You always do keep us waiting half an hour whenever we start to go anywhere," said Germaine firmly.

The millionaire bustled out of the room. With a gesture of impatience Germaine dropped into a chair. Irma stood waiting by the drawing-room door. Sonia sat down by the bureau.

There came a sharp patter of rain against the windows.

"Rain! It only wanted that! It's going to be perfectly beastly!" cried Germaine.

"Oh, well, you must make the best of it. At any rate you're well wrapped up, and the night is warm enough, though it is raining," said the Duke. "Still, I could have wished that Lupin confined his operations to fine weather." He paused, and added cheerfully, "But, after all, it will lay the dust."

They sat for three or four minutes in a dull silence, listening to the pattering of the rain against the panes. The Duke took his cigarette-case from his pocket and lighted a cigarette.

Suddenly he lost his bored air; his face lighted up; and he said joyfully: "Of course, why didn't I think of it? Why should we start from a pit of gloom like this? Let us have the proper illumination which our enterprise deserves."

With that he set about lighting all the lamps in the hall. There were lamps on stands, lamps on brackets, lamps on tables, and lamps which hung from the roof—old-fashioned lamps with new reservoirs, new lamps of what is called chaste design, brass lamps, silver lamps, and lamps in porcelain. The Duke lighted them one after another, patiently, missing none, with a cold perseverance. The operation was punctuated by exclamations from Germaine. They were all to the effect that she could not understand how he could be such a fool. The Duke paid no attention whatever to her. His face illumined with boyish glee, he lighted lamp after lamp.

Sonia watched him with a smiling admiration of the childlike enthusiasm with which he performed the task. Even the stolid face of the ox-eyed Irma relaxed into grins, which she smoothed quickly out with a respectful hand.

The Duke had just lighted the twenty-second lamp when in bustled the millionaire.

"What's this? What's this?" he cried, stopping short, blinking.

"Just some more of Jacques' foolery!" cried Germaine in tones of the last exasperation.

"But, my dear Duke!—my dear Duke! The oil!—the oil!" cried the millionaire, in a tone of bitter distress. "Do you think it's my object in life to swell the Rockefeller millions? We never have more than six lamps burning unless we are holding a reception."

"I think it looks so cheerful," said the Duke, looking round on his handiwork with a beaming smile of satisfaction. "But where are the cars? Jean seems a deuce of a time bringing them round. Does he expect us to go to the garage through this rain? We'd better hurry him up. Come on; you've got a good carrying voice."

He caught the millionaire by the arm, hurried him through the outer hall, opened the big door of the chateau, and said: "Now shout!"

The millionaire looked at him, shrugged his shoulders, and said: "You don't beat about the bush when you want anything."

"Why should I?" said the Duke simply. "Shout, my good chap—shout!"

The millionaire raised his voice in a terrific bellow of "Jean! Jean! Firmin! Firmin!"

There was no answer.

7

THE THEFT OF THE MOTOR-CARS

The night was very black; the rain pattered in their faces.

Again the millionaire bellowed: "Jean! Firmin! Firmin! Jean!"

No answer came out of the darkness, though his bellow echoed and re-echoed among the out-buildings and stables away on the left.

He turned and looked at the Duke and said uneasily, "What on earth can they be doing?"

"I can't conceive," said the Duke. "I suppose we must go and hunt them out."

"What! In this darkness, with these burglars about?" said the millionaire, starting back.

"If we don't, nobody else will," said the Duke. "And all the time that rascal Lupin is stealing nearer and nearer your pictures. So buck up, and come along!"

He seized the reluctant millionaire by the arm and drew him down the steps. They took their way to the stables. A dim light shone from the open door of the motor-house. The Duke went into it first, and stopped short.

"Well, I'll be hanged!" he cried,

Instead of three cars the motor-house held but one—the hundred horse-power Mercrac. It was a racing car, with only two seats. On them sat two figures, Jean and Firmin.

"What are you sitting there for? You idle dogs!" bellowed the millionaire.

Neither of the men answered, nor did they stir. The light from the lamp gleamed on their fixed eyes, which stared at their infuriated master.

"What on earth is this?" said the Duke; and seizing the lamp which stood beside the car, he raised it so that its light fell on the two figures. Then it was clear what had happened: they were trussed like two fowls, and gagged.

The Duke pulled a penknife from his pocket, opened the blade, stepped into the car and set Firmin free. Firmin coughed and spat and swore. The Duke cut the bonds of Jean.

"Well," said the Duke, in a tone of cutting irony, "what new game is this? What have you been playing at?"

"It was those Charolais—those cursed Charolais!" growled Firmin.

"They came on us unawares from behind," said Jean.

"They tied us up, and gagged us—the swine!" said Firmin.

"And then—they went off in the two cars," said Jean.

"Went off in the two cars?" cried the millionaire, in blank stupefaction.

The Duke burst into a shout of laughter.

"Well, your dear friend Lupin doesn't do things by halves," he cried. "This is the funniest thing I ever heard of."

"Funny!" howled the millionaire. "Funny! Where does the fun come in? What about my pictures and the coronet?"

The Duke laughed his laugh out; then changed on the instant to a man of action.

"Well, this means a change in our plans," he said. "I must get to Paris in this car here."

"It's such a rotten old thing," said the millionaire. "You'll never do it."

"Never mind," said the Duke. "I've got to do it somehow. I daresay it's better than you think. And after all, it's only a matter of two hundred miles." He paused, and then said in an anxious tone: "All the same I don't like leaving you and Germaine in the chateau. These rogues have probably only taken the cars out of reach just to prevent your getting to Paris. They'll leave them in some field and come back."

"You're not going to leave us behind. I wouldn't spend the night in the chateau for a million francs. There's always the train," said the millionaire.

"The train! Twelve hours in the train—with all those changes! You don't mean that you will actually go to Paris by train?" said the Duke.

"I do," said the millionaire. "Come along—I must go and tell Germaine; there's no time to waste," and he hurried off to the chateau.

"Get the lamps lighted, Jean, and make sure that the tank's full. As for the engine, I must humour it and trust to luck. I'll get her to Paris somehow," said the Duke.

He went back to the chateau, and Firmin followed him.

When the Duke came into the great hall he found Germaine and her father indulging in recriminations. She was declaring that nothing would induce her to make the journey by train; her father was declaring that she should. He bore down her opposition by the mere force of his magnificent voice.

When at last there came a silence, Sonia said quietly: "But is there a train? I know there's a train at midnight; but is there one before?"

"A time-table—where's a time-table?" said the millionaire.

"Now, where did I see a time-table?" said the Duke. "Oh, I know; there's one in the drawer of that Oriental cabinet." Crossing to the cabinet, he opened the drawer, took out the time-table, and handed it to M. Gournay-Martin.

The millionaire took it and turned over the leaves quickly, ran his eye down a page, and said, "Yes, thank goodness, there is a train. There's one at a quarter to nine."

"And what good is it to us? How are we to get to the station?" said Germaine.

They looked at one another blankly. Firmin, who had followed the Duke into the hall, came to the rescue.

"There's the luggage-cart," he said.

"The luggage-cart!" cried Germaine contemptuously.

"The very thing!" said the millionaire. "I'll drive it myself. Off you go, Firmin; harness a horse to it."

Firmin went clumping out of the hall.

It was perhaps as well that he went, for the Duke asked what time it was; and since the watches of Germaine and her father differed still, there ensued an altercation in which, had Firmin been there, he would doubtless have taken part.

The Duke cut it short by saying: "Well, I don't think I'll wait to see you start for the station. It won't take you more than half an hour. The cart is light. You needn't start yet. I'd better get off as soon as the car is ready. It isn't as though I could trust it."

"One moment," said Germaine. "Is there a dining-car on the train? I'm not going to be starved as well as have my night's rest cut to pieces."

"Of course there isn't a dining-car," snapped her father. "We must eat something now, and take something with us."

"Sonia, Irma, quick! Be off to the larder and see what you can find. Tell Mother Firmin to make an omelette. Be quick!"

Sonia went towards the door of the hall, followed by Irma.

"Good-night, and bon voyage, Mademoiselle Sonia," said the Duke.

"Good-night, and bon voyage, your Grace," said Sonia.

The Duke opened the door of the hall for her; and as she went out, she said anxiously, in a low voice: "Oh, do—do be careful. I hate to think of your hurrying to Paris on a night like this. Please be careful."

"I will be careful," said the Duke.

The honk of the motor-horn told him that Jean had brought the car to the door of the chateau. He came down the room, kissed Germaine's hands, shook hands with the millionaire, and bade them good-night. Then he went out to the car. They heard it start; the rattle of it grew fainter and fainter down the long avenue and died away.

M. Gournay-Martin arose, and began putting out lamps. As he did so, he kept casting fearful glances at the window, as if he feared lest, now that the Duke had gone, the burglars should dash in upon him.

There came a knock at the door, and Jean appeared on the threshold.

"His Grace told me that I was to come into the house, and help Firmin look after it," he said.

The millionaire gave him instructions about the guarding of the house. Firmin, since he was an old soldier, was to occupy the post of honour, and guard the hall, armed with his gun. Jean was to guard the two drawing-rooms, as being less likely points of attack. He also was to have a gun; and the millionaire went with him to the gun-room and gave him one and a dozen cartridges. When they came back to the hall, Sonia called them into the dining-room; and there, to the accompaniment of an unsubdued grumbling from Germaine at having to eat cold food at eight at night, they made a hasty but excellent meal, since the chef had left an elaborate cold supper ready to be served.

They had nearly finished it when Jean came in, his gun on his arm, to say that Firmin had harnessed the horse to the luggage-cart, and it was awaiting them at the door of the chateau.

"Send him in to me, and stand by the horse till we come out," said the millionaire.

Firmin came clumping in.

The millionaire gazed at him solemnly, and said: "Firmin, I am relying on you. I am leaving you in a position of honour and danger—a position which an old soldier of France loves."

Firmin did his best to look like an old soldier of France. He pulled himself up out of the slouch which long years of loafing through woods with a gun on his arm had given him. He lacked also the old soldier of France's fiery gaze. His eyes were lack-lustre.

"I look for anything, Firmin—burglary, violence, an armed assault," said the millionaire.

"Don't be afraid, sir. I saw the war of '70," said Firmin boldly, rising to the occasion.

"Good!" said the millionaire. "I confide the chateau to you. I trust you with my treasures."

He rose, and saying "Come along, we must be getting to the station," he led the way to the door of the chateau.

The luggage-cart stood rather high, and they had to bring a chair out of the hall to enable the girls to climb into it. Germaine did not forget to give her real opinion of the advantages of a seat formed by a plank resting on the sides of the cart. The millionaire climbed heavily up in front, and took the reins.

"Never again will I trust only to motor-cars. The first thing I'll do after I've made sure that my collections are safe will be to buy carriages—something roomy," he said gloomily, as he realized the discomfort of his seat.

He turned to Jean and Firmin, who stood on the steps of the chateau watching the departure of their master, and said: "Sons of France, be brave—be brave!"

The cart bumped off into the damp, dark night.

Jean and Firmin watched it disappear into the darkness. Then they came into the chateau and shut the door.

Firmin looked at Jean, and said gloomily: "I don't like this. These burglars stick at nothing. They'd as soon cut your throat as look at you."

"It can't be helped," said Jean. "Besides, you've got the post of honour. You guard the hall. I'm to look after the drawing-rooms. They're not likely to break in through the drawing-rooms. And I shall lock the door between them and the hall."

"No, no; you won't lock that door!" cried Firmin.

"But I certainly will," said Jean. "You'd better come and get a gun."

They went to the gun-room, Firmin still protesting against the locking of the door between the drawing-rooms and the hall. He chose his gun; and they went into the kitchen. Jean took two bottles of wine, a rich-looking pie, a sweet, and carried them to the drawing-room. He came back into the hall, gathered together an armful of papers and magazines, and went back to the drawing-room. Firmin kept trotting after him, like a little dog with a somewhat heavy footfall.

On the threshold of the drawing-room Jean paused and said: "The important thing with burglars is to fire first, old cock. Good-night. Pleasant dreams."

He shut the door and turned the key. Firmin stared at the decorated panels blankly. The beauty of the scheme of decoration did not, at the moment, move him to admiration.

He looked fearfully round the empty hall and at the windows, black against the night. Under the patter of the rain he heard footsteps—distinctly. He went hastily clumping down the hall, and along the passage to the kitchen.

His wife was setting his supper on the table.

"My God!" he said. "I haven't been so frightened since '70." And he mopped his glistening forehead with a dish-cloth. It was not a clean dish-cloth; but he did not care.

"Frightened? What of?" said his wife.

"Burglars! Cut-throats!" said Firmin.

He told her of the fears of M. Gournay-Martin, and of his own appointment to the honourable and dangerous post of guard of the chateau.

"God save us!" said his wife. "You lock the door of that beastly hall, and come into the kitchen. Burglars won't bother about the kitchen."

"But the master's treasures!" protested Firmin. "He confided them to me. He said so distinctly."

"Let the master look after his treasures himself," said Madame Firmin, with decision. "You've only one throat; and I'm not going to have it cut. You sit down and eat your supper. Go and lock that door first, though."

Firmin locked the door of the hall; then he locked the door of the kitchen; then he sat down, and began to eat his supper. His appetite was hearty, but none the less he derived little pleasure from the meal. He kept stopping with the food poised on his fork, midway between the plate and his mouth, for several seconds at a time, while he listened with straining ears for the sound of burglars breaking in the windows of the hall. He was much too far from those windows to hear anything that happened to them, but that did not prevent him from straining his ears. Madame Firmin ate her supper with an air of perfect ease. She felt sure that burglars would not bother with the kitchen.

Firmin's anxiety made him terribly thirsty. Tumbler after tumbler of wine flowed down the throat for which he feared. When he had finished his supper he went on satisfying his thirst. Madame Firmin lighted his pipe for him, and went and washed up the supper-dishes in the scullery. Then she came back, and sat down on the other side of the hearth, facing him. About the middle of his third bottle of wine, Firmin's cold, relentless courage was suddenly restored to him. He began to talk firmly about his duty to his master, his resolve to die, if need were, in defence of his interests, of his utter contempt for burglars—probably Parisians. But he did not go into the hall. Doubtless the pleasant warmth of the kitchen fire held him in his chair.

He had described to his wife, with some ferocity, the cruel manner in which he would annihilate the first three burglars who entered the hall, and was proceeding to describe his method of dealing with the fourth, when there came a loud knocking on the front door of the chateau.

Stricken silent, turned to stone, Firmin sat with his mouth open, in the midst of an unfinished word. Madame Firmin scuttled to the kitchen door she had left unlocked on her return from the scullery, and locked it. She turned, and they stared at one another.

The heavy knocker fell again and again and again. Between the knocking there was a sound like the roaring of lions. Husband and wife stared at one another with white faces. Firmin picked up his gun with trembling hands, and the movement seemed to set his teeth chattering. They chattered like castanets.

The knocking still went on, and so did the roaring.

It had gone on at least for five minutes, when a slow gleam of comprehension lightened Madame Firmin's face.

"I believe it's the master's voice," she said.

"The master's voice!" said Firmin, in a hoarse, terrified whisper.

"Yes," said Madame Firmin. And she unlocked the thick door and opened it a few inches.

The barrier removed, the well-known bellow of the millionaire came distinctly to their ears. Firmin's courage rushed upon him in full flood. He clumped across the room, brushed his wife aside, and trotted to the door of the chateau. He unlocked it, drew the bolts, and threw it open. On the steps stood the millionaire, Germaine, and Sonia. Irma stood at the horse's head.

"What the devil have you been doing?" bellowed the millionaire. "What do you keep me standing in the rain for? Why didn't you let me in?"

"B-b-b-burglars—I thought you were b-b-b-burglars," stammered Firmin.

"Burglars!" howled the millionaire. "Do I sound like a burglar?"

At the moment he did not; he sounded more like a bull of Bashan. He bustled past Firmin to the door of the hall.

"Here! What's this locked for?" he bellowed.

"I—I—locked it in case burglars should get in while I was opening the front door," stammered Firmin.

The millionaire turned the key, opened the door, and went into the hall. Germaine followed him. She threw off her dripping coat, and said with some heat: "I can't conceive why you didn't make sure that there was a train at a quarter to nine. I will not go to Paris to-night. Nothing shall induce me to take that midnight train!"

"Nonsense!" said the millionaire. "Nonsense—you'll have to go! Where's that infernal time-table?" He rushed to the table on to which he had thrown the time-table after looking up the train, snatched it up, and looked at the cover. "Why, hang it!" he cried. "It's for June—June, 1903!"

"Oh!" cried Germaine, almost in a scream. "It's incredible! It's one of Jacques' jokes!"

8

THE DUKE ARRIVES

The morning was gloomy, and the police-station with its bare, white-washed walls—their white expanse was only broken by notice-boards to which were pinned portraits of criminals with details of their appearance, their crime, and the reward offered for their apprehension—with its shabby furniture, and its dingy fireplace, presented a dismal and sordid appearance entirely in keeping with the September grey. The inspector sat at his desk, yawning after a night which had passed without an arrest. He was waiting to be relieved. The policeman at the door and the two policemen sitting on a bench by the wall yawned in sympathy.

The silence of the street was broken by the rattle of an uncommonly noisy motor-car. It stopped before the door of the police-station, and the eyes of the inspector and his men turned, idly expectant, to the door of the office.

It opened, and a young man in motor-coat and cap stood on the threshold.

He looked round the office with alert eyes, which took in everything, and said, in a brisk, incisive voice: "I am the Duke of Charmerace. I am here on behalf of M. Gournay-Martin. Last evening he received a letter from Arsène Lupin saying he was going to break into his Paris house this very morning."

At the name of Arsène Lupin the inspector sprang from his chair, the policemen from their bench. On the instant they were wide awake, attentive, full of zeal.

"The letter, your Grace!" said the inspector briskly.

The Duke pulled off his glove, drew the letter from the breast-pocket of his under-coat, and handed it to the inspector.

The inspector glanced through it, and said. "Yes, I know the handwriting well." Then he read it carefully, and added, "Yes, yes: it's his usual letter."

"There's no time to be lost," said the Duke quickly. "I ought to have been here hours ago—hours. I had a break-down. I'm afraid I'm too late as it is."

"Come along, your Grace—come along, you," said the inspector briskly.

The four of them hurried out of the office and down the steps of the police-station. In the roadway stood a long grey racing-car, caked with muds—grey mud, brown mud, red mud—from end to end. It looked as if it had brought samples of the soil of France from many districts.

"Come along; I'll take you in the car. Your men can trot along beside us," said the Duke to the inspector.

He slipped into the car, the inspector jumped in and took the seat beside him, and they started. They went slowly, to allow the two policemen to keep up with them. Indeed, the car could not have made any great pace, for the tyre of the off hind-wheel was punctured and deflated.

In three minutes they came to the Gournay-Martin house, a wide-fronted mass of undistinguished masonry, in an undistinguished row of exactly the same pattern. There were no signs that any one was living in it. Blinds were drawn, shutters were up over all the windows, upper and lower. No smoke came from any of its chimneys, though indeed it was full early for that.

Pulling a bunch of keys from his pocket, the Duke ran up the steps. The inspector followed him. The Duke looked at the bunch, picked out the latch-key, and fitted it into the lock. It did not open it. He drew it out and tried another key and another. The door remained locked.

"Let me, your Grace," said the inspector. "I'm more used to it. I shall be quicker."

The Duke handed the keys to him, and, one after another, the inspector fitted them into the lock. It was useless. None of them opened the door.

"They've given me the wrong keys," said the Duke, with some vexation. "Or no—stay—I see what's happened. The keys have been changed."

"Changed?" said the inspector. "When? Where?"

"Last night at Charmerace," said the Duke. "M. Gournay-Martin declared that he saw a burglar slip out of one of the windows of the hall of the chateau, and we found the lock of the bureau in which the keys were kept broken."

The inspector seized the knocker, and hammered on the door.

"Try that door there," he cried to his men, pointing to a side-door on the right, the tradesmen's entrance, giving access to the back of the house. It was locked. There came no sound of movement in the house in answer to the inspector's knocking.

"Where's the concierge?" he said.

The Duke shrugged his shoulders. "There's a housekeeper, too—a woman named Victoire," he said. "Let's hope we don't find them with their throats cut."

"That isn't Lupin's way," said the inspector. "They won't have come to much harm."

"It's not very likely that they'll be in a position to open doors," said the Duke drily.

"Hadn't we better have it broken open and be done with it?"

The inspector hesitated.

"People don't like their doors broken open," he said. "And M. Gournay-Martin—"

"Oh, I'll take the responsibility of that," said the Duke.

"Oh, if you say so, your Grace," said the inspector, with a brisk relief. "Henri, go to Ragoneau, the locksmith in the Rue Theobald. Bring him here as quickly as ever you can get him."

"Tell him it's a couple of louis if he's here inside of ten minutes," said the Duke.

The policeman hurried off. The inspector bent down and searched the steps carefully. He searched the roadway. The Duke lighted a cigarette and watched him. The house of the millionaire stood next but one to the corner of a street which ran at right angles to the one in which it stood, and the corner house was empty. The inspector searched the road, then he went round the corner. The other policeman went along the road, searching in the opposite direction. The Duke leant against the door and smoked on patiently. He showed none of the weariness of a man who has spent the night in a long and anxious drive in a rickety motor-car. His eyes were bright and clear; he looked as fresh as if he had come from his bed after a long night's rest. If he had not found the South Pole, he had at any rate brought back fine powers of endurance from his expedition in search of it.

The inspector came back, wearing a disappointed air.

"Have you found anything?" said the Duke.

"Nothing," said the inspector.

He came up the steps and hammered again on the door. No one answered his knock. There was a clatter of footsteps, and Henri and the locksmith, a burly, bearded man, his bag of tools slung over his shoulder, came hurrying up. He was not long getting to work, but it was not an easy job. The lock was strong. At the end of five minutes he said that he might spend an hour struggling with the lock itself; should he cut away a piece of the door round it?

"Cut away," said the Duke.

The locksmith changed his tools, and in less than three minutes he had cut away a square piece from the door, a square in which the lock was fixed, and taken it bodily away.

The door opened. The inspector drew his revolver, and entered the house. The Duke followed him. The policemen drew their revolvers, and followed the Duke. The big hall was but dimly lighted. One of the policemen quickly threw back the shutters of the windows and let in the light. The hall was empty, the furniture in perfect order; there were no signs of burglary there.

"The concierge?" said the inspector, and his men hurried through the little door on the right which opened into the concierge's rooms. In half a minute one of them came out and said: "Gagged and bound, and his wife too."

"But the rooms which were to be plundered are upstairs," said the Duke—"the big drawing-rooms on the first floor. Come on; we may be just in time. The scoundrels may not yet have got away."

He ran quickly up the stairs, followed by the inspector, and hurried along the corridor to the door of the big drawing-room. He threw it open, and stopped dead on the threshold. He had arrived too late.

The room was in disorder. Chairs were overturned, there were empty spaces on the wall where the finest pictures of the millionaire had been hung. The window facing the door was wide open. The shutters were broken; one of them was hanging crookedly from only its bottom hinge. The top of a ladder rose above the window-sill, and beside it, astraddle the sill, was an Empire card-table, half inside the room, half out. On the hearth-rug, before a large tapestry fire-screen, which masked the wide fireplace, built in imitation of the big, wide fireplaces of our ancestors, and rose to the level of the chimney-piece—a magnificent chimney-piece in carved oak-were some chairs tied together ready to be removed.

The Duke and the inspector ran to the window, and looked down into the garden. It was empty. At the further end of it, on the other side of its wall, rose the scaffolding of a house a-building. The burglars had found every convenience to their hand—a strong ladder, an egress through the door in the garden wall, and then through the gap formed by the house in process of erection, which had rendered them independent of the narrow passage between the walls of the gardens, which debouched into a side-street on the right.

The Duke turned from the window, glanced at the wall opposite, then, as if something had caught his eye, went quickly to it.

"Look here," he said, and he pointed to the middle of one of the empty spaces in which a picture had hung.

There, written neatly in blue chalk, were the words:

ARSÈNE LUPIN

"This is a job for Guerchard," said the inspector. "But I had better get an examining magistrate to take the matter in hand first." And he ran to the telephone.

The Duke opened the folding doors which led into the second drawing-room. The shutters of the windows were open, and it was plain that Arsène Lupin had plundered it also of everything that had struck his fancy. In the gaps between the pictures on the walls was again the signature "Arsène Lupin."

The inspector was shouting impatiently into the telephone, bidding a servant wake her master instantly. He did not leave the telephone till he was sure that she had done so, that her master was actually awake, and had been informed of the crime. The Duke sat down in an easy chair and waited for him.

When he had finished telephoning, the inspector began to search the two rooms for traces of the burglars. He found nothing, not even a finger-mark.

When he had gone through the two rooms he said, "The next thing to do is to find the house-keeper. She may be sleeping still—she may not even have heard the noise of the burglars."

"I find all this extremely interesting," said the Duke; and he followed the inspector out of the room.

The inspector called up the two policemen, who had been freeing the concierge and going through the rooms on the ground-floor. They did not then examine any more of the rooms on the first floor to discover if they also had been plundered. They went straight up to the top of the house, the servants' quarters.

The inspector called, "Victoire! Victoire!" two or three times; but there was no answer.

They opened the door of room after room and looked in, the inspector taking the rooms on the right, the policemen the rooms on the left.

"Here we are," said one of the policemen. "This room's been recently occupied." They looked in, and saw that the bed was unmade. Plainly Victoire had slept in it.

"Where can she be?" said the Duke.

"Be?" said the inspector. "I expect she's with the burglars—an accomplice."

"I gather that M. Gournay-Martin had the greatest confidence in her," said the Duke.

"He'll have less now," said the inspector drily. "It's generally the confidential ones who let their masters down."

The inspector and his men set about a thorough search of the house. They found the other rooms undisturbed. In half an hour they had established the fact that the burglars had confined their attention to the two drawing-rooms. They found no traces of them; and they did not find Victoire. The concierge could throw no light on her disappearance. He and his wife had been taken by surprise in their sleep and in the dark.

They had been gagged and bound, they declared, without so much as having set eyes on their assailants. The Duke and the inspector came back to the plundered drawing-room.

The inspector looked at his watch and went to the telephone.

"I must let the Prefecture know," he said.

"Be sure you ask them to send Guerchard," said the Duke.

"Guerchard?" said the inspector doubtfully.

"M. Formery, the examining magistrate, does not get on very well with Guerchard."

"What sort of a man is M. Formery? Is he capable?" said the Duke.

"Oh, yes—yes. He's very capable," said the inspector quickly. "But he doesn't have very good luck."

"M. Gournay-Martin particularly asked me to send for Guerchard if I arrived too late, and found the burglary already committed," said the Duke. "It seems that there is war to the knife between Guerchard and this Arsène Lupin. In that case Guerchard will leave no stone unturned to catch the rascal and recover the stolen treasures. M. Gournay-Martin felt that Guerchard was the man for this piece of work very strongly indeed."

"Very good, your Grace," said the inspector. And he rang up the Prefecture of Police.

The Duke heard him report the crime and ask that Guerchard should be sent. The official in charge at the moment seemed to make some demur.

The Duke sprang to his feet, and said in an anxious tone, "Perhaps I'd better speak to him myself."

He took his place at the telephone and said, "I am the Duke of Charmerace. M. Gournay-Martin begged me to secure the services of M. Guerchard. He laid the greatest stress on my securing them, if on reaching Paris I found that the crime had already been committed."

The official at the other end of the line hesitated. He did not refuse on the instant as he had refused the inspector. It may be that he reflected that M. Gournay-Martin was a millionaire and a man of influence; that the Duke of Charmerace was a Duke; that he, at any rate, had nothing whatever to gain by running counter to their wishes. He said that Chief-Inspector Guerchard was not at the Prefecture, that he was off duty; that he would send down two detectives, who were on duty, at once, and summon Chief-Inspector Guerchard with all speed. The Duke thanked him and rang off.

"That's all right," he said cheerfully, turning to the inspector. "What time will M. Formery be here?"

"Well, I don't expect him for another hour," said the inspector. "He won't come till he's had his breakfast. He always makes a good breakfast before setting out to start an inquiry, lest he shouldn't find time to make one after he's begun it."

"Breakfast—breakfast—that's a great idea," said the Duke. "Now you come to remind me, I'm absolutely famished. I got some supper on my way late last night; but I've had nothing since. I suppose nothing interesting will happen till M. Formery comes; and I may as well get some food. But I don't want to leave the house. I think I'll see what the concierge can do for me."

So saying, he went downstairs and interviewed the concierge. The concierge seemed to be still doubtful whether he was standing on his head or his heels, but he undertook to supply the needs of the Duke. The Duke gave him a louis, and he hurried off to get food from a restaurant.

The Duke went upstairs to the bathroom and refreshed himself with a cold bath. By the time he had bathed and dressed the concierge had a meal ready for him in the dining-room. He ate it with the heartiest appetite. Then he sent out for a barber and was shaved.

He then repaired to the pillaged drawing-room, disposed himself in the most restful attitude on a sofa, and lighted an excellent cigar. In the middle of it the inspector came to him. He was not wearing a very cheerful air; and he told the Duke that he had found no clue to the perpetrators of the crime, though M. Dieusy and M. Bonavent, the detectives from the Prefecture of Police, had joined him in the search.

The Duke was condoling with him on this failure when they heard a knocking at the front door, and then voices on the stairs.

"Ah! Here is M. Formery!" said the inspector cheerfully. "Now we can get on."

9

M. FORMERY OPENS THE INQUIRY

The examining magistrate came into the room. He was a plump and pink little man, with very bright eyes. His bristly hair stood up straight all over his head, giving it the appearance of a broad, dapple-grey clothes-brush. He appeared to be of the opinion that Nature had given the world the toothbrush as a model of what a moustache should be; and his own was clipped to that pattern.

"The Duke of Charmerace, M. Formery," said the inspector.

The little man bowed and said, "Charmed, charmed to make your acquaintance, your Grace—though the occasion—the occasion is somewhat painful. The treasures of M. Gournay-Martin are known to all the world. France will deplore his losses." He paused, and added hastily, "But we shall recover them—we shall recover them."

The Duke rose, bowed, and protested his pleasure at making the acquaintance of M. Formery.

"Is this the scene of the robbery, inspector?" said M. Formery; and he rubbed his hands together with a very cheerful air.

"Yes, sir," said the inspector. "These two rooms seem to be the only ones touched, though of course we can't tell till M. Gournay-Martin arrives. Jewels may have been stolen from the bedrooms."

"I fear that M. Gournay-Martin won't be of much help for some days," said the Duke. "When I left him he was nearly distracted; and he won't be any better after a night journey to Paris from Charmerace. But probably these are the only two rooms touched, for in them M. Gournay-Martin had gathered together the gems of his collection. Over the doors hung some pieces of Flemish tapestry—marvels—the composition admirable—the colouring delightful."

"It is easy to see that your Grace was very fond of them," said M. Formery.

"I should think so," said the Duke. "I looked on them as already belonging to me, for my father-in-law was going to give them to me as a wedding present."

"A great loss—a great loss. But we will recover them, sooner or later, you can rest assured of it. I hope you have touched nothing in this room. If anything has been moved it may put me off the scent altogether. Let me have the details, inspector."

The inspector reported the arrival of the Duke at the police-station with Arsène Lupin's letter to M. Gournay-Martin; the discovery that the keys had been changed and would not open the door of the house; the opening of it by the locksmith; the discovery of the concierge and his wife gagged and bound.

"Probably accomplices," said M. Formery.

"Does Lupin always work with accomplices?" said the Duke. "Pardon my ignorance—but I've been out of France for so long—before he attained to this height of notoriety."

"Lupin—why Lupin?" said M. Formery sharply.

"Why, there is the letter from Lupin which my future father-in-law received last night; its arrival was followed by the theft of his two swiftest motor-cars; and then, these signatures on the wall here," said the Duke in some surprise at the question.

"Lupin! Lupin! Everybody has Lupin on the brain!" said M. Formery impatiently. "I'm sick of hearing his name. This letter and these signatures are just as likely to be forgeries as not."

"I wonder if Guerchard will take that view," said the Duke.

"Guerchard? Surely we're not going to be cluttered up with Guerchard. He has Lupin on the brain worse than any one else."

"But M. Gournay-Martin particularly asked me to send for Guerchard if I arrived too late to prevent the burglary. He would never forgive me if I had neglected his request: so I telephoned for him—to the Prefecture of Police," said the Duke.

"Oh, well, if you've already telephoned for him. But it was unnecessary—absolutely unnecessary," said M. Formery sharply.

"I didn't know," said the Duke politely.

"Oh, there was no harm in it—it doesn't matter," said M. Formery in a discontented tone with a discontented air.

He walked slowly round the room, paused by the windows, looked at the ladder, and scanned the garden:

"Arsène Lupin," he said scornfully. "Arsène Lupin doesn't leave traces all over the place. There's nothing but traces. Are we going to have that silly Lupin joke all over again?"

"I think, sir, that this time joke is the word, for this is a burglary pure and simple," said the inspector.

"Yes, it's plain as daylight," said M. Formery "The burglars came in by this window, and they went out by it."

He crossed the room to a tall safe which stood before the unused door. The safe was covered with velvet, and velvet curtains hung before its door. He drew the curtains, and tried the handle of the door of the safe. It did not turn; the safe was locked.

"As far as I can see, they haven't touched this," said M. Formery.

"Thank goodness for that," said the Duke. "I believe, or at least my fiancee does, that M. Gournay-Martin keeps the most precious thing in his collection in that safe—the coronet."

"What! The famous coronet of the Princesse de Lamballe?" said M. Formery.

"Yes," said the Duke.

"But according to your report, inspector, the letter signed 'Lupin' announced that he was going to steal the coronet also."

"It did—in so many words," said the Duke.

"Well, here is a further proof that we're not dealing with Lupin. That rascal would certainly have put his threat into execution, M. Formery," said the inspector.

"Who's in charge of the house?" said M. Formery.

"The concierge, his wife, and a housekeeper—a woman named Victoire," said the inspector.

"I'll see to the concierge and his wife presently. I've sent one of your men round for their dossier. When I get it I'll question them. You found them gagged and bound in their bedroom?"

"Yes, M. Formery; and always this imitation of Lupin—a yellow gag, blue cords, and the motto, 'I take, therefore I am,' on a scrap of cardboard—his usual bag of tricks."

"Then once again they're going to touch us up in the papers. It's any odds on it," said M. Formery gloomily. "Where's the housekeeper? I should like to see her."

"The fact is, we don't know where she is," said the inspector.

"You don't know where she is?" said M. Formery.

"We can't find her anywhere," said the inspector.

"That's excellent, excellent. We've found the accomplice," said M. Formery with lively delight; and he rubbed his hands together. "At least, we haven't found her, but we know her."

"I don't think that's the case," said the Duke. "At least, my future father-in-law and my fiancee had both of them the greatest confidence in her. Yesterday she telephoned to us at the Chateau de Charmerace. All the jewels were left in her charge, and the wedding presents as they were sent in."

"And these jewels and wedding presents—have they been stolen too?" said M. Formery.

"They don't seem to have been touched," said the Duke, "though of course we can't tell till M. Gournay-Martin arrives.

As far as I can see, the burglars have only touched these two drawing-rooms."

"That's very annoying," said M. Formery.

"I don't find it so," said the Duke, smiling.

"I was looking at it from the professional point of view," said M. Formery. He turned to the inspector and added, "You can't have searched thoroughly. This housekeeper must be somewhere about—if she's really trustworthy. Have you looked in every room in the house?"

"In every room—under every bed—in every corner and every cupboard," said the inspector.

"Bother!" said M. Formery. "Are there no scraps of torn clothes, no blood-stains, no traces of murder, nothing of interest?"

"Nothing!" said the inspector.

"But this is very regrettable," said M. Formery. "Where did she sleep? Was her bed unmade?"

"Her room is at the top of the house," said the inspector. "The bed had been slept in, but she does not appear to have taken away any of her clothes."

"Extraordinary! This is beginning to look a very complicated business," said M. Formery gravely.

"Perhaps Guerchard will be able to throw a little more light on it," said the Duke.

M. Formery frowned and said, "Yes, yes. Guerchard is a good assistant in a business like this. A little visionary, a little fanciful—wrong-headed, in fact; but, after all, he IS Guerchard. Only, since Lupin is his bugbear, he's bound to find some means of muddling us up with that wretched animal. You're going to see Lupin mixed up with all this to a dead certainty, your Grace."

The Duke looked at the signatures on the wall. "It seems to me that he is pretty well mixed up with it already," he said quietly.

"Believe me, your Grace, in a criminal affair it is, above all things, necessary to distrust appearances. I am growing more and more confident that some ordinary burglars have committed this crime and are trying to put us off the scent by diverting our attention to Lupin."

The Duke stooped down carelessly and picked up a book which had fallen from a table.

"Excuse me, but please—please—do not touch anything," said M. Formery quickly.

"Why, this is odd," said the Duke, staring at the floor.

"What is odd?" said M. Formery.

"Well, this book looks as if it had been knocked off the table by one of the burglars. And look here; here's a footprint under it—a footprint on the carpet," said the Duke.

M. Formery and the inspector came quickly to the spot. There, where the book had fallen, plainly imprinted on the carpet, was a white footprint. M. Formery and the inspector stared at it.

"It looks like plaster. How did plaster get here?" said M. Formery, frowning at it.

"Well, suppose the robbers came from the garden," said the Duke.

"Of course they came from the garden, your Grace. Where else should they come from?" said M. Formery, with a touch of impatience in his tone.

"Well, at the end of the garden they're building a house," said the Duke.

"Of course, of course," said M. Formery, taking him up quickly. "The burglars came here with their boots covered with plaster. They've swept away all the other marks of their feet from the carpet; but whoever did the sweeping was too slack to lift up that book and sweep under it. This footprint, however, is not of great importance, though it is corroborative of all the other evidence we have that they came and went by the garden.

There's the ladder, and that table half out of the window. Still, this footprint may turn out useful, after all. You had better take the measurements of it, inspector. Here's a foot-rule for you. I make a point of carrying this foot-rule about with me, your Grace. You would be surprised to learn how often it has come in useful."

He took a little ivory foot-rule from his waist-coat pocket, and gave it to the inspector, who fell on his knees and measured the footprint with the greatest care.

"I must take a careful look at that house they're building. I shall find a good many traces there, to a dead certainty," said M. Formery.

The inspector entered the measurements of the footprint in his note-book. There came the sound of a knocking at the front door.

"I shall find footprints of exactly the same dimensions as this one at the foot of some heap of plaster beside that house," said M. Formery; with an air of profound conviction, pointing through the window to the house building beyond the garden.

A policeman opened the door of the drawing-room and saluted.

"If you please, sir, the servants have arrived from Charmerace," he said.

"Let them wait in the kitchen and the servants' offices," said M. Formery. He stood silent, buried in profound meditation, for a couple of minutes. Then he turned to the Duke and said, "What was that you said about a theft of motor-cars at Charmerace?"

"When he received the letter from Arsène Lupin, M. Gournay-Martin decided to start for Paris at once," said the Duke. "But when we sent for the cars we found that they had just been stolen. M. Gournay-Martin's chauffeur and another servant were in the garage gagged and bound. Only an old car, a hundred horse-power Mercrac, was left. I drove it to Paris, leaving M. Gournay-Martin and his family to come on by train."

"Very important—very important indeed," said M. Formery. He thought for a moment, and then added. "Were the motor-cars the only things stolen? Were there no other thefts?"

"Well, as a matter of fact, there was another theft, or rather an attempt at theft," said the Duke with some hesitation. "The rogues who stole the motor-cars presented themselves at the chateau under the name of Charolais—a father and three sons—on the pretext of buying the hundred-horse-power Mercrac. M. Gournay-Martin had advertised it for sale in the Rennes Advertiser. They were waiting in the big hall of the chateau, which the family uses as the chief living-room, for the return of M. Gournay-Martin. He came; and as they left the hall one of them attempted to steal a pendant set with pearls which I had given to Mademoiselle Gournay-Martin half an hour before. I caught him in the act and saved the pendant."

"Good! Good! Wait—we have one of the gang—wait till I question him," said M. Formery, rubbing his hands; and his eyes sparkled with joy.

"Well, no; I'm afraid we haven't," said the Duke in an apologetic tone.

"What! We haven't? Has he escaped from the police? Oh, those country police!" cried M. Formery.

"No; I didn't charge him with the theft," said the Duke.

"You didn't charge him with the theft?" cried M. Formery, astounded.

"No; he was very young and he begged so hard. I had the pendant. I let him go," said the Duke.

"Oh, your Grace, your Grace! Your duty to society!" cried M. Formery.

"Yes, it does seem to have been rather weak," said the Duke; "but there you are. It's no good crying over spilt milk."

M. Formery folded his arms and walked, frowning, backwards and forwards across the room.

He stopped, raised his hand with a gesture commanding attention, and said, "I have no hesitation in saying that there is a connection—an intimate connection—between the thefts at Charmerace and this burglary!"

The Duke and the inspector gazed at him with respectful eyes—at least, the eyes of the inspector were respectful; the Duke's eyes twinkled.

"I am gathering up the threads," said M. Formery. "Inspector, bring up the concierge and his wife. I will question them on the scene of the crime. Their dossier should be here. If it is, bring it up with them; if not, no matter; bring them up without it."

The inspector left the drawing-room. M. Formery plunged at once into frowning meditation.

"I find all this extremely interesting," said the Duke.

"Charmed! Charmed!" said M. Formery, waving his hand with an absent-minded air.

The inspector entered the drawing-room followed by the concierge and his wife. He handed a paper to M. Formery. The concierge, a bearded man of about sixty, and his wife, a somewhat bearded woman of about fifty-five, stared at M. Formery with fascinated, terrified eyes. He sat down in a chair, crossed his legs, read the paper through, and then scrutinized them keenly.

"Well, have you recovered from your adventure?" he said.

"Oh, yes, sir," said the concierge. "They hustled us a bit, but they did not really hurt us."

"Nothing to speak of, that is," said his wife. "But all the same, it's a disgraceful thing that an honest woman can't sleep in peace in her bed of a night without being disturbed by rascals like that. And if the police did their duty things like this wouldn't happen. And I don't care who hears me say it."

"You say that you were taken by surprise in your sleep?" said M. Formery. "You say you saw nothing, and heard nothing?"

"There was no time to see anything or hear anything. They trussed us up like greased lightning," said the concierge.

"But the gag was the worst," said the wife. "To lie there and not be able to tell the rascals what I thought about them!"

"Didn't you hear the noise of footsteps in the garden?" said M. Formery.

"One can't hear anything that happens in the garden from our bedroom," said the concierge.

"Even the night when Mlle. Germaine's great Dane barked from twelve o'clock till seven in the morning, all the household was kept awake except us; but bless you, sir, we slept like tops," said his wife proudly.

"If they sleep like that it seems rather a waste of time to have gagged them," whispered the Duke to the inspector.

The inspector grinned, and whispered scornfully, "Oh, them common folks; they do sleep like that, your Grace."

"Didn't you hear any noise at the front door?" said M. Formery.

"No, we heard no noise at the door," said the concierge.

"Then you heard no noise at all the whole night?" said M. Formery.

"Oh, yes, sir, we heard noise enough after we'd been gagged," said the concierge.

"Now, this is important," said M. Formery. "What kind of a noise was it?"

"Well, it was a bumping kind of noise," said the concierge. "And there was a noise of footsteps, walking about the room."

"What room? Where did these noises come from?" said M. Formery.

"From the room over our heads—the big drawing-room," said the concierge.

"Didn't you hear any noise of a struggle, as if somebody was being dragged about—no screaming or crying?" said M. Formery.

The concierge and his wife looked at one another with inquiring eyes.

"No, I didn't," said the concierge.

"Neither did I," said his wife.

M. Formery paused. Then he said, "How long have you been in the service of M. Gournay-Martin?"

"A little more than a year," said the concierge.

M. Formery looked at the paper in his hand, frowned, and said severely, "I see you've been convicted twice, my man."

"Yes, sir, but—"

"My husband's an honest man, sir—perfectly honest," broke in his wife. "You've only to ask M. Gournay-Martin; he'll—"

"Be so good as to keep quiet, my good woman," said M. Formery; and, turning to her husband, he went on: "At your first conviction you were sentenced to a day's imprisonment with costs; at your second conviction you got three days' imprisonment."

"I'm not going to deny it, sir," said the concierge; "but it was an honourable imprisonment."

"Honourable?" said M. Formery.

"The first time, I was a gentleman's servant, and I got a day's imprisonment for crying, 'Hurrah for the General Strike!'—on the first of May."

"You were a valet? In whose service?" said M. Formery.

"In the service of M. Genlis, the Socialist leader."

"And your second conviction?" said M. Formery.

"It was for having cried in the porch of Ste. Clotilde, 'Down with the cows!'—meaning the police, sir," said the concierge.

"And were you in the service of M. Genlis then?" said M. Formery.

"No, sir; I was in the service of M. Bussy-Rabutin, the Royalist deputy."

"You don't seem to have very well-defined political convictions," said M. Formery.

"Oh, yes, sir, I have," the concierge protested. "I'm always devoted to my masters; and I have the same opinions that they have—always."

"Very good; you can go," said M. Formery.

The concierge and his wife left the room, looking as if they did not quite know whether to feel relieved or not.

"Those two fools are telling the exact truth, unless I'm very much mistaken," said M. Formery.

"They look honest enough people," said the Duke.

"Well, now to examine the rest of the house," said M. Formery.

"I'll come with you, if I may," said the Duke.

"By all means, by all means," said M. Formery.

"I find it all so interesting," said the Duke.

10

GUERCHARD ASSISTS

Leaving a policeman on guard at the door of the drawing-room M. Formery, the Duke, and the inspector set out on their tour of inspection. It was a long business, for M. Formery examined every room with the most scrupulous care—with more care, indeed, than he had displayed in his examination of the drawing-rooms. In particular he lingered long in the bedroom of Victoire, discussing the possibilities of her having been murdered and carried away by the burglars along with their booty. He seemed, if anything, disappointed at finding no blood-stains, but to find real consolation in the thought that she might have been strangled. He found the inspector in entire agreement with every theory he enunciated, and he grew more and more disposed to regard him as a zealous and trustworthy officer. Also he was not at all displeased at enjoying this opportunity of impressing the Duke with his powers of analysis and synthesis. He was unaware that, as a rule, the Duke's eyes did not usually twinkle as they twinkled during this solemn and deliberate progress through the house of M. Gournay-Martin. M. Formery had so exactly the air of a sleuthhound; and he was even noisier.

Having made this thorough examination of the house, M. Formery went out into the garden and set about examining that. There were footprints on the turf about the foot of the ladder, for the grass was close-clipped, and the rain had penetrated and softened the soil; but there were hardly as many footprints as might have been expected, seeing that the burglars must have made many journeys in the course of robbing the drawing-rooms of so many objects of art, some of them of considerable weight. The footprints led to a path of hard gravel; and M. Formery led the way down it, out of the door in the wall at the bottom of the garden, and into the space round the house which was being built.

As M. Formery had divined, there was a heap, or, to be exact, there were several heaps of plaster about the bottom of the scaffolding. Unfortunately, there were also hundreds of footprints. M. Formery looked at them with longing eyes; but he did not suggest that the inspector should hunt about for a set of footprints of the size of the one he had so carefully measured on the drawing-room carpet.

While they were examining the ground round the half-built house a man came briskly down the stairs from the second floor of the house of M. Gournay-Martin. He was an ordinary-looking man, almost insignificant, of between forty and fifty, and of rather more than middle height. He had an ordinary, rather shapeless mouth, an ordinary nose, an ordinary chin, an ordinary forehead, rather low, and ordinary ears. He was wearing an ordinary top-hat, by no means new. His clothes were the ordinary clothes of a fairly well-to-do citizen; and his boots had been chosen less to set off any slenderness his feet might possess than for their comfortable roominess. Only his eyes relieved his face from insignificance. They were extraordinarily alert eyes, producing in those on whom they rested the somewhat uncomfortable impression that the depths of their souls were being penetrated. He was the famous Chief-Inspector Guerchard, head of the Detective Department of the Prefecture of Police, and sworn foe of Arsène Lupin.

The policeman at the door of the drawing-room saluted him briskly. He was a fine, upstanding, red-faced young fellow, adorned by a rich black moustache of extraordinary fierceness.

"Shall I go and inform M. Formery that you have come, M. Guerchard?" he said.

"No, no; there's no need to take the trouble," said Guerchard in a gentle, rather husky voice. "Don't bother any one about me—I'm of no importance."

"Oh, come, M. Guerchard," protested the policeman.

"Of no importance," said M. Guerchard decisively. "For the present, M. Formery is everything. I'm only an assistant."

He stepped into the drawing-room and stood looking about it, curiously still. It was almost as if the whole of his being was concentrated in the act of seeing—as if all the other functions of his mind and body were in suspension.

"M. Formery and the inspector have just been up to examine the housekeeper's room. It's right at the top of the house—on the second floor. You take the servants' staircase. Then it's right at the end of the passage on the left. Would you like me to take you up to it, sir?" said the policeman eagerly. His heart was in his work.

"Thank you, I know where it is—I've just come from it," said Guerchard gently.

A grin of admiration widened the already wide mouth of the policeman, and showed a row of very white, able-looking teeth.

"Ah, M. Guerchard!" he said, "You're cleverer than all the examining magistrates in Paris put together!"

"You ought not to say that, my good fellow. I can't prevent you thinking it, of course; but you ought not to say it," said Guerchard with husky gentleness; and the faintest smile played round the corners of his mouth.

He walked slowly to the window, and the policeman walked with him.

"Have you noticed this, sir?" said the policeman, taking hold of the top of the ladder with a powerful hand. "It's probable that the burglars came in and went away by this ladder."

"Thank you," said Guerchard.

"They have even left this card-table on the window-sill," said the policeman; and he patted the card-table with his other powerful hand.

"Thank you, thank you," said Guerchard.

"They don't think it's Lupin's work at all," said the policeman. "They think that Lupin's letter announcing the burglary and these signatures on the walls are only a ruse."

"Is that so?" said Guerchard.

"Is there any way I can help you, sir?" said policeman.

"Yes," said Guerchard. "Take up your post outside that door and admit no one but M. Formery, the inspector, Bonavent, or Dieusy, without consulting me." And he pointed to the drawing-room door.

"Shan't I admit the Duke of Charmerace? He's taking a great interest in this affair," said the policeman.

"The Duke of Charmerace? Oh, yes—admit the Duke of Charmerace," said Guerchard.

The policeman went to his post of responsibility, a proud man.

Hardly had the door closed behind him when Guerchard was all activity—activity and eyes. He examined the ladder, the gaps on the wall from which the pictures had been taken, the signatures of Arsène Lupin. The very next thing he did was to pick up the book which the Duke had set on the top of the footprint again, to preserve it; and he measured, pacing it, the distance between the footprint and the window.

The result of this measuring did not appear to cause him any satisfaction, for he frowned, measured the distance again, and then stared out of the window with a perplexed air, thinking hard. It was curious that, when he concentrated himself on a process of reasoning, his eves seemed to lose something of their sharp brightness and grew a little dim.

At last he seemed to come to some conclusion. He turned away from the window, drew a small magnifying-glass from his pocket, dropped on his hands and knees, and began to examine the surface of the carpet with the most minute care.

He examined a space of it nearly six feet square, stopped, and gazed round the room. His eyes rested on the fireplace, which he could see under the bottom of the big tapestried fire-screen which was raised on legs about a foot high, fitted with big casters. His eyes filled with interest; without rising, he crawled quickly across the room, peeped round the edge of the screen and rose, smiling.

He went on to the further drawing-room and made the same careful examination of it, again examining a part of the surface of the carpet with his magnifying-glass. He came back to the window to which the ladder had been raised and examined very carefully the broken shutter. He whistled softly to himself, lighted a cigarette, and leant against the side of the window. He looked out of it, with dull eyes which saw nothing, the while his mind worked upon the facts he had discovered.

He had stood there plunged in reflection for perhaps ten minutes, when there came a sound of voices and footsteps on the stairs. He awoke from his absorption, seemed to prick his ears, then slipped a leg over the window-ledge, and disappeared from sight down the ladder.

The door opened, and in came M. Formery, the Duke, and the inspector. M. Formery looked round the room with eyes which seemed to expect to meet a familiar sight, then walked to the other drawing-room and looked round that. He turned to the policeman, who had stepped inside the drawing-room, and said sharply, "M. Guerchard is not here."

"I left him here," said the policeman. "He must have disappeared. He's a wonder."

"Of course," said M. Formery. "He has gone down the ladder to examine that house they're building. He's just following in our tracks and doing all over again the work we've already done. He might have saved himself the trouble. We could have told him all he wants to know. But there! He very likely would not be satisfied till he had seen everything for himself."

"He may see something which we have missed," said the Duke.

M. Formery frowned, and said sharply "That's hardly likely. I don't think that your Grace realizes to what a perfection constant practice brings one's power of observation. The inspector and I will cheerfully eat anything we've missed—won't we, inspector?" And he laughed heartily at his joke.

"It might always prove a large mouthful," said the Duke with an ironical smile.

M. Formery assumed his air of profound reflection, and walked a few steps up and down the room, frowning:

"The more I think about it," he said, "the clearer it grows that we have disposed of the Lupin theory. This is the work of far less expert rogues than Lupin. What do you think, inspector?"

"Yes; I think you have disposed of that theory, sir," said the inspector with ready acquiescence.

"All the same, I'd wager anything that we haven't disposed of it to the satisfaction of Guerchard," said M. Formery.

"Then he must be very hard to satisfy," said the Duke.

"Oh, in any other matter he's open to reason," said M. Formery; "but Lupin is his fixed idea; it's an obsession—almost a mania."

"But yet he never catches him," said the Duke.

"No; and he never will. His very obsession by Lupin hampers him. It cramps his mind and hinders its working," said M. Formery.

He resumed his meditative pacing, stopped again, and said:

"But considering everything, especially the absence of any traces of violence, combined with her entire disappearance, I have come to another conclusion. Victoire is the key to the mystery. She is the accomplice. She never slept in her bed. She unmade it to put us off the scent. That, at any rate, is something gained, to have found the accomplice. We shall have this good news, at least, to tell M. Gournay-Martin on his arrival."

"Do you really think that she's the accomplice?" said the Duke.

"I'm dead sure of it," said M. Formery. "We will go up to her room and make another thorough examination of it."

Guerchard's head popped up above the window-sill:

"My dear M. Formery," he said, "I beg that you will not take the trouble."

M. Formery's mouth opened: "What! You, Guerchard?" he stammered.

"Myself," said Guerchard; and he came to the top of the ladder and slipped lightly over the window-sill into the room.

He shook hands with M. Formery and nodded to the inspector. Then he looked at the Duke with an air of inquiry.

"Let me introduce you," said M. Formery. "Chief-Inspector Guerchard, head of the Detective Department—the Duke of Charmerace."

The Duke shook hands with Guerchard, saying, "I'm delighted to make your acquaintance, M. Guerchard. I've been expecting your coming with the greatest interest. Indeed it was I who begged the officials at the Prefecture of Police to put this case in your hands. I insisted on it."

"What were you doing on that ladder?" said M. Formery, giving Guerchard no time to reply to the Duke.

"I was listening," said Guerchard simply—"listening. I like to hear people talk when I'm engaged on a case. It's a distraction—and it helps. I really must congratulate you, my dear M. Formery, on the admirable manner in which you have conducted this inquiry."

M. Formery bowed, and regarded him with a touch of suspicion.

"There are one or two minor points on which we do not agree, but on the whole your method has been admirable," said Guerchard.

"Well, about Victoire," said M. Formery. "You're quite sure that an examination, a more thorough examination, of her room, is unnecessary?"

"Yes, I think so," said Guerchard. "I have just looked at it myself."

The door opened, and in came Bonavent, one of the detectives who had come earlier from the Prefecture. In his hand he carried a scrap of cloth.

He saluted Guerchard, and said to M. Formery, "I have just found this scrap of cloth on the edge of the well at the bottom of the garden. The concierge's wife tells me that it has been torn from Victoire's dress."

"I feared it," said M. Formery, taking the scrap of cloth from him. "I feared foul play. We must go to the well at once, send some one down it, or have it dragged."

He was moving hastily to the door, when Guerchard said, in his husky, gentle voice, "I don't think there is any need to look for Victoire in the well."

"But this scrap of cloth," said M. Formery, holding it out to him.

"Yes, yes, that scrap of cloth," said Guerchard. And, turning to the Duke, he added, "Do you know if there's a dog or cat in the house, your Grace? I suppose that, as the fiance of Mademoiselle Gournay-Martin, you are familiar with the house?"

"What on earth—" said M. Formery.

"Excuse me," interrupted Guerchard. "But this is important—very important."

"Yes, there is a cat," said the Duke. "I've seen a cat at the door of the concierge's rooms."

"It must have been that cat which took this scrap of cloth to the edge of the well," said Guerchard gravely.

"This is ridiculous—preposterous!" cried M. Formery, beginning to flush. "Here we're dealing with a most serious crime—a murder—the murder of Victoire—and you talk about cats!"

"Victoire has not been murdered," said Guerchard; and his husky voice was gentler than ever, only just audible.

"But we don't know that—we know nothing of the kind," said M. Formery.

"I do," said Guerchard.

"You?" said M. Formery.

"Yes," said Guerchard.

"Then how do you explain her disappearance?"

"If she had disappeared I shouldn't explain it," said Guerchard.

"But since she has disappeared?" cried M. Formery, in a tone of exasperation.

"She hasn't," said Guerchard.

"You know nothing about it!" cried M. Formery, losing his temper.

"Yes, I do," said Guerchard, with the same gentleness.

"Come, do you mean to say that you know where she is?" cried M. Formery.

"Certainly," said Guerchard.

"Do you mean to tell us straight out that you've seen her?" cried M. Formery.

"Oh, yes; I've seen her," said Guerchard.

"You've seen her—when?" cried M. Formery.

Guerchard paused to consider. Then he said gently:

"It must have been between four and five minutes ago."

"But hang it all, you haven't been out of this room!" cried M. Formery.

"No, I haven't," said Guerchard.

"And you've seen her?" cried M. Formery.

"Yes," said Guerchard, raising his voice a little.

"Well, why the devil don't you tell us where she is? Tell us!" cried M. Formery, purple with exasperation.

"But you won't let me get a word out of my mouth," protested Guerchard with aggravating gentleness.

"Well, speak!" cried M. Formery; and he sank gasping on to a chair.

"Ah, well, she's here," said Guerchard.

"Here! How did she GET here?" said M. Formery.

"On a mattress," said Guerchard.

M. Formery sat upright, almost beside himself, glaring furiously at Guerchard:

"What do you stand there pulling all our legs for?" he almost howled.

"Look here," said Guerchard.

He walked across the room to the fireplace, pushed the chairs which stood bound together on the hearth-rug to one side of the fireplace, and ran the heavy fire-screen on its casters to the other side of it, revealing to their gaze the wide, old-fashioned fireplace itself. The iron brazier which held the coals had been moved into the corner, and a mattress lay on the floor of the fireplace. On the mattress lay the figure of a big, middle-aged woman, half-dressed. There was a yellow gag in her mouth; and her hands and feet were bound together with blue cords.

"She is sleeping soundly," said Guerchard. He stooped and picked up a handkerchief, and smelt it. "There's the handkerchief they chloroformed her with. It still smells of chloroform."

They stared at him and the sleeping woman.

"Lend a hand, inspector," he said. "And you too, Bonavent. She looks a good weight."

The three of them raised the mattress, and carried it and the sleeping woman to a broad couch, and laid them on it. They staggered under their burden, for truly Victoire was a good weight.

M. Formery rose, with recovered breath, but with his face an even richer purple. His eyes were rolling in his head, as if they were not under proper control.

He turned on the inspector and cried savagely, "You never examined the fireplace, inspector!"

"No, sir," said the downcast inspector.

"It was unpardonable—absolutely unpardonable!" cried M. Formery. "How is one to work with subordinates like this?"

"It was an oversight," said Guerchard.

M. Formery turned to him and said, "You must admit that it was materially impossible for me to see her."

"It was possible if you went down on all fours," said Guerchard.

"On all fours?" said M. Formery.

"Yes; on all fours you could see her heels sticking out beyond the mattress," said Guerchard simply.

M. Formery shrugged his shoulders: "That screen looked as if it had stood there since the beginning of the summer," he said.

"The first thing, when you're dealing with Lupin, is to distrust appearances," said Guerchard.

"Lupin!" cried M. Formery hotly. Then he bit his lip and was silent.

He walked to the side of the couch and looked down on the sleeping Victoire, frowning: "This upsets everything," he said. "With these new conditions, I've got to begin all over again, to find a new explanation of the affair. For the moment—for the moment, I'm thrown completely off the track. And you, Guerchard?"

"Oh, well," said Guerchard, "I have an idea or two about the matter still."

"Do you really mean to say that it hasn't thrown you off the track too?" said M. Formery, with a touch of incredulity in his tone.

"Well, no—not exactly," said Guerchard. "I wasn't on that track, you see."

"No, of course not—of course not. You were on the track of Lupin," said M. Formery; and his contemptuous smile was tinged with malice.

The Duke looked from one to the other of them with curious, searching eyes: "I find all this so interesting," he said.

"We do not take much notice of these checks; they do not depress us for a moment," said M. Formery, with some return of his old grandiloquence. "We pause hardly for an instant; then we begin to reconstruct—to reconstruct."

"It's perfectly splendid of you," said the Duke, and his limpid eyes rested on M. Formery's self-satisfied face in a really affectionate gaze; they might almost be said to caress it.

Guerchard looked out of the window at a man who was carrying a hod-full of bricks up one of the ladders set against the scaffolding of the building house. Something in this honest workman's simple task seemed to amuse him, for he smiled.

Only the inspector, thinking of the unexamined fireplace, looked really depressed.

"We shan't get anything out of this woman till she wakes," said M. Formery, "When she does, I shall question her closely and fully. In the meantime, she may as well be carried up to her bedroom to sleep off the effects of the chloroform."

Guerchard turned quickly: "Not her own bedroom, I think," he said gently.

"Certainly not—of course, not her own bedroom," said M. Formery quickly.

"And I think an officer at the door of whatever bedroom she does sleep in," said Guerchard.

"Undoubtedly—most necessary," said M. Formery gravely. "See to it, inspector. You can take her away."

The inspector called in a couple of policemen, and with their aid he and Bonavent raised the sleeping woman, a man at each corner of the mattress, and bore her from the room.

"And now to reconstruct," said M. Formery; and he folded his arms and plunged into profound reflection.

The Duke and Guerchard watched him in silence.

11

THE FAMILY ARRIVES

In carrying out Victoire, the inspector had left the door of the drawing-room open. After he had watched M. Formery reflect for two minutes, Guerchard faded—to use an expressive Americanism—through it. The Duke felt in the breast-pocket of his coat, murmured softly, "My cigarettes," and followed him.

He caught up Guerchard on the stairs and said, "I will come with you, if I may, M. Guerchard. I find all these investigations extraordinarily interesting. I have been observing M. Formery's methods—I should like to watch yours, for a change."

"By all means," said Guerchard. "And there are several things I want to hear about from your Grace. Of course it might be an advantage to discuss them together with M. Formery, but—" and he hesitated.

"It would be a pity to disturb M. Formery in the middle of the process of reconstruction," said the Duke; and a faint, ironical smile played round the corners of his sensitive lips.

Guerchard looked at him quickly: "Perhaps it would," he said.

They went through the house, out of the back door, and into the garden. Guerchard moved about twenty yards from the house, then he stopped and questioned the Duke at great length. He questioned him first about the Charolais, their appearance, their actions, especially about Bernard's attempt to steal the pendant, and the theft of the motor-cars.

"I have been wondering whether M. Charolais might not have been Arsène Lupin himself," said the Duke.

"It's quite possible," said Guerchard. "There seem to be no limits whatever to Lupin's powers of disguising himself. My colleague, Ganimard, has come across him at least three times that he knows of, as a different person. And no single time could he be sure that it was the same man. Of course, he had a feeling that he was in contact with some one he had met before, but that was all. He had no certainty. He may have met him half a dozen times besides without knowing him. And the photographs of him—they're all different. Ganimard declares that Lupin is so extraordinarily successful in his disguises because he is a great actor. He actually becomes for the time being the person he pretends to be. He thinks and feels absolutely like that person. Do you follow me?"

"Oh, yes; but he must be rather fluid, this Lupin," said the Duke; and then he added thoughtfully, "It must be awfully risky to come so often into actual contact with men like Ganimard and you."

"Lupin has never let any consideration of danger prevent him doing anything that caught his fancy. He has odd fancies, too. He's a humourist of the most varied kind—grim, ironic, farcical, as the mood takes him. He must be awfully trying to live with," said Guerchard.

"Do you think humourists are trying to live with?" said the Duke, in a meditative tone. "I think they brighten life a good deal; but of course there are people who do not like them—the middle-classes."

"Yes, yes, they're all very well in their place; but to live with they must be trying," said Guerchard quickly.

He went on to question the Duke closely and at length about the household of M. Gournay-Martin, saying that Arsène Lupin worked with the largest gang a burglar had ever captained, and it was any odds that he had introduced one, if not more, of that gang into it. Moreover, in the case of a big affair like this, Lupin himself often played two or three parts under as many disguises.

"If he was Charolais, I don't see how he could be one of M. Gournay-Martin's household, too," said the Duke in some perplexity.

"I don't say that he WAS Charolais," said Guerchard. "It is quite a moot point. On the whole, I'm inclined to think that he was not. The theft of the motor-cars was a job for a subordinate. He would hardly bother himself with it."

The Duke told him all that he could remember about the millionaire's servants—and, under the clever questioning of the detective, he was surprised to find how much he did remember—all kinds of odd details about them which he had scarcely been aware of observing.

The two of them, as they talked, afforded an interesting contrast: the Duke, with his air of distinction and race, his ironic expression, his mobile features, his clear enunciation and well-modulated voice, his easy carriage of an accomplished fencer—a fencer with muscles of steel—seemed to be a man of another kind from the slow-moving detective, with his husky voice, his common, slurring enunciation, his clumsily moulded features, so ill adapted to the expression of emotion and intelligence. It was a contrast almost between the hawk and the mole, the warrior and the workman. Only in their eyes were they alike; both of them had the keen, alert eyes of observers. Perhaps the most curious thing of all was that, in spite of the fact that he had for so much of his life been an idler, trifling away his time in the pursuit of pleasure, except when he had made his expedition to the South Pole, the Duke gave one the impression of being a cleverer man, of a far finer brain, than the detective who had spent so much of his life sharpening his wits on the more intricate problems of crime.

When Guerchard came to the end of his questions, the Duke said: "You have given me a very strong feeling that it is going to be a deuce of a job to catch Lupin. I don't wonder that, so far, you have none of you laid hands on him."

"But we have!" cried Guerchard quickly. "Twice Ganimard has caught him. Once he had him in prison, and actually brought him to trial. Lupin became another man, and was let go from the very dock."

"Really? It sounds absolutely amazing," said the Duke.

"And then, in the affair of the Blue Diamond, Ganimard caught him again. He has his weakness, Lupin—it's women. It's a very common weakness in these masters of crime. Ganimard and Holmlock Shears, in that affair, got the better of him by using his love for a woman—'the fair-haired lady,' she was called—to nab him."

"A shabby trick," said the Duke.

"Shabby?" said Guerchard in a tone of utter wonder. "How can anything be shabby in the case of a rogue like this?"

"Perhaps not—perhaps not—still—" said the Duke, and stopped.

The expression of wonder faded from Guerchard's face, and he went on, "Well, Holmlock Shears recovered the Blue Diamond, and Ganimard nabbed Lupin. He held him for ten minutes, then Lupin escaped."

"What became of the fair-haired lady?" said the Duke.

"I don't know. I have heard that she is dead," said Guerchard. "Now I come to think of it, I heard quite definitely that she died."

"It must be awful for a woman to love a man like Lupin—the constant, wearing anxiety," said the Duke thoughtfully.

"I dare say. Yet he can have his pick of sweethearts. I've been offered thousands of francs by women—women of your Grace's world and wealthy Viennese—to make them acquainted with Lupin," said Guerchard.

"You don't surprise me," said the Duke with his ironic smile. "Women never do stop to think—where one of their heroes is concerned. And did you do it?"

"How could I? If I only could! If I could find Lupin entangled with a woman like Ganimard did—well—" said Guerchard between his teeth.

"He'd never get out of YOUR clutches," said the Duke with conviction.

"I think not—I think not," said Guerchard grimly. "But come, I may as well get on."

He walked across the turf to the foot of the ladder and looked at the footprints round it. He made but a cursory examination of them, and took his way down the garden-path, out of the door in the wall into the space about the house that was building. He was not long examining it, and he went right through it out into the street on which the house would face when it was finished. He looked up and down it, and began to retrace his footsteps.

"I've seen all I want to see out here. We may as well go back to the house," he said to the Duke.

"I hope you've seen what you expected to see," said the Duke.

"Exactly what I expected to see—exactly," said Guerchard.

"That's as it should be," said the Duke.

They went back to the house and found M. Formery in the drawing-room, still engaged in the process of reconstruction.

"The thing to do now is to hunt the neighbourhood for witnesses of the departure of the burglars with their booty. Loaded as they were with such bulky objects, they must have had a big conveyance. Somebody must have noticed it. They must have wondered why it was standing in front of a half-built house. Somebody may have actually seen the burglars loading it, though it was so early in the morning. Bonavent had better inquire at every house in the street on which that half-built house faces. Did you happen to notice the name of it?" said M. Formery.

"It's Sureau Street," said Guerchard. "But Dieusy has been hunting the neighbourhood for someone who saw the burglars loading their conveyance, or saw it waiting to be loaded, for the last hour."

"Good," said M. Formery. "We are getting on."

M. Formery was silent. Guerchard and the Duke sat down and lighted cigarettes.

"You found plenty of traces," said M. Formery, waving his hand towards the window.

"Yes; I've found plenty of traces," said Guerchard.

"Of Lupin?" said M. Formery, with a faint sneer.

"No; not of Lupin," said Guerchard.

A smile of warm satisfaction illumined M. Formery's face:

"What did I tell you?" he said. "I'm glad that you've changed your mind about that."

"I have hardly changed my mind," said Guerchard, in his husky, gentle voice.

There came a loud knocking on the front door, the sound of excited voices on the stairs. The door opened, and in burst M. Gournay-Martin. He took one glance round the devastated room, raised his clenched hands towards the ceiling, and bellowed, "The scoundrels! The dirty scoundrels!" And his voice stuck in his throat. He tottered across the room to a couch, dropped heavily to it, gazed round the scene of desolation, and burst into tears.

Germaine and Sonia came into the room. The Duke stepped forward to greet them.

"Do stop crying, papa. You're as hoarse as a crow as it is," said Germaine impatiently. Then, turning on the Duke with a frown, she said: "I think that joke of yours about the train was simply disgraceful, Jacques. A joke's a joke, but to send us out to the station on a night like last night, through all that heavy rain, when you knew all the time that there was no quarter-to-nine train—it was simply disgraceful."

"I really don't know what you're talking about," said the Duke quietly. "Wasn't there a quarter-to-nine train?"

"Of course there wasn't," said Germaine. "The time-table was years old. I think it was the most senseless attempt at a joke I ever heard of."

"It doesn't seem to me to be a joke at all," said the Duke quietly. "At any rate, it isn't the kind of a joke I make—it would be detestable. I never thought to look at the date of the time-table. I keep a box of cigarettes in that drawer, and I have noticed the time-table there. Of course, it may have been lying there for years. It was stupid of me not to look at the date."

"I said it was a mistake. I was sure that his Grace would not do anything so unkind as that," said Sonia.

The Duke smiled at her.

"Well, all I can say is, it was very stupid of you not to look at the date," said Germaine.

M. Gournay-Martin rose to his feet and wailed, in the most heartrending fashion: "My pictures! My wonderful pictures! Such investments! And my cabinets! My Renaissance cabinets! They can't be replaced! They were unique! They were worth a hundred and fifty thousand francs."

M. Formery stepped forward with an air and said, "I am distressed, M. Gournay-Martin—truly distressed by your loss. I am M. Formery, examining magistrate."

"It is a tragedy, M. Formery—a tragedy!" groaned the millionaire.

"Do not let it upset you too much. We shall find your masterpieces—we shall find them. Only give us time," said M. Formery in a tone of warm encouragement.

The face of the millionaire brightened a little.

"And, after all, you have the consolation, that the burglars did not get hold of the gem of your collection. They have not stolen the coronet of the Princesse de Lamballe," said M. Formery.

"No," said the Duke. "They have not touched this safe. It is unopened."

"What has that got to do with it?" growled the millionaire quickly. "That safe is empty."

"Empty ... but your coronet?" cried the Duke.

"Good heavens! Then they HAVE stolen it," cried the millionaire hoarsely, in a panic-stricken voice.

"But they can't have—this safe hasn't been touched," said the Duke.

"But the coronet never was in that safe. It was—have they entered my bedroom?" said the millionaire.

"No," said M. Formery.

"They don't seem to have gone through any of the rooms except these two," said the Duke.

"Ah, then my mind is at rest about that. The safe in my bedroom has only two keys. Here is one." He took a key from his waistcoat pocket and held it out to them. "And the other is in this safe."

The face of M. Formery was lighted up with a splendid satisfaction. He might have rescued the coronet with his own hands. He cried triumphantly, "There, you see!"

"See? See?" cried the millionaire in a sudden bellow. "I see that they have robbed me—plundered me. Oh, my pictures! My wonderful pictures! Such investments!"

12

THE THEFT OF THE PENDANT

They stood round the millionaire observing his anguish, with eyes in which shone various degrees of sympathy. As if no longer able to bear the sight of such woe, Sonia slipped out of the room.

The millionaire lamented his loss and abused the thieves by turns, but always at the top of his magnificent voice.

Suddenly a fresh idea struck him. He clapped his hand to his brow and cried: "That eight hundred pounds! Charolais will never buy the Mercrac now! He was not a bona fide purchaser!"

The Duke's lips parted slightly and his eyes opened a trifle wider than their wont. He turned sharply on his heel, and almost sprang into the other drawing-room. There he laughed at his ease.

M. Formery kept saying to the millionaire: "Be calm, M. Gournay-Martin. Be calm! We shall recover your masterpieces. I pledge you my word. All we need is time. Have patience. Be calm!"

His soothing remonstrances at last had their effect. The millionaire grew calm:

"Guerchard?" he said. "Where is Guerchard?"

M. Formery presented Guerchard to him.

"Are you on their track? Have you a clue?" said the millionaire.

"I think," said M. Formery in an impressive tone, "that we may now proceed with the inquiry in the ordinary way."

He was a little piqued by the millionaire's so readily turning from him to the detective. He went to a writing-table, set some sheets of paper before him, and prepared to make notes on the answers to his questions. The Duke came back into the drawing-room; the inspector was summoned. M. Gournay-Martin sat down on a couch with his hands on his knees and gazed gloomily at M. Formery. Germaine, who was sitting on a couch near the door, waiting with an air of resignation for her father to cease his lamentations, rose and moved to a chair nearer the writing-table. Guerchard kept moving restlessly about the room, but noiselessly. At last he came to a standstill, leaning against the wall behind M. Formery.

M. Formery went over all the matters about which he had already questioned the Duke. He questioned the millionaire and his daughter about the Charolais, the theft of the motor-cars, and the attempted theft of the pendant. He questioned them at less length about the composition of their household—the servants and their characters. He elicited no new fact.

He paused, and then he said, carelessly as a mere matter of routine: "I should like to know, M. Gournay-Martin, if there has ever been any other robbery committed at your house?"

"Three years ago this scoundrel Lupin—" the millionaire began violently.

"Yes, yes; I know all about that earlier burglary. But have you been robbed since?" said M. Formery, interrupting him.

"No, I haven't been robbed since that burglary; but my daughter has," said the millionaire.

"Your daughter?" said M. Formery.

"Yes; I have been robbed two or three times during the last three years," said Germaine.

"Dear me! But you ought to have told us about this before. This is extremely interesting, and most important," said M. Formery, rubbing his hands, "I suppose you suspect Victoire?"

"No, I don't," said Germaine quickly. "It couldn't have been Victoire. The last two thefts were committed at the chateau when Victoire was in Paris in charge of this house."

M. Formery seemed taken aback, and he hesitated, consulting his notes. Then he said: "Good—good. That confirms my hypothesis."

"What hypothesis?" said M. Gournay-Martin quickly.

"Never mind—never mind," said M. Formery solemnly. And, turning to Germaine, he went on: "You say, Mademoiselle, that these thefts began about three years ago?"

"Yes, I think they began about three years ago in August."

"Let me see. It was in the month of August, three years ago, that your father, after receiving a threatening letter like the one he received last night, was the victim of a burglary?" said M. Formery.

"Yes, it was—the scoundrels!" cried the millionaire fiercely.

"Well, it would be interesting to know which of your servants entered your service three years ago," said M. Formery.

"Victoire has only been with us a year at the outside," said Germaine.

"Only a year?" said M. Formery quickly, with an air of some vexation. He paused and added, "Exactly—exactly. And what was the nature of the last theft of which you were the victim?"

"It was a pearl brooch—not unlike the pendant which his Grace gave me yesterday," said Germaine.

"Would you mind showing me that pendant? I should like to see it," said M. Formery.

"Certainly—show it to him, Jacques. You have it, haven't you?" said Germaine, turning to the Duke.

"Me? No. How should I have it?" said the Duke in some surprise. "Haven't you got it?"

"I've only got the case—the empty case," said Germaine, with a startled air.

"The empty case?" said the Duke, with growing surprise.

"Yes," said Germaine. "It was after we came back from our useless journey to the station. I remembered suddenly that I had started without the pendant. I went to the bureau and picked up the case; and it was empty."

"One moment—one moment," said M. Formery. "Didn't you catch this young Bernard Charolais with this case in his hands, your Grace?"

"Yes," said the Duke. "I caught him with it in his pocket."

"Then you may depend upon it that the young rascal had slipped the pendant out of its case and you only recovered the empty case from him," said M. Formery triumphantly.

"No," said the Duke. "That is not so. Nor could the thief have been the burglar who broke open the bureau to get at the keys. For long after both of them were out of the house I took a cigarette from the box which stood on the bureau beside the case which held the pendant. And it occurred to me that the young rascal might have played that very trick on me. I opened the case and the pendant was there."

"It has been stolen!" cried the millionaire; "Of course it has been stolen."

"Oh, no, no," said the Duke. "It hasn't been stolen. Irma, or perhaps Mademoiselle Kritchnoff, has brought it to Paris for Germaine."

"Sonia certainly hasn't brought it. It was she who suggested to me that you had seen it lying on the bureau, and slipped it into your pocket," said Germaine quickly.

"Then it must be Irma," said the Duke.

"We had better send for her and make sure," said M. Formery. "Inspector, go and fetch her."

The inspector went out of the room and the Duke questioned Germaine and her father about the journey, whether it had been very uncomfortable, and if they were very tired by it. He learned that they had been so fortunate as to find sleeping compartments on the train, so that they had suffered as little as might be from their night of travel.

M. Formery looked through his notes; Guerchard seemed to be going to sleep where he stood against the wall.

The inspector came back with Irma. She wore the frightened, half-defensive, half-defiant air which people of her class wear when confronted by the authorities. Her big, cow's eyes rolled uneasily.

"Oh, Irma—" Germaine began.

M. Formery cut her short, somewhat brusquely. "Excuse me, excuse me. I am conducting this inquiry," he said. And then, turning to Irma, he added, "Now, don't be frightened, Mademoiselle Irma; I want to ask you a question or two. Have you brought up to Paris the pendant which the Duke of Charmerace gave your mistress yesterday?"

"Me, sir? No, sir. I haven't brought the pendant," said Irma.

"You're quite sure?" said M. Formery.

"Yes, sir; I haven't seen the pendant. Didn't Mademoiselle Germaine leave it on the bureau?" said Irma.

"How do you know that?" said M. Formery.

"I heard Mademoiselle Germaine say that it had been on the bureau. I thought that perhaps Mademoiselle Kritchnoff had put it in her bag."

"Why should Mademoiselle Kritchnoff put it in her bag?" said the Duke quickly.

"To bring it up to Paris for Mademoiselle Germaine," said Irma.

"But what made you think that?" said Guerchard, suddenly intervening.

"Oh, I thought Mademoiselle Kritchnoff might have put it in her bag because I saw her standing by the bureau," said Irma.

"Ah, and the pendant was on the bureau?" said M. Formery.

"Yes, sir," said Irma.

There was a silence. Suddenly the atmosphere of the room seemed to have become charged with an oppression—a vague menace. Guerchard seemed to have become wide awake again. Germaine and the Duke looked at one another uneasily.

"Have you been long in the service of Mademoiselle Gournay-Martin?" said M. Formery.

"Six months, sir," said Irma.

"Very good, thank you. You can go," said M. Formery. "I may want you again presently."

Irma went quickly out of the room with an air of relief.

M. Formery scribbled a few words on the paper before him and then said: "Well, I will proceed to question Mademoiselle Kritchnoff."

"Mademoiselle Kritchnoff is quite above suspicion," said the Duke quickly.

"Oh, yes, quite," said Germaine.

"How long has Mademoiselle Kritchnoff been in your service, Mademoiselle?" said Guerchard.

"Let me think," said Germaine, knitting her brow.

"Can't you remember?" said M. Formery.

"Just about three years," said Germaine.

"That's exactly the time at which the thefts began," said M. Formery.

"Yes," said Germaine, reluctantly.

"Ask Mademoiselle Kritchnoff to come here, inspector," said M. Formery.

"Yes, sir," said the inspector.

"I'll go and fetch her—I know where to find her," said the Duke quickly, moving toward the door.

"Please, please, your Grace," protested Guerchard. "The inspector will fetch her."

The Duke turned sharply and looked at him: "I beg your pardon, but do you—" he said.

"Please don't be annoyed, your Grace," Guerchard interrupted. "But M. Formery agrees with me—it would be quite irregular."

"Yes, yes, your Grace," said M. Formery. "We have our method of procedure. It is best to adhere to it—much the best. It is the result of years of experience of the best way of getting the truth."

"Just as you please," said the Duke, shrugging his shoulders.

The inspector came into the room: "Mademoiselle Kritchnoff will be here in a moment. She was just going out."

"She was going out?" said M. Formery. "You don't mean to say you're letting members of the household go out?"

"No, sir," said the inspector. "I mean that she was just asking if she might go out."

M. Formery beckoned the inspector to him, and said to him in a voice too low for the others to hear:

"Just slip up to her room and search her trunks."

"There is no need to take the trouble," said Guerchard, in the same low voice, but with sufficient emphasis.

"No, of course not. There's no need to take the trouble," M. Formery repeated after him.

The door opened, and Sonia came in. She was still wearing her travelling costume, and she carried her cloak on her arm. She stood looking round her with an air of some surprise; perhaps there was even a touch of fear in it. The long journey of the night before did not seem to have dimmed at all her delicate beauty. The Duke's eyes rested on her in an inquiring, wondering, even searching gaze. She looked at him, and her own eyes fell.

"Will you come a little nearer, Mademoiselle?" said M. Formery. "There are one or two questions—"

"Will you allow me?" said Guerchard, in a tone of such deference that it left M. Formery no grounds for refusal.

M. Formery flushed and ground his teeth. "Have it your own way!" he said ungraciously.

"Mademoiselle Kritchnoff," said Guerchard, in a tone of the most good-natured courtesy, "there is a matter on which M. Formery needs some information. The pendant which the Duke of Charmerace gave Mademoiselle Gournay-Martin yesterday has been stolen."

"Stolen? Are you sure?" said Sonia in a tone of mingled surprise and anxiety.

"Quite sure," said Guerchard. "We have exactly determined the conditions under which the theft was committed. But we have every reason to believe that the culprit, to avoid detection, has hidden the pendant in the travelling-bag or trunk of somebody else in order to—"

"My bag is upstairs in my bedroom, sir," Sonia interrupted quickly. "Here is the key of it."

In order to free her hands to take the key from her wrist-bag, she set her cloak on the back of a couch. It slipped off it, and fell to the ground at the feet of the Duke, who had not returned to his place beside Germaine. While she was groping in her bag for the key, and all eyes were on her, the Duke, who had watched her with a curious intentness ever since her entry into the room, stooped quietly down and picked up the cloak. His hand slipped into the pocket of it; his fingers touched a hard object wrapped in tissue-paper. They closed round it, drew it from the pocket, and, sheltered by the cloak, transferred it to his own. He set the cloak on the back of the sofa, and very softly moved back to his place by Germaine's side. No one in the room observed the movement, not even Guerchard: he was watching Sonia too intently.

Sonia found the key, and held it out to Guerchard.

He shook his head and said: "There is no reason to search your bag—none whatever. Have you any other luggage?"

She shrank back a little from his piercing eyes, almost as if their gaze scared her.

"Yes, my trunk ... it's upstairs in my bedroom too ... open."

She spoke in a faltering voice, and her troubled eyes could not meet those of the detective.

"You were going out, I think," said Guerchard gently.

"I was asking leave to go out. There is some shopping that must be done," said Sonia.

"You do not see any reason why Mademoiselle Kritchnoff should not go out, M. Formery, do you?" said Guerchard.

"Oh, no, none whatever; of course she can go out," said M. Formery.

Sonia turned round to go.

"One moment," said Guerchard, coming forward. "You've only got that wrist-bag with you?"

"Yes," said Sonia. "I have my money and my handkerchief in it." And she held it out to him.

Guerchard's keen eyes darted into it; and he muttered, "No point in looking in that. I don't suppose any one would have had the audacity—" and he stopped.

Sonia made a couple of steps toward the door, turned, hesitated, came back to the couch, and picked up her cloak.

There was a sudden gleam in Guerchard's eyes—a gleam of understanding, expectation, and triumph. He stepped forward, and holding out his hands, said: "Allow me."

"No, thank you," said Sonia. "I'm not going to put it on."

"No ... but it's possible ... someone may have ... have you felt in the pockets of it? That one, now? It seems as if that one—"

He pointed to the pocket which had held the packet.

Sonia started back with an air of utter dismay; her eyes glanced wildly round the room as if seeking an avenue of escape; her fingers closed convulsively on the pocket.

"But this is abominable!" she cried. "You look as if—"

"I beg you, mademoiselle," interrupted Guerchard. "We are sometimes obliged—"

"Really, Mademoiselle Sonia," broke in the Duke, in a singularly clear and piercing tone, "I cannot see why you should object to this mere formality."

"Oh, but—but—" gasped Sonia, raising her terror-stricken eyes to his.

The Duke seemed to hold them with his own; and he said in the same clear, piercing voice, "There isn't the slightest reason for you to be frightened."

Sonia let go of the cloak, and Guerchard, his face all alight with triumph, plunged his hand into the pocket. He drew it out empty, and stared at it, while his face fell to an utter, amazed blankness.

"Nothing? Nothing?" he muttered under his breath. And he stared at his empty hand as if he could not believe his eyes.

By a violent effort he forced an apologetic smile on his face, and said to Sonia: "A thousand apologies, mademoiselle."

He handed the cloak to her. Sonia took it and turned to go. She took a step towards the door, and tottered.

The Duke sprang forward and caught her as she was falling.

"Do you feel faint?" he said in an anxious voice.

"Thank you, you just saved me in time," muttered Sonia.

"I'm really very sorry," said Guerchard.

"Thank you, it was nothing. I'm all right now," said Sonia, releasing herself from the Duke's supporting arm.

She drew herself up, and walked quietly out of the room.

Guerchard went back to M. Formery at the writing-table.

"You made a clumsy mistake there, Guerchard," said M. Formery, with a touch of gratified malice in his tone.

Guerchard took no notice of it: "I want you to give orders that nobody leaves the house without my permission," he said, in a low voice.

"No one except Mademoiselle Kritchnoff, I suppose," said M. Formery, smiling.

"She less than any one," said Guerchard quickly.

"I don't understand what you're driving at a bit," said M. Formery. "Unless you suppose that Mademoiselle Kritchnoff is Lupin in disguise."

Guerchard laughed softly: "You will have your joke, M. Formery," he said.

"Well, well, I'll give the order," said M. Formery, somewhat mollified by the tribute to his humour.

He called the inspector to him and whispered a word in his ear. Then he rose and said: "I think, gentlemen, we ought to go and examine the bedrooms, and, above all, make sure that the safe in M. Gournay-Martin's bedroom has not been tampered with."

"I was wondering how much longer we were going to waste time here talking about that stupid pendant," grumbled the millionaire; and he rose and led the way.

"There may also be some jewel-cases in the bedrooms," said M. Formery.

"There are all the wedding presents. They were in charge of Victoire." said Germaine quickly. "It would be dreadful if they had been stolen. Some of them are from the first families in France."

"They would replace them ... those paper-knives," said the Duke, smiling.

Germaine and her father led the way. M. Formery, Guerchard, and the inspector followed them. At the door the Duke paused, stopped, closed it on them softly. He came back to the window, put his hand in his pocket, and drew out the packet wrapped in tissue-paper.

He unfolded the paper with slow, reluctant fingers, and revealed the pendant.

13

LUPIN WIRES

The Duke stared at the pendant, his eyes full of wonder and pity.

"Poor little girl!" he said softly under his breath.

He put the pendant carefully away in his waistcoat-pocket and stood staring thoughtfully out of the window.

The door opened softly, and Sonia came quickly into the room, closed the door, and leaned back against it. Her face was a dead white; her skin had lost its lustre of fine porcelain, and she stared at him with eyes dim with anguish.

In a hoarse, broken voice, she muttered: "Forgive me! Oh, forgive me!"

"A thief—you?" said the Duke, in a tone of pitying wonder.

Sonia groaned.

"You mustn't stop here," said the Duke in an uneasy tone, and he looked uneasily at the door.

"Ah, you don't want to speak to me any more," said Sonia, in a heartrending tone, wringing her hands.

"Guerchard is suspicious of everything. It is dangerous for us to be talking here. I assure you that it's dangerous," said the Duke.

"What an opinion must you have of me! It's dreadful—cruel!" wailed Sonia.

"For goodness' sake don't speak so loud," said the Duke, with even greater uneasiness. "You MUST think of Guerchard."

"What do I care?" cried Sonia. "I've lost the liking of the only creature whose liking I wanted. What does anything else matter? What DOES it matter?"

"We'll talk somewhere else presently. That'll be far safer," said the Duke.

"No, no, we must talk now!" cried Sonia. "You must know... I must tell ... Oh, dear! ... Oh, dear! ... I don't know how to tell you... And then it is so unfair... she ... Germaine ... she has everything," she panted. "Yesterday, before me, you gave her that pendant, ... she smiled ... she was proud of it... I saw her pleasure... Then I took it—I took it—I took it! And if I could, I'd take her fortune, too... I hate her! Oh, how I hate her!"

"What!" said the Duke.

"Yes, I do ... I hate her!" said Sonia; and her eyes, no longer gentle, glowed with the sombre resentment, the dull rage of the weak who turn on Fortune. Her gentle voice was harsh with rebellious wrath.

"You hate her?" said the Duke quickly.

"I should never have told you that... But now I dare... I dare speak out... It's you! ... It's you—" The avowal died on her lips. A burning flush crimsoned her cheeks and faded as quickly as it came: "I hate her!" she muttered.

"Sonia—" said the Duke gently.

"Oh! I know that it's no excuse... I know that you're thinking 'This is a very pretty story, but it's not her first theft'; ... and it's true—it's the tenth, ... perhaps it's the twentieth... It's true—I am a thief." She paused, and the glow deepened in her eyes. "But there's one thing you must believe—you shall believe; since you came, since I've known you, since the first day you set eyes on me, I have stolen no more ... till yesterday when you gave her the pendant before me. I could not bear it ... I could not." She paused and looked at him with eyes that demanded an assent.

"I believe you," said the Duke gravely.

She heaved a deep sigh of relief, and went on more quietly—some of its golden tone had returned to her voice: "And then, if you knew how it began ... the horror of it," she said.

"Poor child!" said the Duke softly.

"Yes, you pity me, but you despise me—you despise me beyond words. You shall not! I will not have it!" she cried fiercely.

"Believe me, no," said the Duke, in a soothing tone.

"Listen," said Sonia. "Have you ever been alone—alone in the world? ... Have you ever been hungry? Think of it ... in this big city where I was starving in sight of bread ... bread in the shops ... One only had to stretch out one's hand to touch it ... a penny loaf. Oh, it's commonplace!" she broke off: "Quite commonplace!"

"Go on: tell me," said the Duke curtly.

"There was one way I could make money and I would not do it: no, I would not," she went on. "But that day I was dying ... understand, I was dying ... I went to the rooms of a man I knew a little. It was my last resource. At first I was glad ... he gave me food and wine ... and then, he talked to me ... he offered me money."

"What!" cried the Duke; and a sudden flame of anger flared up in his eyes.

"No; I could not ... and then I robbed him... I preferred to ... it was more decent. Ah, I had excuses then. I began to steal to remain an honest woman ... and I've gone on stealing to keep up appearances. You see ... I joke about it." And she laughed, the faint, dreadful, mocking laugh of a damned soul. "Oh, dear! Oh, dear!" she cried; and, burying her face in her hands, she burst into a storm of weeping.

"Poor child," said the Duke softly. And he stared gloomily on the ground, overcome by this revelation of the tortures of the feeble in the underworld beneath the Paris he knew.

"Oh, you do pity me ... you do understand ... and feel," said Sonia, between her sobs.

The Duke raised his head and gazed at her with eyes full of an infinite sympathy and compassion.

"Poor little Sonia," he said gently. "I understand."

She gazed at him with incredulous eyes, in which joy and despair mingled, struggling.

He came slowly towards her, and stopped short. His quick ear had caught the sound of a footstep outside the door.

"Quick! Dry your eyes! You must look composed. The other room!" he cried, in an imperative tone.

He caught her hand and drew her swiftly into the further drawing-room.

With the quickness which came of long practice in hiding her feelings Sonia composed her face to something of its usual gentle calm. There was even a faint tinge of colour in her cheeks; they had lost their dead whiteness. A faint light shone in her eyes; the anguish had cleared from them. They rested on the Duke with a look of ineffable gratitude. She sat down on a couch. The Duke went to the window and lighted a cigarette. They heard the door of the outer drawing-room open, and there was a pause. Quick footsteps crossed the room, and Guerchard stood in the doorway. He looked from one to the other with keen and eager eyes. Sonia sat staring rather listlessly at the carpet. The Duke turned, and smiled at him.

"Well, M. Guerchard," he said. "I hope the burglars have not stolen the coronet."

"The coronet is safe, your Grace," said Guerchard.

"And the paper-knives?" said the Duke.

"The paper-knives?" said Guerchard with an inquiring air.

"The wedding presents," said the Duke.

"Yes, your Grace, the wedding presents are safe," said Guerchard.

"I breathe again," said the Duke languidly.

Guerchard turned to Sonia and said, "I was looking for you, Mademoiselle, to tell you that M. Formery has changed his mind. It is impossible for you to go out. No one will be allowed to go out."

"Yes?" said Sonia, in an indifferent tone.

"We should be very much obliged if you would go to your room," said Guerchard. "Your meals will be sent up to you."

"What?" said Sonia, rising quickly; and she looked from Guerchard to the Duke. The Duke gave her the faintest nod.

"Very well, I will go to my room," she said coldly.

They accompanied her to the door of the outer drawing-room. Guerchard opened it for her and closed it after her.

"Really, M. Guerchard," said the Duke, shrugging his shoulders. "This last measure—a child like that!"

"Really, I'm very sorry, your Grace; but it's my trade, or, if you prefer it, my duty. As long as things are taking place here which I am still the only one to perceive, and which are not yet clear to me, I must neglect no precaution."

"Of course, you know best," said the Duke. "But still, a child like that—you're frightening her out of her life."

Guerchard shrugged his shoulders, and went quietly out of the room.

The Duke sat down in an easy chair, frowning and thoughtful. Suddenly there struck on his ears the sound of a loud roaring and heavy bumping on the stairs, the door flew open, and M. Gournay-Martin stood on the threshold waving a telegram in his hand.

M. Formery and the inspector came hurrying down the stairs behind him, and watched his emotion with astonished and wondering eyes.

"Here!" bellowed the millionaire. "A telegram! A telegram from the scoundrel himself! Listen! Just listen:"

> "A thousand apologies for not having been able to keep my promise about the coronet. Had an appointment at the Acacias. Please have coronet ready in your room to-night. Will come without fail to fetch it, between a quarter to twelve and twelve o'clock."
> "Yours affectionately," "ARSÈNE LUPIN."

"There! What do you think of that?"

"If you ask me, I think he's humbug," said the Duke with conviction.

"Humbug! You always think it's humbug! You thought the letter was humbug; and look what has happened!" cried the millionaire.

"Give me the telegram, please," said M. Formery quickly.

The millionaire gave it to him; and he read it through.

"Find out who brought it, inspector," he said.

The inspector hurried to the top of the staircase and called to the policeman in charge of the front door. He came back to the drawing-room and said: "It was brought by an ordinary post-office messenger, sir."

"Where is he?" said M. Formery. "Why did you let him go?"

"Shall I send for him, sir?" said the inspector.

"No, no, it doesn't matter," said M. Formery; and, turning to M. Gournay-Martin and the Duke, he said, "Now we're really going to have trouble with Guerchard. He is going to muddle up everything. This telegram will be the last straw. Nothing will persuade him now that this is not Lupin's work. And just consider, gentlemen: if Lupin had come last night, and if he had really set his heart on the coronet, he would have stolen it then, or at any rate he would have tried to open the safe in M. Gournay-Martin's bedroom, in which the coronet actually is, or this safe here"—he went to the safe and rapped on the door of it—"in which is the second key."

"That's quite clear," said the inspector.

"If, then, he did not make the attempt last night, when he had a clear field—when the house was empty—he certainly will not make the attempt now when we are warned, when the police are on the spot, and the house is surrounded. The idea is childish, gentlemen"—he leaned against the door of the safe—"absolutely childish, but Guerchard is mad on this point; and I foresee that his madness is going to hamper us in the most idiotic way."

He suddenly pitched forward into the middle of the room, as the door of the safe opened with a jerk, and Guerchard shot out of it.

"What the devil!" cried M. Formery, gaping at him.

"You'd be surprised how clearly you hear everything in these safes—you'd think they were too thick," said Guerchard, in his gentle, husky voice.

"How on earth did you get into it?" cried M. Formery.

"Getting in was easy enough. It's the getting out that was awkward. These jokers had fixed up some kind of a spring so that I nearly shot out with the door," said Guerchard, rubbing his elbow.

"But how did you get into it? How the deuce DID you get into it?" cried M. Formery.

"Through the little cabinet into which that door behind the safe opens. There's no longer any back to the safe; they've cut it clean out of it—a very neat piece of work. Safes like this should always be fixed against a wall, not stuck in front of a door. The backs of them are always the weak point."

"And the key? The key of the safe upstairs, in my bedroom, where the coronet is—is the key there?" cried M. Gournay-Martin.

Guerchard went back into the empty safe, and groped about in it. He came out smiling.

"Well, have you found the key?" cried the millionaire.

"No. I haven't; but I've found something better," said Guerchard.

"What is it?" said M. Formery sharply.

"I'll give you a hundred guesses," said Guerchard with a tantalizing smile.

"What is it?" said M. Formery.

"A little present for you," said Guerchard.

"What do you mean?" cried M. Formery angrily.

Guerchard held up a card between his thumb and forefinger and said quietly:

"The card of Arsène Lupin."

14

GUERCHARD PICKS UP THE TRUE SCENT

The millionaire gazed at the card with stupefied eyes, the inspector gazed at it with extreme intelligence, the Duke gazed at it with interest, and M. Formery gazed at it with extreme disgust.

"It's part of the same ruse—it was put there to throw us off the scent. It proves nothing—absolutely nothing," he said scornfully.

"No; it proves nothing at all," said Guerchard quietly.

"The telegram is the important thing—this telegram," said M. Gournay-Martin feverishly. "It concerns the coronet. Is it going to be disregarded?"

"Oh, no, no," said M. Formery in a soothing tone. "It will be taken into account. It will certainly be taken into account."

M. Gournay-Martin's butler appeared in the doorway of the drawing-room: "If you please, sir, lunch is served," he said.

At the tidings some of his weight of woe appeared to be lifted from the head of the millionaire. "Good!" he said, "Good! Gentlemen, you will lunch with me, I hope."

"Thank you," said M. Formery. "There is nothing else for us to do, at any rate at present, and in the house. I am not quite satisfied about Mademoiselle Kritchnoff—at least Guerchard is not. I propose to question her again—about those earlier thefts."

"I'm sure there's nothing in that," said the Duke quickly.

"No, no; I don't think there is," said M. Formery. "But still one never knows from what quarter light may come in an affair like this. Accident often gives us our best clues."

"It seems rather a shame to frighten her—she's such a child," said the Duke.

"Oh, I shall be gentle, your Grace—as gentle as possible, that is. But I look to get more from the examination of Victoire. She was on the scene. She has actually seen the rogues at work; but till she recovers there is nothing more to be done, except to wait the discoveries of the detectives who are working outside; and they will report here. So in the meantime we shall be charmed to lunch with you, M. Gournay-Martin."

They went downstairs to the dining-room and found an elaborate and luxurious lunch, worthy of the hospitality of a millionaire, awaiting them. The skill of the cook seemed to have been quite unaffected by the losses of his master. M. Formery, an ardent lover of good things, enjoyed himself immensely. He was in the highest spirits. Germaine, a little upset by the night-journey, was rather querulous. Her father was plunged in a gloom which lifted for but a brief space at the appearance of a fresh delicacy. Guerchard ate and drank seriously, answering the questions of the Duke in a somewhat absent-minded fashion. The Duke himself seemed to have lost his usual flow of good spirits, and at times his brow was knitted in an anxious frown. His questions to Guerchard showed a far less keen interest in the affair.

To him the lunch seemed very long and very tedious; but at last it came to an end. M. Gournay-Martin seemed to have been much cheered by the wine he had drunk. He was almost hopeful. M. Formery, who had not by any means trifled with the champagne, was raised to the very height of sanguine certainty.

Their coffee and liqueurs were served in the smoking-room. Guerchard lighted a cigar, refused a liqueur, drank his coffee quickly, and slipped out of the room.

The Duke followed him, and in the hall said: "I will continue to watch you unravel the threads of this mystery, if I may, M. Guerchard."

Good Republican as Guerchard was, he could not help feeling flattered by the interest of a Duke; and the excellent lunch he had eaten disposed him to feel the honour even more deeply.

"I shall be charmed," he said. "To tell the truth, I find the company of your Grace really quite stimulating."

"It must be because I find it all so extremely interesting," said the Duke.

They went up to the drawing-room and found the red-faced young policeman seated on a chair by the door eating a lunch, which had been sent up to him from the millionaire's kitchen, with a very hearty appetite.

They went into the drawing-room. Guerchard shut the door and turned the key: "Now," he said, "I think that M. Formery will give me half an hour to myself. His cigar ought to last him at least half an hour. In that time I shall know what the burglars really did with their plunder—at least I shall know for certain how they got it out of the house."

"Please explain," said the Duke. "I thought we knew how they got it out of the house." And he waved his hand towards the window.

"Oh, that!—that's childish," said Guerchard contemptuously. "Those are traces for an examining magistrate. The ladder, the table on the window-sill, they lead nowhere. The only people who came up that ladder were the two men who brought it from the scaffolding. You can see their footsteps. Nobody went down it at all. It was mere waste of time to bother with those traces."

"But the footprint under the book?" said the Duke.

"Oh, that," said Guerchard. "One of the burglars sat on the couch there, rubbed plaster on the sole of his boot, and set his foot down on the carpet. Then he dusted the rest of the plaster off his boot and put the book on the top of the footprint."

"Now, how do you know that?" said the astonished Duke.

"It's as plain as a pike-staff," said Guerchard. "There must have been several burglars to move such pieces of furniture. If the soles of all of them had been covered with plaster, all the sweeping in the world would not have cleared the carpet of the tiny fragments of it. I've been over the carpet between the footprint and the window with a magnifying glass. There are no fragments of plaster on it. We dismiss the footprint. It is a mere blind, and a very fair blind too—for an examining magistrate."

"I understand," said the Duke.

"That narrows the problem, the quite simple problem, how was the furniture taken out of the room. It did not go through that window down the ladder. Again, it was not taken down the stairs, and out of the front door, or the back. If it had been, the concierge and his wife would have heard the noise. Besides that, it would have been carried down into a main street, in which there are people at all hours. Somebody would have been sure to tell a policeman that this house was being emptied. Moreover, the police were continually patrolling the main streets, and, quickly as a man like Lupin would do the job, he could not do it so quickly that a policeman would not have seen it. No; the furniture was not taken down the stairs or out of the front door. That narrows the problem still more. In fact, there is only one mode of egress left."

"The chimney!" cried the Duke.

"You've hit it," said Guerchard, with a husky laugh. "By that well-known logical process, the process of elimination, we've excluded all methods of egress except the chimney."

He paused, frowning, in some perplexity; and then he said uneasily: "What I don't like about it is that Victoire was set in the fireplace. I asked myself at once what was she doing there. It was unnecessary that she should be drugged and set in the fireplace—quite unnecessary."

"It might have been to put off an examining magistrate," said the Duke. "Having found Victoire in the fireplace, M. Formery did not look for anything else."

"Yes, it might have been that," said Guerchard slowly. "On the other hand, she might have been put there to make sure that I did not miss the road the burglars took. That's the worst of having to do with Lupin. He knows me to the bottom of my mind. He has something up his sleeve—some surprise for me. Even now, I'm nowhere near the bottom of the mystery. But come along, we'll take the road the burglars took. The inspector has put my lantern ready for me."

As he spoke he went to the fireplace, picked up a lantern which had been set on the top of the iron fire-basket, and lighted it. The Duke stepped into the great fireplace beside him. It was four feet deep, and between eight and nine feet broad. Guerchard threw the light from the lantern on to the back wall of it. Six feet from the floor the soot from the fire stopped abruptly, and there was a dappled patch of bricks, half of them clean and red, half of them blackened by soot, five feet broad, and four feet high.

"The opening is higher up than I thought," said Guerchard. "I must get a pair of steps."

He went to the door of the drawing-room and bade the young policeman fetch him a pair of steps. They were brought quickly. He took them from the policeman, shut the door, and locked it again. He set the steps in the fireplace and mounted them.

"Be careful," he said to the Duke, who had followed him into the fireplace, and stood at the foot of the steps. "Some of these bricks may drop inside, and they'll sting you up if they fall on your toes."

The Duke stepped back out of reach of any bricks that might fall.

Guerchard set his left hand against the wall of the chimney-piece between him and the drawing-room, and pressed hard with his right against the top of the dappled patch of bricks. At the first push, half a dozen of them fell with a bang on to the floor of the next house. The light came flooding in through the hole, and shone on Guerchard's face and its smile of satisfaction. Quickly he pushed row after row of bricks into the next house until he had cleared an opening four feet square.

"Come along," he said to the Duke, and disappeared feet foremost through the opening.

The Duke mounted the steps, and found himself looking into a large empty room of the exact size and shape of the drawing-room of M. Gournay-Martin, save that it had an ordinary modern fireplace instead of one of the antique pattern of that in which he stood. Its chimney-piece was a few inches below the opening. He stepped out on to the chimney-piece and dropped lightly to the floor.

"Well," he said, looking back at the opening through which he had come. "That's an ingenious dodge."

"Oh, it's common enough," said Guerchard. "Robberies at the big jewellers' are sometimes worked by these means. But what is uncommon about it, and what at first sight put me off the track, is that these burglars had the cheek to pierce the wall with an opening large enough to enable them to remove the furniture of a house."

"It's true," said the Duke. "The opening's as large as a good-sized window. Those burglars seem capable of everything—even of a first-class piece of mason's work."

"Oh, this has all been prepared a long while ago. But now I'm really on their track. And after all, I haven't really lost any time. Dieusy wasted no time in making inquiries in Sureau Street; he's been working all this side of the house."

Guerchard drew up the blinds, opened the shutters, and let the daylight flood the dim room. He came back to the fireplace and looked down at the heap of bricks, frowning:

"I made a mistake there," he said. "I ought to have taken those bricks down carefully, one by one."

Quickly he took brick after brick from the pile, and began to range them neatly against the wall on the left. The Duke watched him for two or three minutes, then began to help him. It did not take them long, and under one of the last few bricks Guerchard found a fragment of a gilded picture-frame.

"Here's where they ought to have done their sweeping," he said, holding it up to the Duke.

"I tell you what," said the Duke, "I shouldn't wonder if we found the furniture in this house still."

"Oh, no, no!" said Guerchard. "I tell you that Lupin would allow for myself or Ganimard being put in charge of the case; and he would know that we should find the opening in the chimney. The furniture was taken straight out into the side-street on to which this house opens." He led the way out of the room on to the landing and went down the dark staircase into the hall. He opened the shutters of the hall windows, and let in the light. Then he examined the hall. The dust lay thick on the tiled floor. Down the middle of it was a lane formed by many feet. The footprints were faint, but still plain in the layer of dust. Guerchard came back to the stairs and began to examine them. Half-way up the flight he stooped, and picked up a little spray of flowers: "Fresh!" he said. "These have not been long plucked."

"Salvias," said the Duke.

"Salvias they are," said Guerchard. "Pink salvias; and there is only one gardener in France who has ever succeeded in getting this shade—M. Gournay-Martin's gardener at Charmerace. I'm a gardener myself."

"Well, then, last night's burglars came from Charmerace. They must have," said the Duke.

"It looks like it," said Guerchard.

"The Charolais," said the Duke.

"It looks like it," said Guerchard.

"It must be," said the Duke. "This IS interesting—if only we could get an absolute proof."

"We shall get one presently," said Guerchard confidently.

"It is interesting," said the Duke in a tone of lively enthusiasm. "These clues—these tracks which cross one another—each fact by degrees falling into its proper place—extraordinarily interesting." He paused and took out his cigarette-case: "Will you have a cigarette?" he said.

"Are they caporal?" said Guerchard.

"No, Egyptians—Mercedes."

"Thank you," said Guerchard; and he took one.

The Duke struck a match, lighted Guerchard's cigarette, and then his own:

"Yes, it's very interesting," he said. "In the last quarter of an hour you've practically discovered that the burglars came from Charmerace—that they were the Charolais—that they came in by the front door of this house, and carried the furniture out of it."

"I don't know about their coming in by it," said Guerchard. "Unless I'm very much mistaken, they came in by the front door of M. Gournay-Martin's house."

"Of course," said the Duke. "I was forgetting. They brought the keys from Charmerace."

"Yes, but who drew the bolts for them?" said Guerchard. "The concierge bolted them before he went to bed. He told me so. He was telling the truth—I know when that kind of man is telling the truth."

"By Jove!" said the Duke softly. "You mean that they had an accomplice?"

"I think we shall find that they had an accomplice. But your Grace is beginning to draw inferences with uncommon quickness. I believe that you would make a first-class detective yourself—with practice, of course—with practice."

"Can I have missed my true career?" said the Duke, smiling. "It's certainly a very interesting game."

"Well, I'm not going to search this barracks myself," said Guerchard. "I'll send in a couple of men to do it; but I'll just take a look at the steps myself."

So saying, he opened the front door and went out and examined the steps carefully.

"We shall have to go back the way we came," he said, when he had finished his examination. "The drawing-room door is locked. We ought to find M. Formery hammering on it." And he smiled as if he found the thought pleasing.

They went back up the stairs, through the opening, into the drawing-room of M. Gournay-Martin's house. Sure enough, from the other side of the locked door came the excited voice of M. Formery, crying:

"Guerchard! Guerchard! What are you doing? Let me in! Why don't you let me in?"

Guerchard unlocked the door; and in bounced M. Formery, very excited, very red in the face.

"Hang it all, Guerchard! What on earth have you been doing?" he cried. "Why didn't you open the door when I knocked?"

"I didn't hear you," said Guerchard. "I wasn't in the room."

"Then where on earth have you been?" cried M. Formery.

Guerchard looked at him with a faint, ironical smile, and said in his gentle voice, "I was following the real track of the burglars."

15

THE EXAMINATION OF SONIA

M. Formery gasped: "The real track?" he muttered.

"Let me show you," said Guerchard. And he led him to the fireplace, and showed him the opening between the two houses.

"I must go into this myself!" cried M. Formery in wild excitement.

Without more ado he began to mount the steps. Guerchard followed him. The Duke saw their heels disappear up the steps. Then he came out of the drawing-room and inquired for M. Gournay-Martin. He was told that the millionaire was up in his bedroom; and he went upstairs, and knocked at the door of it.

M. Gournay-Martin bade him enter in a very faint voice, and the Duke found him lying on the bed. He was looking depressed, even exhausted, the shadow of the blusterous Gournay-Martin of the day before. The rich rosiness of his cheeks had faded to a moderate rose-pink.

"That telegram," moaned the millionaire. "It was the last straw. It has overwhelmed me. The coronet is lost."

"What, already?" said the Duke, in a tone of the liveliest surprise.

"No, no; it's still in the safe," said the millionaire. "But it's as good as lost—before midnight it will be lost. That fiend will get it."

"If it's in this safe now, it won't be lost before midnight," said the Duke. "But are you sure it's there now?"

"Look for yourself," said the millionaire, taking the key of the safe from his waistcoat pocket, and handing it to the Duke.

The Duke opened the safe. The morocco case which held the coronet lay on the middle shell in front of him. He glanced at the millionaire, and saw that he had closed his eyes in the exhaustion of despair. Whistling softly, the Duke opened the case, took out the diadem, and examined it carefully, admiring its admirable workmanship. He put it back in the case, turned to the millionaire, and said thoughtfully:

"I can never make up my mind, in the case of one of these old diadems, whether one ought not to take out the stones and have them re-cut. Look at this emerald now. It's a very fine stone, but this old-fashioned cutting does not really do it justice."

"Oh, no, no: you should never interfere with an antique, historic piece of jewellery. Any alteration decreases its value—its value as an historic relic," cried the millionaire, in a shocked tone.

"I know that," said the Duke, "but the question for me is, whether one ought not to sacrifice some of its value to increasing its beauty."

"You do have such mad ideas," said the millionaire, in a tone of peevish exasperation.

"Ah, well, it's a nice question," said the Duke.

He snapped the case briskly, put it back on the shelf, locked the safe, and handed the key to the millionaire. Then he strolled across the room and looked down into the street, whistling softly.

"I think—I think—I'll go home and get out of these motoring clothes. And I should like to have on a pair of boots that were a trifle less muddy," he said slowly.

M. Gournay-Martin sat up with a jerk and cried, "For Heaven's sake, don't you go and desert me, my dear chap! You don't know what my nerves are like!"

"Oh, you've got that sleuth-hound, Guerchard, and the splendid Formery, and four other detectives, and half a dozen ordinary policemen guarding you. You can do without my feeble arm. Besides, I shan't be gone more than half an hour—three-quarters at the outside. I'll bring back my evening clothes with me, and dress for dinner here. I don't suppose that anything fresh will happen between now and midnight; but I want to be on the spot, and hear the information as it comes in fresh. Besides, there's Guerchard. I positively cling to Guerchard. It's an education, though perhaps not a liberal education, to go about with him," said the Duke; and there was a sub-acid irony in his voice.

"Well, if you must, you must," said M. Gournay-Martin grumpily.

"Good-bye for the present, then," said the Duke. And he went out of the room and down the stairs. He took his motor-cap from the hall-table, and had his hand on the latch of the door, when the policeman in charge of it said, "I beg your pardon, sir, but have you M. Guerchard's permission to leave the house?"

"M. Guerchard's permission?" said the Duke haughtily. "What has M. Guerchard to do with me? I am the Duke of Charmerace." And he opened the door.

"It was M. Formery's orders, your Grace," stammered the policeman doubtfully.

"M. Formery's orders?" said the Duke, standing on the top step. "Call me a taxi-cab, please."

The concierge, who stood beside the policeman, ran down the steps and blew his whistle. The policeman gazed uneasily at the Duke, shifting his weight from one foot to the other; but he said no more.

A taxi-cab came up to the door, the Duke went down the steps, stepped into it, and drove away.

Three-quarters of an hour later he came back, having changed into clothes more suited to a Paris drawing-room. He went up to the drawing-room, and there he found Guerchard, M. Formery, and the inspector, who had just completed their tour of inspection of the house next door and had satisfied themselves that the stolen treasures were not in it. The inspector and his men had searched it thoroughly just to make sure; but, as Guerchard had foretold, the burglars had not taken the chance of the failure of the police to discover the opening between the two houses. M. Formery told the Duke about their tour of inspection at length. Guerchard went to the telephone and told the exchange to put him through to Charmerace. He was informed that the trunk line was very busy and that he might have to wait half an hour.

The Duke inquired if any trace of the burglars, after they had left with their booty, had yet been found. M. Formery told him that, so far, the detectives had failed to find a single trace. Guerchard said that he had three men at work on the search, and that he was hopeful of getting some news before long.

"The layman is impatient in these matters," said M. Formery, with an indulgent smile. "But we have learnt to be patient, after long experience."

He proceeded to discuss with Guerchard the new theories with which the discovery of the afternoon had filled his mind. None of them struck the Duke as being of great value, and he listened to them with a somewhat absent-minded air. The coming examination of Sonia weighed heavily on his spirit. Guerchard answered only in monosyllables to the questions and suggestions thrown out by M. Formery. It seemed to the Duke that he paid very little attention to him, that his mind was still working hard on the solution of the mystery, seeking the missing facts which would bring him to the bottom of it. In the middle of one of M. Formery's more elaborate dissertations the telephone bell rang.

Guerchard rose hastily and went to it. They heard him say: "Is that Charmerace? ... I want the gardener... Out? When will he be back? ... Tell him to ring me up at M. Gournay-Martin's house in Paris the moment he gets back... Detective-Inspector Guerchard ... Guerchard ... Detective-Inspector."

He turned to them with a frown, and said, "Of course, since I want him, the confounded gardener has gone out for the day. Still, it's of very little importance—a mere corroboration I wanted." And he went back to his seat and lighted another cigarette.

M. Formery continued his dissertation. Presently Guerchard said, "You might go and see how Victoire is, inspector—whether she shows any signs of waking. What did the doctor say?"

"The doctor said that she would not really be sensible and have her full wits about her much before ten o'clock to-night," said the inspector; but he went to examine her present condition.

M. Formery proceeded to discuss the effects of different anesthetics. The others heard him with very little attention.

The inspector came back and reported that Victoire showed no signs of awaking.

"Well, then, M. Formery, I think we might get on with the examination of Mademoiselle Kritchnoff," said Guerchard. "Will you go and fetch her, inspector?"

"Really, I cannot conceive why you should worry that poor child," the Duke protested, in a tone of some indignation.

"It seems to me hardly necessary," said M. Formery.

"Excuse me," said Guerchard suavely, "but I attach considerable importance to it. It seems to me to be our bounden duty to question her fully. One never knows from what quarter light may come."

"Oh, well, since you make such a point of it," said M. Formery. "Inspector, ask Mademoiselle Kritchnoff to come here. Fetch her."

The inspector left the room.

Guerchard looked at the Duke with a faint air of uneasiness: "I think that we had better question Mademoiselle Kritchnoff by ourselves," he said.

M. Formery looked at him and hesitated. Then he said: "Oh, yes, of course, by ourselves."

"Certainly," said the Duke, a trifle haughtily. And he rose and opened the door. He was just going through it when Guerchard said sharply:

"Your Grace—"

The Duke paid no attention to him. He shut the door quickly behind him and sprang swiftly up the stairs. He met the inspector coming down with Sonia. Barring their way for a moment he said, in his kindliest voice: "Now you mustn't be frightened, Mademoiselle Sonia. All you have to do is to try to remember as clearly as you can the circumstances of the earlier thefts at Charmerace. You mustn't let them confuse you."

"Thank you, your Grace, I will try and be as clear as I can," said Sonia; and she gave him an eloquent glance, full of gratitude for the warning; and went down the stairs with firm steps.

The Duke went on up the stairs, and knocked softly at the door of M. Gournay-Martin's bedroom. There was no answer to his knock, and he quietly opened the door and looked in. Overcome by his misfortunes, the millionaire had sunk into a profound sleep and was snoring softly. The Duke stepped inside the room, left the door open a couple of inches, drew a chair to it, and sat down watching the staircase through the opening of the door.

He sat frowning, with a look of profound pity on his face. Once the suspense grew too much for him. He rose and walked up and down the room. His well-bred calm seemed to have deserted him. He muttered curses on Guerchard, M. Formery, and the whole French criminal system, very softly, under his breath. His face was distorted to a mask of fury; and once he wiped the little beads of sweat from his forehead with his handkerchief. Then he recovered himself, sat down in the chair, and resumed his watch on the stairs.

At last, at the end of half an hour, which had seemed to him months long, he heard voices. The drawing-room door shut, and there were footsteps on the stairs. The inspector and Sonia came into view.

He waited till they were at the top of the stairs: then he came out of the room, with his most careless air, and said: "Well, Mademoiselle Sonia, I hope you did not find it so very dreadful, after all."

She was very pale, and there were undried tears on her cheeks. "It was horrible," she said faintly. "Horrible. M. Formery was all right—he believed me; but that horrible detective would not believe a word I said. He confused me. I hardly knew what I was saying."

The Duke ground his teeth softly. "Never mind, it's over now. You had better lie down and rest. I will tell one of the servants to bring you up a glass of wine."

He walked with her to the door of her room, and said: "Try to sleep—sleep away the unpleasant memory."

She went into her room, and the Duke went downstairs and told the butler to take a glass of champagne up to her. Then he went upstairs to the drawing-room. M. Formery was at the table writing. Guerchard stood beside him. He handed what he had written to Guerchard, and, with a smile of satisfaction, Guerchard folded the paper and put it in his pocket.

"Well, M. Formery, did Mademoiselle Kritchnoff throw any fresh light on this mystery?" said the Duke, in a tone of faint contempt.

"No—in fact she convinced ME that she knew nothing whatever about it. M. Guerchard seems to entertain a different opinion. But I think that even he is convinced that Mademoiselle Kritchnoff is not a friend of Arsène Lupin."

"Oh, well, perhaps she isn't. But there's no telling," said Guerchard slowly.

"Arsène Lupin?" cried the Duke. "Surely you never thought that Mademoiselle Kritchnoff had anything to do with Arsène Lupin?"

"I never thought so," said M. Formery. "But when one has a fixed idea ... well, one has a fixed idea." He shrugged his shoulders, and looked at Guerchard with contemptuous eyes.

The Duke laughed, an unaffected ringing laugh, but not a pleasant one: "It's absurd!" he cried.

"There are always those thefts," said Guerchard, with a nettled air.

"You have nothing to go upon," said M. Formery. "What if she did enter the service of Mademoiselle Gournay-Martin just before the thefts began? Besides, after this lapse of time, if she had committed the thefts, you'd find it a job to bring them home to her. It's not a job worth your doing, anyhow—it's a job for an ordinary detective, Guerchard."

"There's always the pendant," said Guerchard. "I am convinced that that pendant is in the house."

"Oh, that stupid pendant! I wish I'd never given it to Mademoiselle Gournay-Martin," said the Duke lightly.

"I have a feeling that if I could lay my hand on that pendant—if I could find who has it, I should have the key to this mystery."

"The devil you would!" said the Duke softly. "That is odd. It is the oddest thing about this business I've heard yet."

"I have that feeling—I have that feeling," said Guerchard quietly.

The Duke smiled.

16

VICTOIRE'S SLIP

They were silent. The Duke walked to the fireplace, stepped into it, and studied the opening. He came out again and said: "Oh, by the way, M. Formery, the policeman at the front door wanted to stop me going out of the house when I went home to change. I take it that M. Guerchard's prohibition does not apply to me?"

"Of course not—of course not, your Grace," said M. Formery quickly.

"I saw that you had changed your clothes, your Grace," said Guerchard. "I thought that you had done it here."

"No," said the Duke, "I went home. The policeman protested; but he went no further, so I did not throw him into the middle of the street."

"Whatever our station, we should respect the law," said M. Formery solemnly.

"The Republican Law, M. Formery? I am a Royalist," said the Duke, smiling at him.

M. Formery shook his head sadly.

"I was wondering," said the Duke, "about M. Guerchard's theory that the burglars were let in the front door of this house by an accomplice. Why, when they had this beautiful large opening, did they want a front door, too?"

"I did not know that that was Guerchard's theory?" said M. Formery, a trifle contemptuously. "Of course they had no need to use the front door."

"Perhaps they had no need to use the front door," said Guerchard; "but, after all, the front door was unbolted, and they did not draw the bolts to put us off the scent. Their false scent was already prepared"—he waved his hand towards the window—"moreover, you must bear in mind that that opening might not have been made when they entered the house. Suppose that, while they were on the other side of the wall, a brick had fallen on to the hearth, and alarmed the concierge. We don't know how skilful they are; they might not have cared to risk it. I'm inclined to think, on the whole, that they did come in through the front door."

M. Formery sniffed contemptuously.

"Perhaps you're right," said the Duke. "But the accomplice?"

"I think we shall know more about the accomplice when Victoire awakes," said Guerchard.

"The family have such confidence in Victoire," said the Duke.

"Perhaps Lupin has, too," said Guerchard grimly.

"Always Lupin!" said M. Formery contemptuously.

There came a knock at the door, and a footman appeared on the threshold. He informed the Duke that Germaine had returned from her shopping expedition, and was awaiting him in her boudoir. He went to her, and tried to persuade her to put in a word for Sonia, and endeavour to soften Guerchard's rigour.

She refused to do anything of the kind, declaring that, in view of the value of the stolen property, no stone must be left unturned to recover it. The police knew what they were doing; they must have a free hand. The Duke did not press her with any great vigour; he realized the futility of an appeal to a nature so shallow, so self-centred, and so lacking in sympathy. He took his revenge by teasing her about the wedding presents which were still flowing in. Her father's business friends were still striving to outdo one another in the costliness of the jewelry they were giving her. The great houses of the Faubourg Saint-Germain were still refraining firmly from anything that savoured of extravagance or ostentation. While he was with her the eleventh paper-knife came—from his mother's friend, the Duchess of Veauleglise. The Duke was overwhelmed with joy at the sight of it, and his delighted comments drove Germaine to the last extremity of exasperation. The result was that she begged him, with petulant asperity, to get out of her sight.

He complied with her request, almost with alacrity, and returned to M. Formery and Guerchard. He found them at a standstill, waiting for reports from the detectives who were hunting outside the house for information about the movements of the burglars with the stolen booty, and apparently finding none. The police were also hunting for the stolen motor-cars, not only in Paris and its environs, but also all along the road between Paris and Charmerace.

At about five o'clock Guerchard grew tired of the inaction, and went out himself to assist his subordinates, leaving M. Formery in charge of the house itself. He promised to be back by half-past seven, to let the examining magistrate, who had an engagement for the evening, get away. The Duke spent his time between the drawing-room, where M. Formery entertained him with anecdotes of his professional skill, and the boudoir, where Germaine was entertaining envious young friends who came to see her wedding presents. The friends of Germaine were always a little ill at ease in the society of the Duke, belonging as they did to that wealthy middle class which has made France what she is. His indifference to the doings of the old friends of his family saddened them; and they were unable to understand his airy and persistent trifling. It seemed to them a discord in the cosmic tune.

The afternoon wore away, and at half-past seven Guerchard had not returned. M. Formery waited for him, fuming, for ten minutes, then left the house in charge of the inspector, and went off to his engagement. M. Gournay-Martin was entertaining two financiers and their wives, two of their daughters, and two friends of the Duke, the Baron de Vernan and the Comte de Vauvineuse, at dinner that night. Thanks to the Duke, the party was of a liveliness to which the gorgeous dining-room had been very little used since it had been so fortunate as to become the property of M. Gournay-Martin.

The millionaire had been looking forward to an evening of luxurious woe, deploring the loss of his treasures—giving their prices—to his sympathetic friends. The Duke had other views; and they prevailed. After dinner the guests went to the smoking-room, since the drawing-rooms were in possession of Guerchard. Soon after ten the Duke slipped away from them, and went to the detective. Guerchard's was not a face at any time full of expression, and all that the Duke saw on it was a subdued dulness.

"Well, M. Guerchard," he said cheerfully, "what luck? Have any of your men come across any traces of the passage of the burglars with their booty?"

"No, your Grace; so far, all the luck has been with the burglars. For all that any one seems to have seen them, they might have vanished into the bowels of the earth through the floor of the cellars in the empty house next door. That means that they were very quick loading whatever vehicle they used with their plunder. I should think, myself, that they first carried everything from this house down into the hall of the house next door; and then, of course, they could be very quick getting them from hall to their van, or whatever it was. But still, some one saw that van—saw it drive up to the house, or waiting at the house, or driving away from it."

"Is M. Formery coming back?" said the Duke.

"Not to-night," said Guerchard. "The affair is in my hands now; and I have my own men on it—men of some intelligence, or, at any rate, men who know my ways, and how I want things done."

"It must be a relief," said the Duke.

"Oh, no, I'm used to M. Formery—to all the examining magistrates in Paris, and in most of the big provincial towns. They do not really hamper me; and often I get an idea from them; for some of them are men of real intelligence."

"And others are not: I understand," said the Duke.

The door opened and Bonavent, the detective, came in.

"The housekeeper's awake, M. Guerchard," he said.

"Good, bring her down here," said Guerchard.

"Perhaps you'd like me to go," said the Duke.

"Oh, no," said Guerchard. "If it would interest you to hear me question her, please stay."

Bonavent left the room. The Duke sat down in an easy chair, and Guerchard stood before the fireplace.

"M. Formery told me, when you were out this afternoon, that he believed this housekeeper to be quite innocent," said the Duke idly.

"There is certainly one innocent in this affair," said Guerchard, grinning.

"Who is that?" said the Duke.

"The examining magistrate," said Guerchard.

The door opened, and Bonavent brought Victoire in. She was a big, middle-aged woman, with a pleasant, cheerful, ruddy face, black-haired, with sparkling brown eyes, which did not seem to have been at all dimmed by her long, drugged sleep. She looked like a well-to-do farmer's wife, a buxom, good-natured, managing woman.

As soon as she came into the room, she said quickly:

"I wish, Mr Inspector, your man would have given me time to put on a decent dress. I must have been sleeping in this one ever since those rascals tied me up and put that smelly handkerchief over my face. I never saw such a nasty-looking crew as they were in my life."

"How many were there, Madame Victoire?" said Guerchard.

"Dozens! The house was just swarming with them. I heard the noise; I came downstairs; and on the landing outside the door here, one of them jumped on me from behind and nearly choked me—to prevent me from screaming, I suppose."

"And they were a nasty-looking crew, were they?" said Guerchard. "Did you see their faces?"

"No, I wish I had! I should know them again if I had; but they were all masked," said Victoire.

"Sit down, Madame Victoire. There's no need to tire you," said Guerchard. And she sat down on a chair facing him.

"Let's see, you sleep in one of the top rooms, Madame Victoire. It has a dormer window, set in the roof, hasn't it?" said Guerchard, in the same polite, pleasant voice.

"Yes; yes. But what has that got to do with it?" said Victoire.

"Please answer my questions," said Guerchard sharply. "You went to sleep in your room. Did you hear any noise on the roof?"

"On the roof? How should I hear it on the roof? There wouldn't be any noise on the roof," said Victoire.

"You heard nothing on the roof?" said Guerchard.

"No; the noise I heard was down here," said Victoire.

"Yes, and you came down to see what was making it. And you were seized from behind on the landing, and brought in here," said Guerchard.

"Yes, that's right," said Madame Victoire.

"And were you tied up and gagged on the landing, or in here?" said Guerchard.

"Oh, I was caught on the landing, and pushed in here, and then tied up," said Victoire.

"I'm sure that wasn't one man's job," said Guerchard, looking at her vigorous figure with admiring eyes.

"You may be sure of that," said Victoire. "It took four of them; and at least two of them have some nice bruises on their shins to show for it."

"I'm sure they have. And it serves them jolly well right," said Guerchard, in a tone of warm approval. "And, I suppose, while those four were tying you up the others stood round and looked on."

"Oh, no, they were far too busy for that," said Victoire.

"What were they doing?" said Guerchard.

"They were taking the pictures off the walls and carrying them out of the window down the ladder," said Victoire.

Guerchard's eyes flickered towards the Duke, but the expression of earnest inquiry on his face never changed.

"Now, tell me, did the man who took a picture from the walls carry it down the ladder himself, or did he hand it through the window to a man who was standing on the top of a ladder ready to receive it?" he said.

Victoire paused as if to recall their action; then she said, "Oh, he got through the window, and carried it down the ladder himself."

"You're sure of that?" said Guerchard.

"Oh, yes, I am quite sure of it—why should I deceive you, Mr Inspector?" said Victoire quickly; and the Duke saw the first shadow of uneasiness on her face.

"Of course not," said Guerchard. "And where were you?"

"Oh, they put me behind the screen."

"No, no, where were you when you came into the room?"

"I was against the door," said Victoire.

"And where was the screen?" said Guerchard. "Was it before the fireplace?"

"No; it was on one side—the left-hand side," said Victoire.

"Oh, will you show me exactly where it stood?" said Guerchard.

Victoire rose, and, Guerchard aiding her, set the screen on the left-hand side of the fireplace.

Guerchard stepped back and looked at it.

"Now, this is very important," he said. "I must have the exact position of the four feet of that screen. Let's see ... some chalk ... of course... You do some dressmaking, don't you, Madame Victoire?"

"Oh, yes, I sometimes make a dress for one of the maids in my spare time," said Victoire.

"Then you've got a piece of chalk on you," said Guerchard.

"Oh, yes," said Victoire, putting her hand to the pocket of her dress.

She paused, took a step backwards, and looked wildly round the room, while the colour slowly faded in her ruddy cheeks.

"What am I talking about?" she said in an uncertain, shaky voice. "I haven't any chalk—I—ran out of chalk the day before yesterday."

"I think you have, Madame Victoire. Feel in your pocket and see," said Guerchard sternly. His voice had lost its suavity; his face its smile: his eyes had grown dangerous.

"No, no; I have no chalk," cried Victoire.

With a sudden leap Guerchard sprang upon her, caught her in a firm grip with his right arm, and his left hand plunged into her pocket.

"Let me go! Let me go! You're hurting," she cried.

Guerchard loosed her and stepped back.

"What's this?" he said; and he held up between his thumb and forefinger a piece of blue chalk.

Victoire drew herself up and faced him gallantly: "Well, what of it?—it is chalk. Mayn't an honest woman carry chalk in her pockets without being insulted and pulled about by every policeman she comes across?" she cried.

"That will be for the examining magistrate to decide," said Guerchard; and he went to the door and called Bonavent. Bonavent came in, and Guerchard said: "When the prison van comes, put this woman in it; and send her down to the station."

"But what have I done?" cried Victoire. "I'm innocent! I declare I'm innocent. I've done nothing at all. It's not a crime to carry a piece of chalk in one's pocket."

"Now, that's a matter for the examining magistrate. You can explain it to him," said Guerchard. "I've got nothing to do with it: so it's no good making a fuss now. Do go quietly, there's a good woman."

He spoke in a quiet, business-like tone. Victoire looked him in the eyes, then drew herself up, and went quietly out of the room.

17

SONIA'S ESCAPE

"One of M. Formery's innocents," said Guerchard, turning to the Duke.

"The chalk?" said the Duke. "Is it the same chalk?"

"It's blue," said Guerchard, holding it out. "The same as that of the signatures on the walls. Add that fact to the woman's sudden realization of what she was doing, and you'll see that they were written with it."

"It is rather a surprise," said the Duke. "To look at her you would think that she was the most honest woman in the world."

"Ah, you don't know Lupin, your Grace," said Guerchard. "He can do anything with women; and they'll do anything for him. And, what's more, as far as I can see, it doesn't make a scrap of difference whether they're honest or not. The fair-haired lady I was telling you about was probably an honest woman; Ganimard is sure of it. We should have found out long ago who she was if she had been a wrong 'un. And Ganimard also swears that when he arrested Lupin on board the Provence some woman, some ordinary, honest woman among the passengers, carried away Lady Garland's jewels, which he had stolen and was bringing to America, and along with them a matter of eight hundred pounds which he had stolen from a fellow-passenger on the voyage."

"That power of fascination which some men exercise on women is one of those mysteries which science should investigate before it does anything else," said the Duke, in a reflective tone. "Now I come to think of it, I had much better have spent my time on that investigation than on that tedious journey to the South Pole. All the same, I'm deucedly sorry for that woman, Victoire. She looks such a good soul."

Guerchard shrugged his shoulders: "The prisons are full of good souls," he said, with cynical wisdom born of experience. "They get caught so much more often than the bad."

"It seems rather mean of Lupin to make use of women like this, and get them into trouble," said the Duke.

"But he doesn't," said Guerchard quickly. "At least he hasn't up to now. This Victoire is the first we've caught. I look on it as a good omen."

He walked across the room, picked up his cloak, and took a card-case from the inner pocket of it. "If you don't mind, your Grace, I want you to show this permit to my men who are keeping the door, whenever you go out of the house. It's just a formality; but I attach considerable importance to it, for I really ought not to make exceptions in favour of any one. I have two men at the door, and they have orders to let nobody out without my written permission. Of course M. Gournay-Martin's guests are different. Bonavent has orders to pass them out. And, if your Grace doesn't mind, it will help me. If you carry a permit, no one else will dream of complaining of having to do so."

"Oh, I don't mind, if it's of any help to you," said the Duke cheerfully.

"Thank you," said Guerchard. And he wrote on his card and handed it to the Duke.

The Duke took it and looked at it. On it was written:

"Pass the Duke of Charmerace." "J. GUERCHARD."

"It's quite military," said the Duke, putting the card into his waistcoat pocket.

There came a knock at the door, and a tall, thin, bearded man came into the room.

"Ah, Dieusy! At last! What news?" cried Guerchard.

Dieusy saluted: "I've learnt that a motor-van was waiting outside the next house—in the side street," he said.

"At what time?" said Guerchard.

"Between four and five in the morning," said Dieusy.

"Who saw it?" said Guerchard.

"A scavenger. He thinks that it was nearly five o'clock when the van drove off."

"Between four and five—nearly five. Then they filled up the opening before they loaded the van. I thought they would," said Guerchard, thoughtfully. "Anything else?"

"A few minutes after the van had gone a man in motoring dress came out of the house," said Dieusy.

"In motoring dress?" said Guerchard quickly.

"Yes. And a little way from the house he threw away his cigarette. The scavenger thought the whole business a little queer, and he picked up the cigarette and kept it. Here it is."

He handed it to Guerchard, whose eyes scanned it carelessly and then glued themselves to it.

"A gold-tipped cigarette ... marked Mercedes ... Why, your Grace, this is one of your cigarettes!"

"But this is incredible!" cried the Duke.

"Not at all," said Guerchard. "It's merely another link in the chain. I've no doubt you have some of these cigarettes at Charmerace."

"Oh, yes, I've had a box on most of the tables," said the Duke.

"Well, there you are," said Guerchard.

"Oh, I see what you're driving at," said the Duke. "You mean that one of the Charolais must have taken a box."

"Well, we know that they'd hardly stick at a box of cigarettes," said Guerchard.

"Yes ... but I thought ..." said the Duke; and he paused.

"You thought what?" said Guerchard.

"Then Lupin ... since it was Lupin who managed the business last night—since you found those salvias in the house next door ... then Lupin came from Charmerace."

"Evidently," said Guerchard.

"And Lupin is one of the Charolais."

"Oh, that's another matter," said Guerchard.

"But it's certain, absolutely certain," said the Duke. "We have the connecting links ... the salvias ... this cigarette."

"It looks very like it. You're pretty quick on a scent, I must say," said Guerchard. "What a detective you would have made! Only ... nothing is certain."

"But it IS. Whatever more do you want? Was he at Charmerace yesterday, or was he not? Did he, or did he not, arrange the theft of the motor-cars?"

"Certainly he did. But he himself might have remained in the background all the while," said Guerchard.

"In what shape? ... Under what mask? ... By Jove, I should like to see this fellow!" said the Duke.

"We shall see him to-night," said Guerchard.

"To-night?" said the Duke.

"Of course we shall; for he will come to steal the coronet between a quarter to twelve and midnight," said Guerchard.

"Never!" said the Duke. "You don't really believe that he'll have the cheek to attempt such a mad act?"

"Ah, you don't know this man, your Grace ... his extraordinary mixture of coolness and audacity. It's the danger that attracts him. He throws himself into the fire, and he doesn't get burnt. For the last ten years I've been saying to myself, 'Here we are:

this time I've got him! ... At last I'm going to nab him.' But I've said that day after day," said Guerchard; and he paused.

"Well?" said the Duke.

"Well, the days pass; and I never nab him. Oh, he is thick, I tell you... He's a joker, he is ... a regular artist"—he ground his teeth—"The damned thief!"

The Duke looked at him, and said slowly, "Then you think that to-night Lupin—"

"You've followed the scent with me, your Grace," Guerchard interrupted quickly and vehemently. "We've picked up each clue together. You've almost seen this man at work... You've understood him. Isn't a man like this, I ask you, capable of anything?"

"He is," said the Duke, with conviction.

"Well, then," said Guerchard.

"Perhaps you're right," said the Duke.

Guerchard turned to Dieusy and said, in a quieter voice, "And when the scavenger had picked up the cigarette, did he follow the motorist?"

"Yes, he followed him for about a hundred yards. He went down into Sureau Street, and turned westwards. Then a motor-car came along; he got into it, and went off."

"What kind of a motor-car?" said Guerchard.

"A big car, and dark red in colour," said Dieusy.

"The Limousine!" cried the Duke.

"That's all I've got so far, sir," said Dieusy.

"Well, off you go," said Guerchard. "Now that you've got started, you'll probably get something else before very long."

Dieusy saluted and went.

"Things are beginning to move," said Guerchard cheerfully. "First Victoire, and now this motor-van."

"They are indeed," said the Duke.

"After all, it ought not to be very difficult to trace that motor-van," said Guerchard, in a musing tone. "At any rate, its movements ought to be easy enough to follow up till about six. Then, of course, there would be a good many others about, delivering goods."

"You seem to have all the possible information you can want at your finger-ends," said the Duke, in an admiring tone.

"I suppose I know the life of Paris as well as anybody," said Guerchard.

They were silent for a while. Then Germaine's maid, Irma, came into the room and said:

"If you please, your Grace, Mademoiselle Kritchnoff would like to speak to you for a moment."

"Oh? Where is she?" said the Duke.

"She's in her room, your Grace."

"Oh, very well, I'll go up to her," said the Duke. "I can speak to her in the library."

He rose and was going towards the door when Guerchard stepped forward, barring his way, and said, "No, your Grace."

"No? Why?" said the Duke haughtily.

"I beg you will wait a minute or two till I've had a word with you," said Guerchard; and he drew a folded sheet of paper from his pocket and held it up.

The Duke looked at Guerchard's face, and he looked at the paper in his hand; then he said: "Oh, very well." And, turning to Irma, he added quietly, "Tell Mademoiselle Kritchnoff that I'm in the drawing-room."

"Yes, your Grace, in the drawing-room," said Irma; and she turned to go.

"Yes; and say that I shall be engaged for the next five minutes—the next five minutes, do you understand?" said the Duke.

"Yes, your Grace," said Irma; and she went out of the door.

"Ask Mademoiselle Kritchnoff to put on her hat and cloak," said Guerchard.

"Yes, sir," said Irma; and she went.

The Duke turned sharply on Guerchard, and said: "Now, why on earth? ... I don't understand."

"I got this from M. Formery," said Guerchard, holding up the paper.

"Well," said the Duke. "What is it?"

"It's a warrant, your Grace," said Guerchard.

"What! ... A warrant! ... Not for the arrest of Mademoiselle Kritchnoff?"

"Yes," said Guerchard.

"Oh, come, it's impossible," said the Duke. "You're never going to arrest that child?"

"I am, indeed," said Guerchard. "Her examination this afternoon was in the highest degree unsatisfactory. Her answers were embarrassed, contradictory, and in every way suspicious."

"And you've made up your mind to arrest her?" said the Duke slowly, knitting his brow in anxious thought.

"I have, indeed," said Guerchard. "And I'm going to do it now. The prison van ought to be waiting at the door." He looked at his watch. "She and Victoire can go together."

"So ... you're going to arrest her ... you're going to arrest her?" said the Duke thoughtfully: and he took a step or two up and down the room, still thinking hard.

"Well, you understand the position, don't you, your Grace?" said Guerchard, in a tone of apology. "Believe me that, personally, I've no animosity against Mademoiselle Kritchnoff. In fact, the child attracts me."

"Yes," said the Duke softly, in a musing tone. "She has the air of a child who has lost its way ... lost its way in life... And that poor little hiding-place she found ... that rolled-up handkerchief ... thrown down in the corner of the little room in the house next door ... it was absolutely absurd."

"What! A handkerchief!" cried Guerchard, with an air of sudden, utter surprise.

"The child's clumsiness is positively pitiful," said the Duke.

"What was in the handkerchief? ... The pearls of the pendant?" cried Guerchard.

"Yes: I supposed you knew all about it. Of course M. Formery left word for you," said the Duke, with an air of surprise at the ignorance of the detective.

"No: I've heard nothing about it," cried Guerchard.

"He didn't leave word for you?" said the Duke, in a tone of greater surprise. "Oh, well, I dare say that he thought to-morrow would do. Of course you were out of the house when he found it. She must have slipped out of her room soon after you went."

"He found a handkerchief belonging to Mademoiselle Kritchnoff. Where is it?" cried Guerchard.

"M. Formery took the pearls, but he left the handkerchief. I suppose it's in the corner where he found it," said the Duke.

"He left the handkerchief?" cried Guerchard. "If that isn't just like the fool! He ought to keep hens; it's all he's fit for!"

He ran to the fireplace, seized the lantern, and began lighting it: "Where is the handkerchief?" he cried.

"In the left-hand corner of the little room on the right on the second floor. But if you're going to arrest Mademoiselle Kritchnoff, why are you bothering about the handkerchief? It can't be of any importance," said the Duke.

"I beg your pardon," said Guerchard. "But it is."

"But why?" said the Duke.

"I was arresting Mademoiselle Kritchnoff all right because I had a very strong presumption of her guilt. But I hadn't the slightest proof of it," said Guerchard.

"What?" cried the Duke, in a horrified tone.

"No, you've just given me the proof; and since she was able to hide the pearls in the house next door, she knew the road which led to it. Therefore she's an accomplice," said Guerchard, in a triumphant tone.

"What? Do you think that, too?" cried the Duke. "Good Heavens! And it's me! ... It's my senselessness! ... It's my fault that you've got your proof!" He spoke in a tone of acute distress.

"It was your duty to give it me," said Guerchard sternly; and he began to mount the steps.

"Shall I come with you? I know where the handkerchief is," said the Duke quickly.

"No, thank you, your Grace," said Guerchard. "I prefer to go alone."

"You'd better let me help you," said the Duke.

"No, your Grace," said Guerchard firmly.

"I must really insist," said the Duke.

"No—no—no," said Guerchard vehemently, with stern decision. "It's no use your insisting, your Grace; I prefer to go alone. I shall only be gone a minute or two."

"Just as you like," said the Duke stiffly.

The legs of Guerchard disappeared up the steps. The Duke stood listening with all his ears. Directly he heard the sound of Guerchard's heels on the floor, when he dropped from the chimney-piece of the next room, he went swiftly to the door, opened it, and went out. Bonavent was sitting on the chair on which the young policeman had sat during the afternoon. Sonia, in her hat and cloak, was half-way down the stairs.

The Duke put his head inside the drawing-room door, and said to the empty room: "Here is Mademoiselle Kritchnoff, M. Guerchard." He held open the door, Sonia came down the stairs, and went through it. The Duke followed her into the drawing-room, and shut the door.

"There's not a moment to lose," he said in a low voice.

"Oh, what is it, your Grace?" said Sonia anxiously.

"Guerchard has a warrant for your arrest."

"Then I'm lost!" cried Sonia, in a panic-stricken voice.

"No, you're not. You must go—at once," said the Duke.

"But how can I go? No one can get out of the house. M. Guerchard won't let them," cried Sonia, panic-stricken.

"We can get over that," said the Duke.

He ran to Guerchard's cloak, took the card-case from the inner pocket, went to the writing-table, and sat down. He took from his waist-coat pocket the permit which Guerchard had given him, and a pencil. Then he took a card from the card-case, set the permit on the table before him, and began to imitate Guerchard's handwriting with an amazing exactness. He wrote on the card:

"Pass Mademoiselle Kritchnoff." "J. GUERCHARD."

Sonia stood by his side, panting quickly with fear, and watched him do it. He had scarcely finished the last stroke, when they heard a noise on the other side of the opening into the empty house. The Duke looked at the fireplace, and his teeth bared in an expression of cold ferocity. He rose with clenched fists, and took a step towards the fireplace.

"Your Grace? Your Grace?" called the voice of Guerchard.

"What is it?" answered the Duke quietly.

"I can't see any handkerchief," said Guerchard. "Didn't you say it was in the left-hand corner of the little room on the right?"

"I told you you'd better let me come with you, and find it," said the Duke, in a tone of triumph. "It's in the right-hand corner of the little room on the left."

"I could have sworn you said the little room on the right," said Guerchard.

They heard his footfalls die away.

"Now, you must get out of the house quickly." said the Duke. "Show this card to the detectives at the door, and they'll pass you without a word."

He pressed the card into her hand.

"But—but—this card?" stammered Sonia.

"There's no time to lose," said the Duke.

"But this is madness," said Sonia. "When Guerchard finds out about this card—that you—you—"

"There's no need to bother about that," interrupted the Duke quickly. "Where are you going to?"

"A little hotel near the Star. I've forgotten the name of it," said Sonia. "But this card—"

"Has it a telephone?" said the Duke.

"Yes—No. 555, Central," said Sonia.

"If I haven't telephoned to you before half-past eight to-morrow morning, come straight to my house," said the Duke, scribbling the telephone number on his shirt-cuff.

"Yes, yes," said Sonia. "But this card... When Guerchard knows ... when he discovers... Oh, I can't let you get into trouble for me."

"I shan't. But go—go," said the Duke, and he slipped his right arm round her and drew her to the door.

"Oh, how good you are to me," said Sonia softly.

The Duke's other arm went round her; he drew her to him, and their lips met.

He loosed her, and opened the door, saying loudly: "You're sure you won't have a cab, Mademoiselle Kritchnoff?"

"No; no, thank you, your Grace. Goodnight," said Sonia. And she went through the door with a transfigured face.

18

THE DUKE STAYS

The Duke shut the door and leant against it, listening anxiously, breathing quickly. There came the bang of the front door. With a deep sigh of relief he left the door, came briskly, smiling, across the room, and put the card-case back into the pocket of Guerchard's cloak. He lighted a cigarette, dropped into an easy chair, and sat waiting with an entirely careless air for the detective's return. Presently he heard quick footsteps on the bare boards of the empty room beyond the opening. Then Guerchard came down the steps and out of the fireplace.

His face wore an expression of extreme perplexity:

"I can't understand it," he said. "I found nothing."

"Nothing?" said the Duke.

"No. Are you sure you saw the handkerchief in one of those little rooms on the second floor—quite sure?" said Guerchard.

"Of course I did," said the Duke. "Isn't it there?"

"No," said Guerchard.

"You can't have looked properly," said the Duke, with a touch of irony in his voice. "If I were you, I should go back and look again."

"No. If I've looked for a thing, I've looked for it. There's no need for me to look a second time. But, all the same, it's rather funny. Doesn't it strike you as being rather funny, your Grace?" said Guerchard, with a worried air.

"It strikes me as being uncommonly funny," said the Duke, with an ambiguous smile.

Guerchard looked at him with a sudden uneasiness; then he rang the bell.

Bonavent came into the room.

"Mademoiselle Kritchnoff, Bonavent. It's quite time," said Guerchard.

"Mademoiselle Kritchnoff?" said Bonavent, with an air of surprise.

"Yes, it's time that she was taken to the police-station."

"Mademoiselle Kritchnoff has gone, sir," said Bonavent, in a tone of quiet remonstrance.

"Gone? What do you mean by gone?" said Guerchard.

"Gone, sir, gone!" said Bonavent patiently.

"But you're mad... Mad!" cried Guerchard.

"No, I'm not mad," said Bonavent.

"Gone! But who let her go?" cried Guerchard.

"The men at the door," said Bonavent.

"The men at the door," said Guerchard, in a tone of stupefaction. "But she had to have my permit ... my permit on my card! Send the fools up to me!"

Bonavent went to the top of the staircase, and called down it. Guerchard followed him. Two detectives came hurrying up the stairs and into the drawing-room.

"What the devil do you mean by letting Mademoiselle Kritchnoff leave the house without my permit, written on my card?" cried Guerchard violently.

"But she had your permit, sir, and it WAS written on your card," stammered one of the detectives.

"It was? ... It was?" said Guerchard. "Then, by Jove, it was a forgery!"

He stood thoughtful for a moment. Then quietly he told his two men to go back to their post. He did not stir for a minute or two, puzzling it out, seeking light.

Then he came back slowly into the drawing-room and looked uneasily at the Duke. The Duke was sitting in his easy chair, smoking a cigarette with a listless air. Guerchard looked at him, and looked at him, almost as if he now saw him for the first time.

"Well?" said the Duke, "Have you sent that poor child off to prison? If I'd done a thing like that I don't think I should sleep very well, M. Guerchard."

"That poor child has just escaped, by means of a forged permit," said Guerchard very glumly.

"By Jove, I AM glad to hear that!" cried the Duke. "You'll forgive my lack of sympathy, M. Guerchard; but she was such a child."

"Not too young to be Lupin's accomplice," said Guerchard drily.

"You really think she is?" said the Duke, in a tone of doubt.

"I'm sure of it," said Guerchard, with decision; then he added slowly, with a perplexed air:

"But how—how—could she get that forged permit?"

The Duke shook his head, and looked as solemn as an owl. Guerchard looked at him uneasily, went out of the drawing-room, and shut the door.

"How long has Mademoiselle Kritchnoff been gone?" he said to Bonavent.

"Not much more than five minutes," said Bonavent. "She came out from talking to you in the drawing-room—"

"Talking to me in the drawing-room!" exclaimed Guerchard.

"Yes," said Bonavent. "She came out and went straight down the stairs and out of the house."

A faint, sighing gasp came from Guerchard's lips. He dashed into the drawing-room, crossed the room quickly to his cloak, picked it up, took the card-case out of the pocket, and counted the cards in it. Then he looked at the Duke.

The Duke smiled at him, a charming smile, almost caressing.

There seemed to be a lump in Guerchard's throat; he swallowed it loudly.

He put the card-case into the breast-pocket of the coat he was wearing. Then he cried sharply, "Bonavent! Bonavent!"

Bonavent opened the door, and stood in the doorway.

"You sent off Victoire in the prison-van, I suppose," said Guerchard.

"Oh, a long while ago, sir," said Bonavent.

"The van had been waiting at the door since half-past nine."

"Since half-past nine? ... But I told them I shouldn't want it till a quarter to eleven. I suppose they were making an effort to be in time for once. Well, it doesn't matter," said Guerchard.

"Then I suppose I'd better send the other prison-van away?" said Bonavent.

"What other van?" said Guerchard.

"The van which has just arrived," said Bonavent.

"What! What on earth are you talking about?" cried Guerchard, with a sudden anxiety in his voice and on his face.

"Didn't you order two prison-vans?" said Bonavent.

Guerchard jumped; and his face went purple with fury and dismay. "You don't mean to tell me that two prison-vans have been here?" he cried.

"Yes, sir," said Bonavent.

"Damnation!" cried Guerchard. "In which of them did you put Victoire? In which of them?"

"Why, in the first, sir," said Bonavent.

"Did you see the police in charge of it? The coachman?"

"Yes, sir," said Bonavent.

"Did you recognize them?" said Guerchard.

"No," said Bonavent; "they must have been new men. They told me they came from the Sante."

"You silly fool!" said Guerchard through his teeth. "A fine lot of sense you've got."

"Why, what's the matter?" said Bonavent.

"We're done, done in the eye!" roared Guerchard. "It's a stroke—a stroke—"

"Of Lupin's!" interposed the Duke softly.

"But I don't understand," said Bonavent.

"You don't understand, you idiot!" cried Guerchard. "You've sent Victoire away in a sham prison-van—a prison-van belonging to Lupin. Oh, that scoundrel! He always has something up his sleeve."

"He certainly shows foresight," said the Duke. "It was very clever of him to foresee the arrest of Victoire and provide against it."

"Yes, but where is the leakage? Where is the leakage?" cried Guerchard, fuming. "How did he learn that the doctor said that she would recover her wits at ten o'clock? Here I've had a guard at the door all day; I've imprisoned the household; all the provisions have been received directly by a man of mine; and here he is, ready to pick up Victoire the very moment she gives herself away! Where is the leakage?"

He turned on Bonavent, and went on: "It's no use your standing there with your mouth open, looking like a fool. Go upstairs to the servants' quarters and search Victoire's room again. That fool of an inspector may have missed something, just as he missed Victoire herself. Get on! Be smart!"

Bonavent went off briskly. Guerchard paced up and down the room, scowling.

"Really, I'm beginning to agree with you, M. Guerchard, that this Lupin is a remarkable man," said the Duke. "That prison-van is extraordinarily neat."

"I'll prison-van him!" cried Guerchard. "But what fools I have to work with. If I could get hold of people of ordinary intelligence it would be impossible to play such a trick as that."

"I don't know about that," said the Duke thoughtfully. "I think it would have required an uncommon fool to discover that trick."

"What on earth do you mean? Why?" said Guerchard.

"Because it's so wonderfully simple," said the Duke. "And at the same time it's such infernal cheek."

"There's something in that," said Guerchard grumpily. "But then, I'm always saying to my men, 'Suspect everything; suspect everybody; suspect, suspect, suspect.' I tell you, your Grace, that there is only one motto for the successful detective, and that is that one word, 'suspect.'"

"It can't be a very comfortable business, then," said the Duke. "But I suppose it has its charms."

"Oh, one gets used to the disagreeable part," said Guerchard.

The telephone bell rang; and he rose and went to it. He put the receiver to his ear and said, "Yes; it's I—Chief-Inspector Guerchard."

He turned and said to the Duke, "It's the gardener at Charmerace, your Grace."

"Is it?" said the Duke indifferently.

Guerchard turned to the telephone. "Are you there?" he said. "Can you hear me clearly? ... I want to know who was in your hot-house yesterday ... who could have gathered some of your pink salvias?"

"I told you that it was I," said the Duke.

"Yes, yes, I know," said Guerchard. And he turned again to the telephone. "Yes, yesterday," he said. "Nobody else? ... No one but the Duke of Charmerace? ... Are you sure?... Quite sure?... Absolutely sure? ... Yes, that's all I wanted to know ... thank you."

He turned to the Duke and said, "Did you hear that, your Grace? The gardener says that you were the only person in his hot-houses yesterday, the only person who could have plucked any pink salvias."

"Does he?" said the Duke carelessly.

Guerchard looked at him, his brow knitted in a faint, pondering frown. Then the door opened, and Bonavent came in: "I've been through Victoire's room," he said, "and all I could find that might be of any use is this—a prayer-book. It was on her dressing-table just as she left it. The inspector hadn't touched it."

"What about it?" said Guerchard, taking the prayer-book.

"There's a photograph in it," said Bonavent. "It may come in useful when we circulate her description; for I suppose we shall try to get hold of Victoire."

Guerchard took the photograph from the prayer-book and looked at it: "It looks about ten years old," he said. "It's a good deal faded for reproduction. Hullo! What have we here?"

The photograph showed Victoire in her Sunday best, and with her a boy of seventeen or eighteen. Guerchard's eyes glued themselves to the face of the boy. He stared at it, holding the portrait now nearer, now further off. His eyes kept stealing covertly from the photograph to the face of the Duke.

The Duke caught one of those covert glances, and a vague uneasiness flickered in his eyes. Guerchard saw it. He came nearer to the Duke and looked at him earnestly, as if he couldn't believe his eyes.

"What's the matter?" said the Duke. "What are you looking at so curiously? Isn't my tie straight?" And he put up his hand and felt it.

"Oh, nothing, nothing," said Guerchard. And he studied the photograph again with a frowning face.

There was a noise of voices and laughter in the hall.

"Those people are going," said the Duke. "I must go down and say good-bye to them." And he rose and went out of the room.

Guerchard stood staring, staring at the photograph.

The Duke ran down the stairs, and said goodbye to the millionaire's guests. After they had gone, M. Gournay-Martin went quickly up the stairs; Germaine and the Duke followed more slowly.

"My father is going to the Ritz to sleep," said Germaine, "and I'm going with him. He doesn't like the idea of my sleeping in this house to-night. I suppose he's afraid that Lupin will make an attack in force with all his gang. Still, if he did, I think that Guerchard could give a good account of himself—he's got men enough in the house, at any rate. Irma tells me it's swarming with them. It would never do for me to be in the house if there were a fight."

"Oh, come, you don't really believe that Lupin is coming to-night?" said the Duke, with a sceptical laugh. "The whole thing is sheer bluff—he has no more intention of coming tonight to steal that coronet than—than I have."

"Oh, well, there's no harm in being on the safe side," said Germaine. "Everybody's agreed that he's a very terrible person. I'll just run up to my room and get a wrap; Irma has my things all packed. She can come round tomorrow morning to the Ritz and dress me."

She ran up the stairs, and the Duke went into the drawing-room. He found Guerchard standing where he had left him, still frowning, still thinking hard.

"The family are off to the Ritz. It's rather a reflection on your powers of protecting them, isn't it?" said the Duke.

"Oh, well, I expect they'd be happier out of the house," said Guerchard. He looked at the Duke again with inquiring, searching eyes.

"What's the matter?" said the Duke. "IS my tie crooked?"

"Oh, no, no; it's quite straight, your Grace," said Guerchard, but he did not take his eyes from the Duke's face.

The door opened, and in came M. Gournay-Martin, holding a bag in his hand. "It seems to be settled that I'm never to sleep in my own house again," he said in a grumbling tone.

"There's no reason to go," said the Duke. "Why ARE you going?"

"Danger," said M. Gournay-Martin. "You read Lupin's telegram: 'I shall come to-night between a quarter to twelve and midnight to take the coronet.' He knows that it was in my bedroom. Do you think I'm going to sleep in that room with the chance of that scoundrel turning up and cutting my throat?"

"Oh, you can have a dozen policemen in the room if you like," said the Duke. "Can't he, M. Guerchard?"

"Certainly," said Guerchard. "I can answer for it that you will be in no danger, M. Gournay-Martin."

"Thank you," said the millionaire. "But all the same, outside is good enough for me."

Germaine came into the room, cloaked and ready to start.

"For once in a way you are ready first, papa," she said. "Are you coming, Jacques?"

"No; I think I'll stay here, on the chance that Lupin is not bluffing," said the Duke. "I don't think, myself, that I'm going to be gladdened by the sight of him—in fact, I'm ready to bet against it. But you're all so certain about it that I really must stay on the chance. And, after all, there's no doubt that he's a man of immense audacity and ready to take any risk."

"Well, at any rate, if he does come he won't find the diadem," said M. Gournay-Martin, in a tone of triumph. "I'm taking it with me—I've got it here." And he held up his bag.

"You are?" said the Duke.

"Yes, I am," said M. Gournay-Martin firmly.

"Do you think it's wise?" said the Duke.

"Why not?" said M. Gournay-Martin.

"If Lupin's really made up his mind to collar that coronet, and if you're so sure that, in spite of all these safeguards, he's going to make the attempt, it seems to me that you're taking a considerable risk. He asked you to have it ready for him in your bedroom. He didn't say which bedroom."

"Good Lord! I never thought of that!" said M. Gournay-Martin, with an air of sudden and very lively alarm.

"His Grace is right," said Guerchard. "It would be exactly like Lupin to send that telegram to drive you out of the house with the coronet to some place where you would be less protected. That is exactly one of his tricks."

"Good Heavens!" said the millionaire, pulling out his keys and unlocking the bag. He opened it, paused hesitatingly, and snapped it to again.

"Half a minute," he said. "I want a word with you, Duke."

He led the way out of the drawing-room door and the Duke followed him. He shut the door and said in a whisper:

"In a case like this, I suspect everybody."

"Everybody suspects everybody, apparently," said the Duke. "Are you sure you don't suspect me?"

"Now, now, this is no time for joking," said the millionaire impatiently. "What do you think about Guerchard?"

"About Guerchard?" said the Duke. "What do you mean?"

"Do you think I can put full confidence in Guerchard?" said M. Gournay-Martin.

"Oh, I think so," said the Duke. "Besides, I shall be here to look after Guerchard. And, though I wouldn't undertake to answer for Lupin, I think I can answer for Guerchard. If he tries to escape with the coronet, I will wring his neck for you with pleasure. It would do me good. And it would do Guerchard good, too."

The millionaire stood reflecting for a minute or two. Then he said, "Very good; I'll trust him."

Hardly had the door closed behind the millionaire and the Duke, when Guerchard crossed the room quickly to Germaine and drew from his pocket the photograph of Victoire and the young man.

"Do you know this photograph of his Grace, mademoiselle?" he said quickly.

Germaine took the photograph and looked at it.

"It's rather faded," she said.

"Yes; it's about ten years old," said Guerchard.

"I seem to know the face of the woman," said Germaine. "But if it's ten years old it certainly isn't the photograph of the Duke."

"But it's like him?" said Guerchard.

"Oh, yes, it's like the Duke as he is now—at least, it's a little like him. But it's not like the Duke as he was ten years ago. He has changed so," said Germaine.

"Oh, has he?" said Guerchard.

"Yes; there was that exhausting journey of his—and then his illness. The doctors gave up all hope of him, you know."

"Oh, did they?" said Guerchard.

"Yes; at Montevideo. But his health is quite restored now."

The door opened and the millionaire and the Duke came into the room. M. Gournay-Martin set his bag upon the table, unlocked it, and with a solemn air took out the case which held the coronet. He opened it; and they looked at it.

"Isn't it beautiful?" he said with a sigh.

"Marvellous!" said the Duke.

M. Gournay-Martin closed the case, and said solemnly:

"There is danger, M. Guerchard, so I am going to trust the coronet to you. You are the defender of my hearth and home—you are the proper person to guard the coronet. I take it that you have no objection?"

"Not the slightest, M. Gournay-Martin," said Guerchard. "It's exactly what I wanted you to ask me to do."

M. Gournay-Martin hesitated. Then he handed the coronet to Guerchard, saying with a frank and noble air, "I have every confidence in you, M. Guerchard."

"Thank you," said Guerchard.

"Good-night," said M. Gournay-Martin.

"Good-night, M. Guerchard," said Germaine.

"I think, after all, I'll change my mind and go with you. I'm very short of sleep," said the Duke. "Good-night, M. Guerchard."

"You're never going too, your Grace!" cried Guerchard.

"Why, you don't want me to stay, do you?" said the Duke.

"Yes," said Guerchard slowly.

"I think I would rather go to bed," said the Duke gaily.

"Are you afraid?" said Guerchard, and there was challenge, almost an insolent challenge, in his tone.

There was a pause. The Duke frowned slightly with a reflective air. Then he drew himself up; and said a little haughtily:

"You've certainly found the way to make me stay, M. Guerchard."

"Yes, yes; stay, stay," said M. Gournay-Martin hastily. "It's an excellent idea, excellent. You're the very man to help M. Guerchard, Duke. You're an intrepid explorer, used to danger and resourceful, absolutely fearless."

"Do you really mean to say you're not going home to bed, Jacques?" said Germaine, disregarding her father's wish with her usual frankness.

"No; I'm going to stay with M. Guerchard," said the Duke slowly.

"Well, you will be fresh to go to the Princess's to-morrow night." said Germaine petulantly. "You didn't get any sleep at all last night, you couldn't have. You left Charmerace at eight o'clock; you were motoring all the night, and only got to Paris at six o'clock this morning."

"Motoring all night, from eight o'clock to six!" muttered Guerchard under his breath.

"Oh, that will be all right," said the Duke carelessly. "This interesting affair is to be over by midnight, isn't it?"

"Well, I warn you that, tired or fresh, you will have to come with me to the Princess's to-morrow night. All Paris will be there—all Paris, that is, who are in Paris."

"Oh, I shall be fresh enough," said the Duke.

They went out of the drawing-room and down the stairs, all four of them. There was an alert readiness about Guerchard, as if he were ready to spring. He kept within a foot of the Duke right to the front door. The detective in charge opened it; and they went down the steps to the taxi-cab which was awaiting them. The Duke kissed Germaine's fingers and handed her into the taxi-cab.

M. Gournay-Martin paused at the cab-door, and turned and said, with a pathetic air, "Am I never to sleep in my own house again?" He got into the cab and drove off.

The Duke turned and came up the steps, followed by Guerchard. In the hall he took his opera-hat and coat from the stand, and went upstairs. Half-way up the flight he paused and said:

"Where shall we wait for Lupin, M. Guerchard? In the drawing-room, or in M. Gournay-Martin's bedroom?"

"Oh, the drawing-room," said Guerchard. "I think it very unlikely that Lupin will look for the coronet in M. Gournay-Martin's bedroom. He would know very well that that is the last place to find it now."

The Duke went on into the drawing-room. At the door Guerchard stopped and said: "I will just go and post my men, your Grace."

"Very good," said the Duke; and he went into the drawing-room.

He sat down, lighted a cigarette, and yawned. Then he took out his watch and looked at it.

"Another twenty minutes," he said.

19

THE DUKE GOES

When Guerchard joined the Duke in the drawing-room, he had lost his calm air and was looking more than a little nervous. He moved about the room uneasily, fingering the bric-a-brac, glancing at the Duke and looking quickly away from him again. Then he came to a standstill on the hearth-rug with his back to the fireplace.

"Do you think it's quite safe to stand there, at least with your back to the hearth? If Lupin dropped through that opening suddenly, he'd catch you from behind before you could wink twice," said the Duke, in a tone of remonstrance.

"There would always be your Grace to come to my rescue," said Guerchard; and there was an ambiguous note in his voice, while his piercing eyes now rested fixed on the Duke's face. They seemed never to leave it; they explored, and explored it.

"It's only a suggestion," said the Duke. "This is rather nervous work, don't you know."

"Yes; and of course you're hardly fit for it," said Guerchard. "If I'd known about your break-down in your car last night, I should have hesitated about asking you—"

"A break-down?" interrupted the Duke.

"Yes, you left Charmerace at eight o'clock last night. And you only reached Paris at six this morning. You couldn't have had a very high-power car?" said Guerchard.

"I had a 100 h.p. car," said the Duke.

"Then you must have had a devil of a break-down," said Guerchard.

"Yes, it was pretty bad, but I've known worse," said the Duke carelessly. "It lost me about three hours: oh, at least three hours. I'm not a first-class repairer, though I know as much about an engine as most motorists."

"And there was nobody there to help you repair it?" said Guerchard.

"No; M. Gournay-Martin could not let me have his chauffeur to drive me to Paris, because he was keeping him to help guard the chateau. And of course there was nobody on the road, because it was two o'clock in the morning."

"Yes, there was no one," said Guerchard slowly.

"Not a soul," said the Duke.

"It was unfortunate," said Guerchard; and there was a note of incredulity in his voice.

"My having to repair the car myself?" said the Duke.

"Yes, of course," said Guerchard, hesitating a little over the assent.

The Duke dropped the end of his cigarette into a tray, and took out his case. He held it out towards Guerchard, and said, "A cigarette? Or perhaps you prefer your caporal?"

"Yes, I do, but all the same I'll have one," said Guerchard, coming quickly across the room. And he took a cigarette from the case, and looked at it.

"All the same, all this is very curious," he said in a new tone, a challenging, menacing, accusing tone.

"What?" said the Duke, looking at him curiously.

"Everything: your cigarettes ... the salvias ... the photograph that Bonavent found in Victoire's prayer-book ... that man in motoring dress ... and finally, your break-down," said Guerchard; and the accusation and the threat rang clearer.

The Duke rose from his chair quickly and said haughtily, in icy tones: "M. Guerchard, you've been drinking!"

He went to the chair on which he had set his overcoat and his hat, and picked them up. Guerchard sprang in front of him, barring his way, and cried in a shaky voice: "No; don't go! You mustn't go!"

"What do you mean?" said the Duke, and paused. "What DO you mean?"

Guerchard stepped back, and ran his hand over his forehead. He was very pale, and his forehead was clammy to his touch:

"No ... I beg your pardon ... I beg your pardon, your Grace ... I must be going mad," he stammered.

"It looks very like it," said the Duke coldly.

"What I mean to say is," said Guerchard in a halting, uncertain voice, "what I mean to say is: help me ... I want you to stay here, to help me against Lupin, you understand. Will you, your Grace?"

"Yes, certainly; of course I will, if you want me to," said the Duke, in a more gentle voice. "But you seem awfully upset, and you're upsetting me too. We shan't have a nerve between us soon, if you don't pull yourself together."

"Yes, yes, please excuse me," muttered Guerchard.

"Very good," said the Duke. "But what is it we're going to do?"

Guerchard hesitated. He pulled out his handkerchief, and mopped his forehead: "Well ... the coronet ... is it in this case?" he said in a shaky voice, and set the case on the table.

"Of course it is," said the Duke impatiently.

Guerchard opened the case, and the coronet sparkled and gleamed brightly in the electric light: "Yes, it is there; you see it?" said Guerchard.

"Yes, I see it; well?" said the Duke, looking at him in some bewilderment, so unlike himself did he seem.

"We're going to wait," said Guerchard.

"What for?" said the Duke.

"Lupin," said Guerchard.

"Lupin? And you actually do believe that, just as in a fairy tale, when that clock strikes twelve, Lupin will enter and take the coronet?"

"Yes, I do; I do," said Guerchard with stubborn conviction. And he snapped the case to.

"This is most exciting," said the Duke.

"You're sure it doesn't bore you?" said Guerchard huskily.

"Not a bit of it," said the Duke, with cheerful derision. "To make the acquaintance of this scoundrel who has fooled you for ten years is as charming a way of spending the evening as I can think of."

"You say that to me?" said Guerchard with a touch of temper.

"Yes," said the Duke, with a challenging smile. "To you."

He sat down in an easy chair by the table. Guerchard sat down in a chair on the other side of it, and set his elbows on it. They were silent.

Suddenly the Duke said, "Somebody's coming."

Guerchard started, and said: "No, I don't hear any one."

Then there came distinctly the sound of a footstep and a knock at the door.

"You've got keener ears than I," said Guerchard grudgingly. "In all this business you've shown the qualities of a very promising detective." He rose, went to the door, and unlocked it.

Bonavent came in: "I've brought you the handcuffs, sir," he said, holding them out. "Shall I stay with you?"

"No," said Guerchard. "You've two men at the back door, and two at the front, and a man in every room on the ground-floor?"

"Yes, and I've got three men on every other floor," said Bonavent, in a tone of satisfaction.

"And the house next door?" said Guerchard.

"There are a dozen men in it," said Bonavent. "No communication between the two houses is possible any longer."

Guerchard watched the Duke's face with intent eyes. Not a shadow flickered its careless serenity.

"If any one tries to enter the house, collar him. If need be, fire on him," said Guerchard firmly. "That is my order; go and tell the others."

"Very good, sir," said Bonavent; and he went out of the room.

"By Jove, we are in a regular fortress," said the Duke.

"It's even more of a fortress than you think, your Grace. I've four men on that landing," said Guerchard, nodding towards the door.

"Oh, have you?" said the Duke, with a sudden air of annoyance.

"You don't like that?" said Guerchard quickly.

"I should jolly well think not," said the Duke. "With these precautions, Lupin will never be able to get into this room at all."

"He'll find it a pretty hard job," said Guerchard, smiling. "Unless he falls from the ceiling, or unless—"

"Unless you're Arsène Lupin," interrupted the Duke.

"In that case, you'd be another, your Grace," said Guerchard.

They both laughed. The Duke rose, yawned, picked up his coat and hat, and said, "Ah, well, I'm off to bed."

"What?" said Guerchard.

"Well," said the Duke, yawning again, "I was staying to see Lupin. As there's no longer any chance of seeing him—"

"But there is ... there is ... so stay," cried Guerchard.

"Do you still cling to that notion?" said the Duke wearily.

"We SHALL see him," said Guerchard.

"Nonsense!" said the Duke.

Guerchard lowered his voice and said with an air of the deepest secrecy: "He's already here, your Grace."

"Lupin? Here?" cried the Duke.

"Yes; Lupin," said Guerchard.

"Where?" cried the astonished Duke.

"He is," said Guerchard.

"As one of your men?" said the Duke eagerly.

"I don't think so," said Guerchard, watching him closely.

"Well, but, well, but—if he's here we've got him... He is going to turn up," said the Duke triumphantly; and he set down his hat on the table beside the coronet.

"I hope so," said Guerchard. "But will he dare to?"

"How do you mean?" said the Duke, with a puzzled air.

"Well, you have said yourself that this is a fortress. An hour ago, perhaps, Lupin was resolved to enter this room, but is he now?"

"I see what you mean," said the Duke, in a tone of disappointment.

"Yes; you see that now it needs the devil's own courage. He must risk everything to gain everything, and throw off the mask. Is Lupin going to throw himself into the wolf's jaws? I dare not think it. What do you think about it?"

Guerchard's husky voice had hardened to a rough harshness; there was a ring of acute anxiety in it, and under the anxiety a faint note of challenge, of a challenge that dare not make itself too distinct. His anxious, challenging eyes burned on the face of the Duke, as if they strove with all intensity to pierce a mask.

The Duke looked at him curiously, as if he were trying to divine what he would be at, but with a careless curiosity, as if it were a matter of indifference to him what the detective's object was; then he said carelessly: "Well, you ought to know better than I. You have known him for ten years ..." He paused, and added with just the faintest stress in his tone, "At least, by reputation."

The anxiety in the detective's face grew plainer, it almost gave him the air of being unnerved; and he said quickly, in a jerky voice: "Yes, and I know his way of acting too. During the last ten years I have learnt to unravel his intrigues—to understand and anticipate his manoeuvres... Oh, his is a clever system! ... Instead of lying low, as you'd expect, he attacks his opponent ... openly... He confuses him—at least, he tries to." He smiled a half-confident, a half-doubtful smile, "It is a mass of entangled, mysterious combinations. I've been caught in them myself again and again. You smile?"

"It interests me so," said the Duke, in a tone of apology.

"Oh, it interests me," said Guerchard, with a snarl. "But this time I see my way clearly. No more tricks—no more secret paths ... We're fighting in the light of day." He paused, and said in a clear, sneering voice, "Lupin has pluck, perhaps, but it's only thief's pluck."

"Oh, is it?" said the Duke sharply, and there was a sudden faint glitter in his eyes.

"Yes; rogues have very poor qualities," sneered Guerchard.

"One can't have everything," said the Duke quietly; but his languid air had fallen from him.

"Their ambushes, their attacks, their fine tactics aren't up to much," said Guerchard, smiling contemptuously.

"You go a trifle too far, I think," said the Duke, smiling with equal contempt.

They looked one another in the eyes with a long, lingering look. They had suddenly the air of fencers who have lost their tempers, and are twisting the buttons off their foils.

"Not a bit of it, your Grace," said Guerchard; and his voice lingered on the words "your Grace" with a contemptuous stress. "This famous Lupin is immensely overrated."

"However, he has done some things which aren't half bad," said the Duke, with his old charming smile.

He had the air of a duelist drawing his blade lovingly through his fingers before he falls to.

"Oh, has he?" said Guerchard scornfully.

"Yes; one must be fair. Last night's burglary, for instance: it is not unheard of, but it wasn't half bad. And that theft of the motorcars: it was a neat piece of work," said the Duke in a gentle, insolent voice, infinitely aggravating.

Guerchard snorted scornfully.

"And a robbery at the British Embassy, another at the Treasury, and a third at M. Lepine's—all in the same week—it wasn't half bad, don't you know?" said the Duke, in the same gentle, irritating voice.

"Oh, no, it wasn't. But—"

"And the time when he contrived to pass as Guerchard—the Great Guerchard—do you remember that?" the Duke interrupted. "Come, come—to give the devil his due—between ourselves—it wasn't half bad."

"No," snarled Guerchard. "But he has done better than that lately... Why don't you speak of that?"

"Of what?" said the Duke.

"Of the time when he passed as the Duke of Charmerace," snapped Guerchard.

"What! Did he do that?" cried the Duke; and then he added slowly, "But, you know, I'm like you—I'm so easy to imitate."

"What would have been amusing, your Grace, would have been to get as far as actual marriage," said Guerchard more calmly.

"Oh, if he had wanted to," said the Duke; and he threw out his hands. "But you know—married life—for Lupin."

"A large fortune ... a pretty girl," said Guerchard, in a mocking tone.

"He must be in love with someone else," said the Duke.

"A thief, perhaps," sneered Guerchard.

"Like himself... And then, if you wish to know what I think, he must have found his fiancee rather trying," said the Duke, with his charming smile.

"After all, it's pitiful—heartrending, you must admit it, that, on the very eve of his marriage, he was such a fool as to throw off the mask. And yet at bottom it's quite logical; it's Lupin coming out through Charmerace. He had to grab at the dowry at the risk of losing the girl," said Guerchard, in a reflective tone; but his eyes were intent on the face of the Duke.

"Perhaps that's what one should call a marriage of reason," said the Duke, with a faint smile.

"What a fall!" said Guerchard, in a taunting voice. "To be expected, eagerly, at the Princess's to-morrow evening, and to pass the evening in a police-station ... to have intended in a month's time, as the Duke of Charmerace, to mount the steps of the Madeleine with all pomp and to fall down the father-in-law's staircase this evening—this very evening"—his voice rose suddenly on a note of savage triumph—"with the handcuffs on! What? Is that a good enough revenge for Guerchard—for that poor old idiot, Guerchard? The rogues' Brummel in a convict's cap! The gentleman-burglar in a gaol! For Lupin it's only a trifling annoyance, but for a duke it's a disaster! Come, in your turn, be frank: don't you find that amusing?"

The Duke rose quietly, and said coldly, "Have you finished?"

"DO you?" cried Guerchard; and he rose and faced him.

"Oh, yes; I find it quite amusing," said the Duke lightly.

"And so do I," cried Guerchard.

"No; you're frightened," said the Duke calmly.

"Frightened!" cried Guerchard, with a savage laugh.

"Yes, you're frightened," said the Duke. "And don't think, policeman, that because I'm familiar with you, I throw off a mask. I don't wear one. I've none to throw off. I AM the Duke of Charmerace."

"You lie! You escaped from the Sante four years ago. You are Lupin! I recognize you now."

"Prove it," said the Duke scornfully.

"I will!" cried Guerchard.

"You won't. I AM the Duke of Charmerace."

Guerchard laughed wildly.

"Don't laugh. You know nothing—nothing, dear boy," said the Duke tauntingly.

"Dear boy?" cried Guerchard triumphantly, as if the word had been a confession.

"What do I risk?" said the Duke, with scathing contempt. "Can you arrest me? ... You can arrest Lupin ... but arrest the Duke of Charmerace, an honourable gentleman, member of the Jockey Club, and of the Union, residing at his house, 34 B, University Street ... arrest the Duke of Charmerace, the fiance of Mademoiselle Gournay-Martin?"

"Scoundrel!" cried Guerchard, pale with sudden, helpless fury.

"Well, do it," taunted the Duke. "Be an ass... Make yourself the laughing-stock of Paris ... call your coppers in. Have you a proof—one single proof? Not one."

"Oh, I shall get them," howled Guerchard, beside himself.

"I think you may," said the Duke coolly. "And you might be able to arrest me next week ... the day after to-morrow perhaps ... perhaps never ... but not to-night, that's certain."

"Oh, if only somebody could hear you!" gasped Guerchard.

"Now, don't excite yourself," said the Duke. "That won't produce any proofs for you... The fact is, M. Formery told you the truth when he said that, when it is a case of Lupin, you lose your head. Ah, that Formery—there is an intelligent man if you like."

"At all events, the coronet is safe ... to-night—"

"Wait, my good chap ... wait," said the Duke slowly; and then he snapped out: "Do you know what's behind that door?" and he flung out his hand towards the door of the inner drawing-room, with a mysterious, sinister air.

"What?" cried Guerchard; and he whipped round and faced the door, with his eyes starting out of his head.

"Get out, you funk!" said the Duke, with a great laugh.

"Hang you!" said Guerchard shrilly.

"I said that you were going to be absolutely pitiable," said the Duke, and he laughed again cruelly.

"Oh, go on talking, do!" cried Guerchard, mopping his forehead.

"Absolutely pitiable," said the Duke, with a cold, disquieting certainty. "As the hand of that clock moves nearer and nearer midnight, you will grow more and more terrified." He paused, and then shouted violently, "Attention!"

Guerchard jumped; and then he swore.

"Your nerves are on edge," said the Duke, laughing.

"Joker!" snarled Guerchard.

"Oh, you're as brave as the next man. But who can stand the anguish of the unknown thing which is bound to happen? ... I'm right. You feel it, you're sure of it. At the end of these few fixed minutes an inevitable, fated event must happen. Don't shrug your shoulders, man; you're green with fear."

The Duke was no longer a smiling, cynical dandy. There emanated from him an impression of vivid, terrible force. His voice had deepened. It thrilled with a consciousness of irresistible power; it was overwhelming, paralyzing. His eyes were terrible.

"My men are outside ... I'm armed," stammered Guerchard.

"Child! Bear in mind ... bear in mind that it is always when you have foreseen everything, arranged everything, made every combination ... bear in mind that it is always then that some accident dashes your whole structure to the ground," said the Duke, in the same deep, thrilling voice. "Remember that it is always at the very moment at which you are going to triumph that he beats you, that he only lets you reach the top of the ladder to throw you more easily to the ground."

"Confess, then, that you are Lupin," muttered Guerchard.

"I thought you were sure of it," said the Duke in a jeering tone.

Guerchard dragged the handcuffs out of his pocket, and said between his teeth, "I don't know what prevents me, my boy."

The Duke drew himself up, and said haughtily, "That's enough."

"What?" cried Guerchard.

"I say that that's enough," said the Duke sternly. "It's all very well for me to play at being familiar with you, but don't you call me 'my boy.'"

"Oh, you won't impose on me much longer," muttered Guerchard; and his bloodshot, haggard eyes scanned the Duke's face in an agony, an anguish of doubting impotence.

"If I'm Lupin, arrest me," said the Duke.

"I'll arrest you in three minutes from now, or the coronet will be untouched," cried Guerchard in a firmer tone.

"In three minutes from now the coronet will have been stolen; and you will not arrest me," said the Duke, in a tone of chilling certainty.

"But I will! I swear I will!" cried Guerchard.

"Don't swear any foolish oaths! ... THERE ARE ONLY TWO MINUTES LEFT," said the Duke; and he drew a revolver from his pocket.

"No, you don't!" cried Guerchard, drawing a revolver in his turn.

"What's the matter?" said the Duke, with an air of surprise. "You haven't forbidden me to shoot Lupin. I have my revolver ready, since he's going to come... THERE'S ONLY A MINUTE LEFT."

"There are plenty of us," said Guerchard; and he went towards the door.

"Funk!" said the Duke scornfully.

Guerchard turned sharply. "Very well," he said, "I'll stick it out alone."

"How rash!" sneered the Duke.

Guerchard ground his teeth. He was panting; his bloodshot eyes rolled in their sockets; the beads of cold sweat stood out on his forehead. He came back towards the table on unsteady feet, trembling from head to foot in the last excitation of the nerves. He kept jerking his head to shake away the mist which kept dimming his eyes.

"At your slightest gesture, at your slightest movement, I'll fire," he said jerkily, and covered the Duke with his revolver.

"I call myself the Duke of Charmerace. You will be arrested to-morrow!" said the Duke, in a compelling, thrilling voice.

"I don't care a curse!" cried Guerchard.

"Only FIFTY SECONDS!" said the Duke.

"Yes, yes," muttered Guerchard huskily. And his eyes shot from the coronet to the Duke, from the Duke to the coronet.

"In fifty seconds the coronet will be stolen," said the Duke.

"No!" cried Guerchard furiously.

"Yes," said the Duke coldly.

"No! No! No!" cried Guerchard.

Their eyes turned to the clock.

To Guerchard the hands seemed to be standing still. He could have sworn at them for their slowness.

Then the first stroke rang out; and the eyes of the two men met like crossing blades. Twice the Duke made the slightest movement. Twice Guerchard started forward to meet it.

At the last stroke both their hands shot out. Guerchard's fell heavily on the case which held the coronet. The Duke's fell on the brim of his hat; and he picked it up.

Guerchard gasped and choked. Then he cried triumphantly:

"I HAVE it; now then, have I won? Have I been fooled this time? Has Lupin got the coronet?"

"It doesn't look like it. But are you quite sure?" said the Duke gaily.

"Sure?" cried Guerchard.

"It's only the weight of it," said the Duke, repressing a laugh. "Doesn't it strike you that it's just a trifle light?"

"What?" cried Guerchard.

"This is merely an imitation." said the Duke, with a gentle laugh.

"Hell and damnation!" howled Guerchard. "Bonavent! Dieusy!"

The door flew open, and half a dozen detectives rushed in.

Guerchard sank into a chair, stupefied, paralyzed; this blow, on the top of the strain of the struggle with the Duke, had broken him.

"Gentlemen," said the Duke sadly, "the coronet has been stolen."

They broke into cries of surprise and bewilderment, surrounding the gasping Guerchard with excited questions.

The Duke walked quietly out of the room.

Guerchard sobbed twice; his eyes opened, and in a dazed fashion wandered from face to face; he said faintly: "Where is he?"

"Where's who?" said Bonavent.

"The Duke—the Duke!" gasped Guerchard.

"Why, he's gone!" said Bonavent.

Guerchard staggered to his feet and cried hoarsely, frantically: "Stop him from leaving the house! Follow him! Arrest him! Catch him before he gets home!"

20

LUPIN COMES HOME

The cold light of the early September morning illumined but dimly the charming smoking-room of the Duke of Charmerace in his house at 34 B, University Street, though it stole in through two large windows. The smoking-room was on the first floor; and the Duke's bedroom opened into it. It was furnished in the most luxurious fashion, but with a taste which nowadays infrequently accompanies luxury. The chairs were of the most comfortable, but their lines were excellent; the couch against the wall, between the two windows, was the last word in the matter of comfort. The colour scheme, of a light greyish-blue, was almost too bright for a man's room; it would have better suited a boudoir. It suggested that the owner of the room enjoyed an uncommon lightness and cheerfulness of temperament. On the walls, with wide gaps between them so that they did not clash, hung three or four excellent pictures. Two ballet-girls by Degas, a group of shepherdesses and shepherds, in pink and blue and white beribboned silk, by Fragonard, a portrait of a woman by Bastien-Lepage, a charming Corot, and two Conder fans showed that the taste of their fortunate owner was at any rate eclectic. At the end of the room was, of all curious things, the opening into the well of a lift. The doors of it were open, though the lift itself was on some other floor. To the left of the opening stood a book-case, its shelves loaded with books of a kind rather suited to a cultivated, thoughtful man than to an idle dandy.

Beside the window, half-hidden, and peering through the side of the curtain into the street, stood M. Charolais. But it was hardly the M. Charolais who had paid M. Gournay-Martin that visit at the Chateau de Charmerace, and departed so firmly in the millionaire's favourite motor-car. This was a paler M. Charolais; he lacked altogether the rich, ruddy complexion of the millionaire's visitor. His nose, too, was thinner, and showed none of the ripe acquaintance with the vintages of the world which had been so plainly displayed on it during its owner's visit to the country. Again, hair and eyebrows were no longer black, but fair; and his hair was no longer curly and luxuriant, but thin and lank. His moustache had vanished, and along with it the dress of a well-to-do provincial man of business. He wore a livery of the Charmeraces, and at that early morning hour had not yet assumed the blue waistcoat which is an integral part of it. Indeed it would have required an acute and experienced observer to recognize in him the bogus purchaser of the Mercrac. Only his eyes, his close-set eyes, were unchanged.

Walking restlessly up and down the middle of the room, keeping out of sight of the windows, was Victoire. She wore a very anxious air, as did Charolais too. By the door stood Bernard Charolais; and his natural, boyish timidity, to judge from his frightened eyes, had assumed an acute phase.

"By the Lord, we're done!" cried Charolais, starting back from the window. "That was the front-door bell."

"No, it was only the hall clock," said Bernard.

"That's seven o'clock! Oh, where can he be?" said Victoire, wringing her hands. "The coup was fixed for midnight... Where can he be?"

"They must be after him," said Charolais. "And he daren't come home." Gingerly he drew back the curtain and resumed his watch.

"I've sent down the lift to the bottom, in case he should come back by the secret entrance," said Victoire; and she went to the opening into the well of the lift and stood looking down it, listening with all her ears.

"Then why, in the devil's name, have you left the doors open?" cried Charolais irritably. "How do you expect the lift to come up if the doors are open?"

"I must be off my head!" cried Victoire.

She stepped to the side of the lift and pressed a button. The doors closed, and there was a grunting click of heavy machinery settling into a new position.

"Suppose we telephone to Justin at the Passy house?" said Victoire.

"What on earth's the good of that?" said Charolais impatiently. "Justin knows no more than we do. How can he know any more?"

"The best thing we can do is to get out," said Bernard, in a shaky voice.

"No, no; he will come. I haven't given up hope," Victoire protested. "He's sure to come; and he may need us."

"But, hang it all! Suppose the police come! Suppose they ransack his papers... He hasn't told us what to do ... we are not ready for them... What are we to do?" cried Charolais, in a tone of despair.

"Well, I'm worse off than you are; and I'm not making a fuss. If the police come they'll arrest me," said Victoire.

"Perhaps they've arrested him," said Bernard, in his shaky voice.

"Don't talk like that," said Victoire fretfully. "Isn't it bad enough to wait and wait, without your croaking like a scared crow?"

She started again her pacing up and down the room, twisting her hands, and now and again moistening her dry lips with the tip of her tongue.

Presently she said: "Are those two plain-clothes men still there watching?" And in her anxiety she came a step nearer the window.

"Keep away from the window!" snapped Charolais. "Do you want to be recognized, you great idiot?" Then he added, more quietly, "They're still there all right, curse them, in front of the cafe... Hullo!"

"What is it, now?" cried Victoire, starting.

"A copper and a detective running," said Charolais. "They are running for all they're worth."

"Are they coming this way?" said Victoire; and she ran to the door and caught hold of the handle.

"No," said Charolais.

"Thank goodness!" said Victoire.

"They're running to the two men watching the house ... they're telling them something. Oh, hang it, they're all running down the street."

"This way? ... Are they coming this way?" cried Victoire faintly; and she pressed her hand to her side.

"They are!" cried Charolais. "They are!" And he dropped the curtain with an oath.

"And he isn't here! Suppose they come... Suppose he comes to the front door! They'll catch him!" cried Victoire.

There came a startling peal at the front-door bell. They stood frozen to stone, their eyes fixed on one another, staring.

The bell had hardly stopped ringing, when there was a slow, whirring noise. The doors of the lift flew open, and the Duke stepped out of it. But what a changed figure from the admirably dressed dandy who had walked through the startled detectives and out of the house of M. Gournay-Martin at midnight! He was pale, exhausted, almost fainting. His eyes were dim in a livid face; his lips were grey. He was panting heavily. He was splashed with mud from head to foot: one sleeve of his coat was torn along half its length. The sole of his left-hand pump was half off; and his cut foot showed white and red through the torn sock.

"The master! The master!" cried Charolais in a tone of extravagant relief; and he danced round the room snapping his fingers.

"You're wounded?" cried Victoire.

"No," said Arsène Lupin.

The front-door bell rang out again, startling, threatening, terrifying.

The note of danger seemed to brace Lupin, to spur him to a last effort.

He pulled himself together, and said in a hoarse but steady voice: "Your waistcoat, Charolais... Go and open the door ... not too quickly ... fumble the bolts... Bernard, shut the book-case. Victoire, get out of sight, do you want to ruin us all? Be smart now, all of you. Be smart!"

He staggered past them into his bedroom, and slammed the door. Victoire and Charolais hurried out of the room, through the anteroom, on to the landing. Victoire ran upstairs, Charolais went slowly down. Bernard pressed the button. The doors of the lift shut and there was a slow whirring as it went down. He pressed another button, and the book-case slid slowly across and hid the opening into the lift-well. Bernard ran out of the room and up the stairs.

Charolais went to the front door and fumbled with the bolts. He bawled through the door to the visitors not to be in such a hurry at that hour in the morning; and they bawled furiously at him to be quick, and knocked and rang again and again. He was fully three minutes fumbling with the bolts, which were already drawn. At last he opened the door an inch or two, and looked out.

On the instant the door was dashed open, flinging him back against the wall; and Bonavent and Dieusy rushed past him, up the stairs, as hard as they could pelt. A brown-faced, nervous, active policeman followed them in and stopped to guard the door.

On the landing the detectives paused, and looked at one another, hesitating.

"Which way did he go?" said Bonavent. "We were on his very heels."

"I don't know; but we've jolly well stopped his getting into his own house; and that's the main thing," said Dieusy triumphantly.

"But are you sure it was him?" said Bonavent, stepping into the anteroom.

"I can swear to it," said Dieusy confidently; and he followed him.

Charolais came rushing up the stairs and caught them up as they were entering the smoking-room:

"Here! What's all this?" he cried. "You mustn't come in here! His Grace isn't awake yet."

"Awake? Awake? Your precious Duke has been galloping all night," cried Dieusy. "And he runs devilish well, too."

The door of the bedroom opened; and Lupin stood on the threshold in slippers and pyjamas.

"What's all this?" he snapped, with the irritation of a man whose sleep has been disturbed; and his tousled hair and eyes dim with exhaustion gave him every appearance of being still heavy with sleep.

The eyes and mouths of Bonavent and Dieusy opened wide; and they stared at him blankly, in utter bewilderment and wonder.

"Is it you who are making all this noise?" said Lupin, frowning at them. "Why, I know you two; you're in the service of M. Guerchard."

"Yes, your Grace," stammered Bonavent.

"Well, what are you doing here? What is it you want?" said Lupin.

"Oh, nothing, your Grace ... nothing ... there's been a mistake," stammered Bonavent.

"A mistake?" said Lupin haughtily. "I should think there had been a mistake. But I take it that this is Guerchard's doing. I'd better deal with him directly. You two can go." He turned to Charolais and added curtly, "Show them out."

Charolais opened the door, and the two detectives went out of the room with the slinking air of whipped dogs. They went down the stairs in silence, slowly, reflectively; and Charolais let them out of the front door.

As they went down the steps Dieusy said: "What a howler! Guerchard risks getting the sack for this!"

"I told you so," said Bonavent. "A duke's a duke."

When the door closed behind the two detectives Lupin tottered across the room, dropped on to the couch with a groan of exhaustion, and closed his eyes. Presently the door opened, Victoire came in, saw his attitude of exhaustion, and with a startled cry ran to his side.

"Oh, dearie! Dearie!" she cried. "Pull yourself together! Oh, do try to pull yourself together." She caught his cold hands and began to rub them, murmuring words of endearment like a mother over a young child. Lupin did not open his eyes; Charolais came in.

"Some breakfast!" she cried. "Bring his breakfast ... he's faint ... he's had nothing to eat this morning. Can you eat some breakfast, dearie?"

"Yes," said Lupin faintly.

"Hurry up with it," said Victoire in urgent, imperative tones; and Charolais left the room at a run.

"Oh, what a life you lead!" said Victoire, or, to be exact, she wailed it. "Are you never going to change? You're as white as a sheet... Can't you speak, dearie?"

at Marathon pace. I walked and walked, and at last I got into Paris, and found myself with still a couple of miles to go. It was all right now; I should soon find a cab. But the luck was dead against me. I heard a man come round the corner of a side-street into a long street I was walking down. He gave a yell, and came bucketing after me. It was that hound Dieusy. He had recognized my figure. Off I went; and the chase began again. I led him a dance, but I couldn't shake him off. All the while I was working my way towards home. Then, just at last, I spurted for all I was worth, got out of his sight, bolted round the corner of the street into the secret entrance, and here I am." He smiled weakly, and added, "Oh, my dear Victoire, what a profession it is!"

21

THE CUTTING OF THE TELEPHONE WIRES

The door opened, and in came Charolais, bearing a tray.

"Here's your breakfast, master," he said.

"Don't call me master—that's how his men address Guerchard. It's a disgusting practice," said Lupin severely.

Victoire and Charolais were quick laying the table. Charolais kept up a running fire of questions as he did it; but Lupin did not trouble to answer them. He lay back, relaxed, drawing deep breaths. Already his lips had lost their greyness, and were pink; there was a suggestion of blood under the skin of his pale face. They soon had the table laid; and he walked to it on fairly steady feet. He sat down; Charolais whipped off a cover, and said:

"Anyhow, you've got out of the mess neatly. It was a jolly smart escape."

"Oh, yes. So far it's all right," said Lupin. "But there's going to be trouble presently—lots of it. I shall want all my wits. We all shall."

He fell upon his breakfast with the appetite but not the manners of a wolf. Charolais went out of the room. Victoire hovered about him, pouring out his coffee and putting sugar into it.

"By Jove, how good these eggs are!" he said. "I think that, of all the thousand ways of cooking eggs, en cocotte is the best."

"Heavens! How empty I was!" he said presently. "What a meal I'm making! It's really a very healthy life, this of mine, Victoire. I feel much better already."

"Oh, yes; it's all very well to talk," said Victoire, in a scolding tone; for since he was better, she felt, as a good woman should, that the time had come to put in a word out of season. "But, all the same, you're trying to kill yourself—that's what you're doing. Just because you're young you abuse your youth. It won't last for ever; and you'll be sorry you used it up before it's time. And this life of lies and thefts and of all kinds of improper things—I suppose it's going to begin all over again. It's no good your getting a lesson. It's just thrown away upon you."

"What I want next is a bath," said Lupin.

"It's all very well your pretending not to listen to me, when you know very well that I'm speaking for your good," she went on, raising her voice a little. "But I tell you that all this is going to end badly. To be a thief gives you no position in the world—no position at all—and when I think of what you made me do the night before last, I'm just horrified at myself."

"We'd better not talk about that—the mess you made of it! It was positively excruciating!" said Lupin.

"And what did you expect? I'm an honest woman, I am!" said Victoire sharply. "I wasn't brought up to do things like that, thank goodness! And to begin at my time of life!"

"It's true, and I often ask myself how you bring yourself to stick to me," said Lupin, in a reflective, quite impersonal tone. "Please pour me out another cup of coffee."

"That's what I'm always asking myself," said Victoire, pouring out the coffee. "I don't know—I give it up. I suppose it is because I'm fond of you."

"Yes, and I'm very fond of you, my dear Victoire," said Lupin, in a coaxing tone.

"And then, look you, there are things that there's no understanding. I often talked to your poor mother about them. Oh, your poor mother! Whatever would she have said to these goings-on?"

Lupin helped himself to another cutlet; his eyes twinkled and he said, "I'm not sure that she would have been very much surprised. I always told her that I was going to punish society for the way it had treated her. Do you think she would have been surprised?"

"Oh, nothing you did would have surprised her," said Victoire. "When you were quite a little boy you were always making us wonder. You gave yourself such airs, and you had such nice manners of your own—altogether different from the other boys. And you were already a bad boy, when you were only seven years old, full of all kinds of tricks; and already you had begun to steal."

"Oh, only sugar," protested Lupin.

"Yes, you began by stealing sugar," said Victoire, in the severe tones of a moralist. "And then it was jam, and then it was pennies. Oh, it was all very well at that age—a little thief is pretty enough. But now—when you're twenty-eight years old."

"Really, Victoire, you're absolutely depressing," said Lupin, yawning; and he helped himself to jam.

"I know very well that you're all right at heart," said Victoire. "Of course you only rob the rich, and you've always been kind to the poor... Yes; there's no doubt about it: you have a good heart."

"I can't help it—what about it?" said Lupin, smiling.

"Well, you ought to have different ideas in your head. Why are you a burglar?"

"You ought to try it yourself, my dear Victoire," said Lupin gently; and he watched her with a humorous eye.

"Goodness, what a thing to say!" cried Victoire.

"I assure you, you ought," said Lupin, in a tone of thoughtful conviction. "I've tried everything. I've taken my degree in medicine and in law. I have been an actor, and a professor of Jiu-jitsu. I have even been a member of the detective force, like that wretched Guerchard. Oh, what a dirty world that is! Then I launched out into society. I have been a duke. Well, I give you my word that not one of these professions equals that of burglar—not even the profession of Duke. There is so much of the unexpected in it, Victoire—the splendid unexpected... And then, it's full of variety, so terrible, so fascinating." His voice sank a little, and he added, "And what fun it is!"

"Fun!" cried Victoire.

"Yes ... these rich men, these swells in their luxury—when one relieves them of a bank-note, how they do howl! ... You should have seen that fat old Gournay-Martin when I relieved him of his treasures—what an agony! You almost heard the death-rattle in his throat. And then the coronet! In the derangement of their minds—and it was sheer derangement, mind you—already prepared at Charmerace, in the derangement of Guerchard, I had only to put out my hand and pluck the coronet. And the joy, the ineffable joy of enraging the police! To see Guerchard's furious eyes when I downed him... And look round you!" He waved his hand round the luxurious room. "Duke of Charmerace! This trade leads to everything ... to everything on condition that one sticks to it ... I tell you, Victoire, that when one cannot be a great artist or a great soldier, the only thing to be is a great thief!"

"Oh, be quiet!" cried Victoire. "Don't talk like that. You're working yourself up; you're intoxicating yourself! And all that, it is not Catholic. Come, at your age, you ought to have one idea in your head which should drive out all these others, which should make you forget all these thefts... Love ... that would change you, I'm sure of it. That would make another man of you. You ought to marry."

"Yes ... perhaps ... that would make another man of me. That's what I've been thinking. I believe you're right," said Lupin thoughtfully.

"Is that true? Have you really been thinking of it?" cried Victoire joyfully.

"Yes," said Lupin, smiling at her eagerness. "I have been thinking about it—seriously."

"No more messing about—no more intrigues. But a real woman ... a woman for life?" cried Victoire.

"Yes," said Lupin softly; and his eyes were shining in a very grave face.

"Is it serious—is it real love, dearie?" said Victoire. "What's she like?"

"She's beautiful," said Lupin.

"Oh, trust you for that. Is she a blonde or a brunette?"

"She's very fair and delicate—like a princess in a fairy tale," said Lupin softly.

"What is she? What does she do?" said Victoire.

"Well, since you ask me, she's a thief," said Lupin with a mischievous smile.

"Good Heavens!" cried Victoire.

"But she's a very charming thief," said Lupin; and he rose smiling.

He lighted a cigar, stretched himself and yawned: "She had ever so much more reason for stealing than ever I had," he said. "And she has always hated it like poison."

"Well, that's something," said Victoire; and her blank and fallen face brightened a little.

Lupin walked up and down the room, breathing out long luxurious puffs of smoke from his excellent cigar, and watching Victoire with a humorous eye. He walked across to his bookshelf, and scanned the titles of his books with an appreciative, almost affectionate smile.

"This is a very pleasant interlude," he said languidly. "But I don't suppose it's going to last very long. As soon as Guerchard recovers from the shock of learning that I spent a quiet night in my ducal bed as an honest duke should, he'll be getting to work with positively furious energy, confound him! I could do with a whole day's sleep—twenty-four solid hours of it."

"I'm sure you could, dearie," said Victoire sympathetically.

"The girl I'm going to marry is Sonia Kritchnoff," he said.

"Sonia? That dear child! But I love her already!" cried Victoire. "Sonia, but why did you say she was a thief? That was a silly thing to say."

"It's my extraordinary sense of humour," said Lupin.

The door opened and Charolais bustled in: "Shall I clear away the breakfast?" he said.

Lupin nodded; and then the telephone bell rang. He put his finger on his lips and went to it.

"Are you there?" he said. "Oh, it's you, Germaine... Good morning... Oh, yes, I had a good night—excellent, thank you... You want to speak to me presently? ... You're waiting for me at the Ritz?"

"Don't go—don't go—it isn't safe," said Victoire, in a whisper.

"All right, I'll be with you in about half an hour, or perhaps three-quarters. I'm not dressed yet ... but I'm ever so much more impatient than you ... good-bye for the present." He put the receiver on the stand.

"It's a trap," said Charolais.

"Never mind, what if it is? Is it so very serious?" said Lupin. "There'll be nothing but traps now; and if I can find the time I shall certainly go and take a look at that one."

"And if she knows everything? If she's taking her revenge ... if she's getting you there to have you arrested?" said Victoire.

"Yes, M. Formery is probably at the Ritz with Gournay-Martin. They're probably all of them there, weighing the coronet," said Lupin, with a chuckle.

He hesitated a moment, reflecting; then he said, "How silly you are! If they wanted to arrest me, if they had the material proof which they haven't got, Guerchard would be here already!"

"Then why did they chase you last night?" said Charolais.

"The coronet," said Lupin. "Wasn't that reason enough? But, as it turned out, they didn't catch me: and when the detectives did come here, they disturbed me in my sleep. And that me was ever so much more me than the man they followed. And then the proofs ... they must have proofs. There aren't any—or rather, what there are, I've got!" He pointed to a small safe let into the wall. "In that safe are the coronet, and, above all, the death certificate of the Duke of Charmerace ... everything that Guerchard must have to induce M. Formery to proceed. But still, there is a risk—I think I'd better have those things handy in case I have to bolt."

He went into his bedroom and came back with the key of the safe and a kit-bag. He opened the safe and took out the coronet, the real coronet of the Princesse de Lamballe, and along with it a pocket-book with a few papers in it. He set the pocket-book on the table, ready to put in his coat-pocket when he should have dressed, and dropped the coronet into the kit-bag.

"I'm glad I have that death certificate; it makes it much safer," he said. "If ever they do nab me, I don't wish that rascal Guerchard to accuse me of having murdered the Duke. It might prejudice me badly. I've not murdered anybody yet."

"That comes of having a good heart," said Victoire proudly.

"Not even the Duke of Charmerace," said Charolais sadly. "And it would have been so easy when he was ill—just one little draught. And he was in such a perfect place—so out of the way—no doctors."

"You do have such disgusting ideas, Charolais," said Lupin, in a tone of severe reproof.

"Instead of which you went and saved his life," said Charolais, in a tone of deep discontent; and he went on clearing the table.

"I did, I did: I had grown quite fond of him," said Lupin, with a meditative air. "For one thing, he was so very like one. I'm not sure that he wasn't even better-looking."

"No; he was just like you," said Victoire, with decision. "Any one would have said you were twin brothers."

"It gave me quite a shock the first time I saw his portrait," said Lupin. "You remember, Charolais? It was three years ago, the day, or rather the night, of the first Gournay-Martin burglary at Charmerace. Do you remember?"

"Do I remember?" said Charolais. "It was I who pointed out the likeness to you. I said, 'He's the very spit of you, master.' And you said, 'There's something to be done with that, Charolais.' And then off you started for the ice and snow and found the Duke, and became his friend; and then he went and died, not that you'd have helped him to, if he hadn't."

"Poor Charmerace. He was indeed grand seigneur. With him a great name was about to be extinguished... Did I hesitate? ... No... I continued it," said Lupin.

He paused and looked at the clock. "A quarter to eight," he said, hesitating. "Shall I telephone to Sonia, or shall I not? Oh, there's no hurry; let the poor child sleep on. She must be worn out after that night-journey and that cursed Guerchard's persecution yesterday. I'll dress first, and telephone to her afterwards. I'd better be getting dressed, by the way. The work I've got to do can't be done in pyjamas. I wish it could; for bed's the place for me. My wits aren't quite as clear as I could wish them to deal with an awkward business like this. Well, I must do the best I can with them."

He yawned and went to the bedroom, leaving the pocket-book on the table.

"Bring my shaving-water, Charolais, and shave me," he said, pausing; and he went into the bedroom and shut the door.

"Ah," said Victoire sadly, "what a pity it is! A few years ago he would have gone to the Crusades; and to-day he steals coronets. What a pity it is!"

"I think myself that the best thing we can do is to pack up our belongings," said Charolais. "And I don't think we've much time to do it either. This particular game is at an end, you may take it from me."

"I hope to goodness it is: I want to get back to the country," said Victoire.

He took up the tray; and they went out of the room. On the landing they separated; she went upstairs and he went down. Presently he came up with the shaving water and shaved his master; for in the house in University Street he discharged the double functions of valet and butler. He had just finished his task when there came a ring at the front-door bell.

"You'd better go and see who it is," said Lupin.

"Bernard is answering the door," said Charolais. "But perhaps I'd better keep an eye on it myself; one never knows."

He put away the razor leisurely, and went. On the stairs he found Bonavent, mounting—Bonavent, disguised in the livery and fierce moustache of a porter from the Ritz.

"Why didn't you come to the servants' entrance?" said Charolais, with the truculent air of the servant of a duke and a stickler for his master's dignity.

"I didn't know that there was one," said Bonavent humbly.

"Well, you ought to have known that there was; and it's plain enough to see. What is it you want?" said Charolais.

"I've brought a letter—a letter for the Duke of Charmerace," said Bonavent.

"Give it to me," said Charolais. "I'll take it to him."

"No, no; I'm to give it into the hands of the Duke himself and to nobody else," said Bonavent.

"Well, in that case, you'll have to wait till he's finished dressing," said Charolais.

They went on up to the stairs into the ante-room. Bonavent was walking straight into the smoking-room.

"Here! Where are you going to? Wait here," said Charolais quickly. "Take a chair; sit down."

Bonavent sat down with a very stolid air, and Charolais looked at him doubtfully, in two minds whether to leave him there alone or not. Before he had decided there came a thundering knock on the front door, not only loud but protracted. Charolais looked round with a scared air; and then ran out of the room and down the stairs.

On the instant Bonavent was on his feet, and very far from stolid. He opened the door of the smoking-room very gently and peered in. It was empty. He slipped noiselessly across the room, a pair of clippers ready in his hand, and cut the wires of the telephone. His quick eye glanced round the room and fell on the pocket-book on the table. He snatched it up, and slipped it into the breast of his tunic. He had scarcely done it—one button of his tunic was still to fasten—when the bedroom door opened, and Lupin came out:

"What do you want?" he said sharply; and his keen eyes scanned the porter with a disquieting penetration.

"I've brought a letter to the Duke of Charmerace, to be given into his own hands," said Bonavent, in a disguised voice.

"Give it to me," said Lupin, holding out his hand.

"But the Duke?" said Bonavent, hesitating.

"I am the Duke," said Lupin.

Bonavent gave him the letter, and turned to go.

"Don't go," said Lupin quietly. "Wait, there may be an answer."

There was a faint glitter in his eyes; but Bonavent missed it.

Charolais came into the room, and said, in a grumbling tone, "A run-away knock. I wish I could catch the brats; I'd warm them. They wouldn't go fetching me away from my work again, in a hurry, I can tell you."

Lupin opened the letter, and read it. As he read it, at first he frowned; then he smiled; and then he laughed joyously. It ran:

"SIR,"

"M. Guerchard has told me everything. With regard to Sonia I have judged you: a man who loves a thief can be nothing but a rogue. I have two pieces of news to announce to you: the death of the Duke of Charmerace, who died three years ago, and my intention of becoming engaged to his cousin and heir, M. de Relzieres, who will assume the title and the arms."

"For Mademoiselle Gournay-Martin,"

"Her maid, IRMA."

"She does write in shocking bad taste," said Lupin, shaking his head sadly. "Charolais, sit down and write a letter for me."

"Me?" said Charolais.

"Yes; you. It seems to be the fashion in financial circles; and I am bound to follow it when a lady sets it. Write me a letter," said Lupin.

Charolais went to the writing-table reluctantly, sat down, set a sheet of paper on the blotter, took a pen in his hand, and sighed painfully.

"Ready?" said Lupin; and he dictated:

"MADEMOISELLE,"

"I have a very robust constitution, and my indisposition will very soon be over. I shall have the honour of sending, this afternoon, my humble wedding present to the future Madame de Relzieres."

"For Jacques de Bartut, Marquis de Relzieres, Prince of Virieux, Duke of Charmerace."

"His butler, ARSÈNE."

"Shall I write Arsène?" said Charolais, in a horrified tone.

"Why not?" said Lupin. "It's your charming name, isn't it?"

Bonavent pricked up his ears, and looked at Charolais with a new interest.

Charolais shrugged his shoulders, finished the letter, blotted it, put it in an envelope, addressed it, and handed it to Lupin.

"Take this to Mademoiselle Gournay-Martin," said Lupin, handing it to Bonavent.

Bonavent took the letter, turned, and had taken one step towards the door when Lupin sprang. His arm went round the detective's neck; he jerked him backwards off his feet, scragging him.

"Stir, and I'll break your neck!" he cried in a terrible voice; and then he said quietly to Charolais, "Just take my pocket-book out of this fellow's tunic."

Charolais, with deft fingers, ripped open the detective's tunic, and took out the pocket-book.

"This is what they call Jiu-jitsu, old chap! You'll be able to teach it to your colleagues," said Lupin. He loosed his grip on Bonavent, and knocked him straight with a thump in the back, and sent him flying across the room. Then he took the pocket-book from Charolais and made sure that its contents were untouched.

"Tell your master from me that if he wants to bring me down he'd better fire the gun himself," said Lupin contemptuously. "Show the gentleman out, Charolais."

Bonavent staggered to the door, paused, and turned on Lupin a face livid with fury.

"He will be here himself in ten minutes," he said.

"Many thanks for the information," said Lupin quietly.

22

THE BARGAIN

Charolais conducted the detective down the stairs and let him out of the front door, cursing and threatening vengeance as he went. Charolais took no notice of his words—he was the well-trained servant. He came back upstairs, and on the landing called to Victoire and Bernard. They came hurrying down; and the three of them went into the smoking-room.

"Now we know where we are," said Lupin, with cheerful briskness. "Guerchard will be here in ten minutes with a warrant for my arrest. All of you clear out."

"It won't be so precious easy. The house is watched," said Charolais. "And I'll bet it's watched back and front."

"Well, slip out by the secret entrance. They haven't found that yet," said Lupin. "And meet me at the house at Passy."

Charolais and Bernard wanted no more telling; they ran to the book-case and pressed the buttons; the book-case slid aside; the doors opened and disclosed the lift. They stepped into it. Victoire had followed them. She paused and said: "And you? Are you coming?"

"In an instant I shall slip out the same way," he said.

"I'll wait for him. You go on," said Victoire; and the lift went down.

Lupin went to the telephone, rang the bell, and put the receiver to his ear.

"You've no time to waste telephoning. They may be here at any moment!" cried Victoire anxiously.

"I must. If I don't telephone Sonia will come here. She will run right into Guerchard's arms. Why the devil don't they answer? They must be deaf!" And he rang the bell again.

"Let's go to her! Let's get out of here!" cried Victoire, more anxiously. "There really isn't any time to waste."

"Go to her? But I don't know where she is. I lost my head last night," cried Lupin, suddenly anxious himself. "Are you there?" he shouted into the telephone. "She's at a little hotel near the Star. ... Are you there? ... But there are twenty hotels near the Star... Are you there? ... Oh, I did lose my head last night. ... Are you there? Oh, hang this telephone! Here I'm fighting with a piece of furniture. And every second is important!"

He picked up the machine, shook it, saw that the wires were cut, and cried furiously: "Ha! They've played the telephone trick on me! That's Guerchard... The swine!"

"And now you can come along!" cried Victoire.

"But that's just what I can't do!" he cried.

"But there's nothing more for you to do here, since you can no longer telephone," said Victoire, bewildered.

Lupin caught her arm and shook her, staring into her face with panic-stricken eyes. "But don't you understand that, since I haven't telephoned, she'll come here?" he cried hoarsely. "Five-and-twenty minutes past eight! At half-past eight she will start—start to come here."

His face had suddenly grown haggard; this new fear had brought back all the exhaustion of the night; his eyes were panic-stricken.

"But what about you?" said Victoire, wringing her hands.

"What about her?" said Lupin; and his voice thrilled with anguished dread.

"But you'll gain nothing by destroying both of you—nothing at all."

"I prefer it," said Lupin slowly, with a suddenly stubborn air.

"But they're coming to take you," cried Victoire, gripping his arm.

"Take me?" cried Lupin, freeing himself quietly from her grip. And he stood frowning, plunged in deep thought, weighing the chances, the risks, seeking a plan, saving devices.

He crossed the room to the writing-table, opened a drawer, and took out a cardboard box about eight inches square and set it on the table.

"They shall never take me alive," he said gloomily.

"Oh, hush, hush!" said Victoire. "I know very well that you're capable of anything ... and they too—they'll destroy you. No, look you, you must go. They won't do anything to her—a child like that—so frail. She'll get off quite easily. You're coming, aren't you?"

"No, I'm not," said Lupin stubbornly.

"Oh, well, if you won't," said Victoire; and with an air of resolution she went to the side of the lift-well, and pressed the buttons. The doors closed; the book-case slid across. She sat down and folded her arms.

"What, you're not going to stop here?" cried Lupin.

"Make me stir if you can. I'm as fond of you as she is—you know I am," said Victoire, and her face set stonily obstinate.

Lupin begged her to go; ordered her to go; he seized her by the shoulder, shook her, and abused her like a pickpocket. She would not stir. He abandoned the effort, sat down, and knitted his brow again in profound and painful thought, working out his plan. Now and again his eyes flashed, once or twice they twinkled. Victoire watched his face with just the faintest hope on her own.

It was past five-and-twenty minutes to nine when the front-door bell rang. They gazed at one another with an unspoken question on their lips. The eyes of Victoire were scared, but in the eyes of Lupin the light of battle was gathering.

"It's her," said Victoire under her breath.

"No," said Lupin. "It's Guerchard."

He sprang to his feet with shining eyes. His lips were curved in a fighting smile. "The game isn't lost yet," he said in a tense, quiet voice. "I'm going to play it to the end. I've a card or two left still—good cards. I'm still the Duke of Charmerace." He turned to her.

"Now listen to me," he said. "Go down and open the door for him."

"What, you want me to?" said Victoire, in a shaky voice.

"Yes, I do. Listen to me carefully. When you have opened the door, slip out of it and watch the house. Don't go too far from it. Look out for Sonia. You'll see her coming. Stop her from entering, Victoire—stop her from entering." He spoke coolly, but his voice shook on the last words.

"But if Guerchard arrests me?" said Victoire.

"He won't. When he comes in, stand behind the door. He will be too eager to get to me to stop for you. Besides, for him you don't count in the game. Once you're out of the house, I'll hold him here for—for half an hour. That will leave a margin. Sonia will hurry here. She should be here in twelve minutes. Get her away to the house at Passy. If I don't come keep her there; she's to live with you. But I shall come."

As he spoke he was pushing her towards the door.

The bell rang again. They were at the top of the stairs.

"And suppose he does arrest me?" said Victoire breathlessly.

"Never mind, you must go all the same," said Lupin. "Don't give up hope—trust to me. Go—go—for my sake."

"I'm going, dearie," said Victoire; and she went down the stairs steadily, with a brave air.

He watched her half-way down the flight; then he muttered: "If only she gets to Sonia in time."

He turned, went into the smoking-room, and shut the door. He sat quietly down in an easy chair, lighted a cigarette, and took up a paper. He heard the noise of the traffic in the street grow louder as the front door was opened. There was a pause; then he heard the door bang. There was the sound of a hasty footstep on the stairs; the door flew open, and Guerchard bounced into the room.

He stopped short in front of the door at the sight of Lupin, quietly reading, smoking at his ease. He had expected to find the bird flown. He stood still, hesitating, shuffling his feet—all his doubts had returned; and Lupin smiled at him over the lowered paper.

Guerchard pulled himself together by a violent effort, and said jerkily, "Good-morning, Lupin."

"Good-morning, M. Guerchard," said Lupin, with an ambiguous smile and all the air of the Duke of Charmerace.

"You were expecting me? ... I hope I haven't kept you waiting," said Guerchard, with an air of bravado.

"No, thank you: the time has passed quite quickly. I have so much to do in the morning always," said Lupin. "I hope you had a good night after that unfortunate business of the coronet. That was a disaster; and so unexpected too."

Guerchard came a few steps into the room, still hesitating:

"You've a very charming house here," he said, with a sneer.

"It's central," said Lupin carelessly. "You must please excuse me, if I cannot receive you as I should like; but all my servants have bolted. Those confounded detectives of yours have frightened them away."

"You needn't bother about that. I shall catch them," said Guerchard.

"If you do, I'm sure I wish you joy of them. Do, please, keep your hat on," said Lupin with ironic politeness.

Guerchard came slowly to the middle of the room, raising his hand to his hat, letting it fall again without taking it off. He sat down slowly facing him, and they gazed at one another with the wary eyes of duellists crossing swords at the beginning of a duel.

"Did you get M. Formery to sign a little warrant?" said Lupin, in a caressing tone full of quiet mockery.

"I did," said Guerchard through his teeth.

"And have you got it on you?" said Lupin.

"I have," said Guerchard.

"Against Lupin, or against the Duke of Charmerace?" said Lupin.

"Against Lupin, called Charmerace," said Guerchard.

"Well, that ought to cover me pretty well. Why don't you arrest me? What are you waiting for?" said Lupin. His face was entirely serene, his eyes were careless, his tone indifferent.

"I'm not waiting for anything," said Guerchard thickly; "but it gives me such pleasure that I wish to enjoy this minute to the utmost, Lupin," said Guerchard; and his eyes gloated on him.

"Lupin, himself," said Lupin, smiling.

"I hardly dare believe it," said Guerchard.

"You're quite right not to," said Lupin.

"Yes, I hardly dare believe it. You alive, here at my mercy?"

"Oh, dear no, not yet," said Lupin.

"Yes," said Guerchard, in a decisive tone. "And ever so much more than you think." He bent forwards towards him, with his hands on his knees, and said, "Do you know where Sonia Kritchnoff is at this moment?"

"What?" said Lupin sharply.

"I ask if you know where Sonia Kritchnoff is?" said Guerchard slowly, lingering over the words.

"Do you?" said Lupin.

"I do," said Guerchard triumphantly.

"Where is she?" said Lupin, in a tone of utter incredulity.

"In a small hotel near the Star. The hotel has a telephone; and you can make sure," said Guerchard.

"Indeed? That's very interesting. What's the number of it?" said Lupin, in a mocking tone.

"555 Central: would you like to telephone to her?" said Guerchard; and he smiled triumphantly at the disabled instrument.

Lupin shook his head with a careless smile, and said, "Why should I telephone to her? What are you driving at?"

"Nothing ... that's all," said Guerchard. And he leant back in his chair with an ugly smile on his face.

"Evidently nothing. For, after all, what has that child got to do with you? You're not interested in her, plainly. She's not big enough game for you. It's me you are hunting ... it's me you hate ... it's me you want. I've played you tricks enough for that, you old scoundrel. So you're going to leave that child in peace? ... You're not going to revenge yourself on her? ... It's all very well for you to be a policeman; it's all very well for you to hate me; but there are things one does not do." There was a ring of menace and appeal in the deep, ringing tones of his voice. "You're not going to do that, Guerchard... You will not do it... Me—yes—anything you like. But her—her you must not touch." He gazed at the detective with fierce, appealing eyes.

"That depends on you," said Guerchard curtly.

"On me?" cried Lupin, in genuine surprise.

"Yes, I've a little bargain to propose to you," said Guerchard.

"Have you?" said Lupin; and his watchful face was serene again, his smile almost pleasant.

"Yes," said Guerchard. And he paused, hesitating.

"Well, what is it you want?" said Lupin. "Out with it! Don't be shy about it."

"I offer you—"

"You offer me?" cried Lupin. "Then it isn't true. You're fooling me."

"Reassure yourself," said Guerchard coldly. "To you personally I offer nothing."

"Then you are sincere," said Lupin. "And putting me out of the question?"

"I offer you liberty."

"Who for? For my concierge?" said Lupin.

"Don't play the fool. You care only for a single person in the world. I hold you through her: Sonia Kritchnoff."

Lupin burst into a ringing, irrepressible laugh:

"Why, you're trying to blackmail me, you old sweep!" he cried.

"If you like to call it so," said Guerchard coldly.

Lupin rose and walked backwards and forwards across the room, frowning, calculating, glancing keenly at Guerchard, weighing him. Twice he looked at the clock.

He stopped and said coldly: "So be it. For the moment you're the stronger... That won't last... But you offer me this child's liberty."

"That's my offer," said Guerchard; and his eyes brightened at the prospect of success.

"Her complete liberty? ... On your word of honour?" said Lupin; and he had something of the air of a cat playing with a mouse.

"On my word of honour," said Guerchard.

"Can you do it?" said Lupin, with a sudden air of doubt; and he looked sharply from Guerchard to the clock.

"I undertake to do it," said Guerchard confidently.

"But how?" said Lupin, looking at him with an expression of the gravest doubt.

"Oh, I'll put the thefts on your shoulders. That will let her out all right," said Guerchard.

"I've certainly good broad shoulders," said Lupin, with a bitter smile. He walked slowly up and down with an air that grew more and more depressed: it was almost the air of a beaten man. Then he stopped and faced Guerchard, and said: "And what is it you want in exchange?"

"Everything," said Guerchard, with the air of a man who is winning. "You must give me back the pictures, tapestry, Renaissance cabinets, the coronet, and all the information about the death of the Duke of Charmerace. Did you kill him?"

"If ever I commit suicide, you'll know all about it, my good Guerchard. You'll be there. You may even join me," said Lupin grimly; he resumed his pacing up and down the room.

"Done for, yes; I shall be done for," he said presently. "The fact is, you want my skin."

"Yes, I want your skin," said Guerchard, in a low, savage, vindictive tone.

"My skin," said Lupin thoughtfully.

"Are you going to do it? Think of that girl," said Guerchard, in a fresh access of uneasy anxiety.

Lupin laughed: "I can give you a glass of port," he said, "but I'm afraid that's all I can do for you."

"I'll throw Victoire in," said Guerchard.

"What?" cried Lupin. "You've arrested Victoire?" There was a ring of utter dismay, almost despair, in his tone.

"Yes; and I'll throw her in. She shall go scot-free. I won't bother with her," said Guerchard eagerly.

The front-door bell rang.

"Wait, wait. Let me think," said Lupin hoarsely; and he strove to adjust his jostling ideas, to meet with a fresh plan this fresh disaster.

He stood listening with all his ears. There were footsteps on the stairs, and the door opened. Dieusy stood on the threshold.

"Who is it?" said Guerchard.

"I accept—I accept everything," cried Lupin in a frantic tone.

"It's a tradesman; am I to detain him?" said Dieusy. "You told me to let you know who came and take instructions."

"A tradesman? Then I refuse!" cried Lupin, in an ecstasy of relief.

"No, you needn't keep him," said Guerchard, to Dieusy.

Dieusy went out and shut the door.

"You refuse?" said Guerchard.

"I refuse," said Lupin.

"I'm going to gaol that girl," said Guerchard savagely; and he took a step towards the door.

"Not for long," said Lupin quietly. "You have no proof."

"She'll furnish the proof all right herself—plenty of proofs," said Guerchard brutally. "What chance has a silly child like that got, when we really start questioning her? A delicate creature like that will crumple up before the end of the third day's cross-examination."

"You swine!" said Lupin.

"You know well enough that I can do it—on my head—with a feeble child like that; and you know your Code; five years is the minimum," said Guerchard, in a tone of relentless brutality, watching him carefully, sticking to his hope.

"By Jove, I could wring your neck!" said Lupin, trembling with fury. By a violent effort he controlled himself, and said thoughtfully, "After all, if I give up everything to you, I shall be free to take it back one of these days."

"Oh, no doubt, when you come out of prison," said Guerchard ironically; and he laughed a grim, jeering laugh.

"I've got to go to prison first," said Lupin quietly.

"Pardon me—if you accept, I mean to arrest you," said Guerchard.

"Manifestly you'll arrest me if you can," said Lupin.

"Do you accept?" said Guerchard. And again his voice quivered with anxiety.

"Well," said Lupin. And he paused as if finally weighing the matter.

"Well?" said Guerchard, and his voice shook.

"Well—no!" said Lupin; and he laughed a mocking laugh.

"You won't?" said Guerchard between his teeth.

"No; you wish to catch me. This is just a ruse," said Lupin, in quiet, measured tones. "At bottom you don't care a hang about Sonia, Mademoiselle Kritchnoff. You will not arrest her. And then, if you did you have no proofs. There ARE no proofs. As for the pendant, you'd have to prove it. You can't prove it. You can't prove that it was in her possession one moment. Where is the pendant?" He paused, and then went on in the same quiet tone: "No, Guerchard; after having kept out of your clutches for the last ten years, I'm not going to be caught to save this child, who is not even in danger. She has a very useful friend in the Duke of Charmerace. I refuse."

Guerchard stared at him, scowling, biting his lips, seeking a fresh point of attack. For the moment he knew himself baffled, but he still clung tenaciously to the struggle in which victory would be so precious.

The front-door bell rang again.

"There's a lot of ringing at your bell this morning," said Guerchard, under his breath; and hope sprang afresh in him.

Again they stood silent, waiting.

Dieusy opened the door, put in his head, and said, "It's Mademoiselle Kritchnoff."

"Collar her! ... Here's the warrant! ... collar her!" shouted Guerchard, with savage, triumphant joy.

"Never! You shan't touch her! By Heaven, you shan't touch her!" cried Lupin frantically; and he sprang like a tiger at Guerchard.

Guerchard jumped to the other side of the table. "Will you accept, then?" he cried.

Lupin gripped the edge of the table with both hands, and stood panting, grinding his teeth, pale with fury. He stood silent and motionless for perhaps half a minute, gazing at Guerchard with burning, murderous eyes. Then he nodded his head.

"Let Mademoiselle Kritchnoff wait," said Guerchard, with a sigh of deep relief. Dieusy went out of the room.

"Now let us settle exactly how we stand," said Lupin, in a clear, incisive voice. "The bargain is this: If I give you the pictures, the tapestry, the cabinets, the coronet, and the death-certificate of the Duke of Charmerace, you give me your word of honour that Mademoiselle Kritchnoff shall not be touched."

"That's it!" said Guerchard eagerly.

"Once I deliver these things to you, Mademoiselle Kritchnoff passes out of the game."

"Yes," said Guerchard.

"Whatever happens afterwards. If I get back anything—if I escape—she goes scot-free," said Lupin.

"Yes," said Guerchard; and his eyes were shining.

"On your word of honour?" said Lupin.

"On my word of honour," said Guerchard.

"Very well," said Lupin, in a quiet, businesslike voice. "To begin with, here in this pocket-book you'll find all the documents relating to the death of the Duke of Charmerace. In it you will also find the receipt of the Plantin furniture repository at Batignolles for the objects of art which I collected at Gournay-Martin's. I sent them to Batignolles because, in my letters asking the owners of valuables to forward them to me, I always make Batignolles the place to which they are to be sent; therefore I knew that you would never look there. They are all in cases; for, while you were making those valuable inquiries yesterday, my men were putting them into cases. You'll not find the receipt in the name of either the Duke of Charmerace or my own. It is in the name of a respected proprietor of Batignolles, a M. Pierre Servien. But he has lately left that charming suburb, and I do not think he will return to it."

Guerchard almost snatched the pocket-book out of his hand. He verified the documents in it with greedy eyes; and then he put them back in it, and stuffed it into the breast-pocket of his coat.

"And where's the coronet?" he said, in an excited voice.

"You're nearly standing on it," said Lupin.

"It's in that kit-bag at your feet, on the top of the change of clothes in it."

Guerchard snatched up the kit-bag, opened it, and took out the coronet.

"I'm afraid I haven't the case," said Lupin, in a tone of regret. "If you remember, I left it at Gournay-Martin's—in your charge."

Guerchard examined the coronet carefully. He looked at the stones in it; he weighed it in his right hand, and he weighed it in his left.

"Are you sure it's the real one?" said Lupin, in a tone of acute but affected anxiety. "Do not—oh, do not let us have any more of these painful mistakes about it. They are so wearing."

"Yes—yes—this is the real one," said Guerchard, with another deep sigh of relief.

"Well, have you done bleeding me?" said Lupin contemptuously.

"Your arms," said Guerchard quickly.

"They weren't in the bond," said Lupin. "But here you are." And he threw his revolver on the table.

Guerchard picked it up and put it into his pocket. He looked at Lupin as if he could not believe his eyes, gloating over him. Then he said in a deep, triumphant tone:

"And now for the handcuffs!"

23

THE END OF THE DUEL

"The handcuffs?" said Lupin; and his face fell. Then it cleared; and he added lightly, "After all, there's nothing like being careful; and, by Jove, with me you need to be. I might get away yet. What luck it is for you that I'm so soft, so little of a Charmerace, so human! Truly, I can't be much of a man of the world, to be in love like this!"

"Come, come, hold out your hands!" said Guerchard, jingling the handcuffs impatiently.

"I should like to see that child for the last time," said Lupin gently.

"All right," said Guerchard.

"Arsène Lupin—and nabbed by you! If you aren't in luck! Here you are!" said Lupin bitterly; and he held out his wrists.

Guerchard snapped the handcuffs on them with a grunt of satisfaction.

Lupin gazed down at them with a bitter face, and said: "Oh, you are in luck! You're not married by any chance?"

"Yes, yes; I am," said Guerchard hastily; and he went quickly to the door and opened it: "Dieusy!" he called. "Dieusy! Mademoiselle Kritchnoff is at liberty. Tell her so, and bring her in here."

Lupin started back, flushed and scowling; he cried: "With these things on my hands! ... No! ... I can't see her!"

Guerchard stood still, looking at him. Lupin's scowl slowly softened, and he said, half to himself, "But I should have liked to see her ... very much ... for if she goes like that ... I shall not know when or where—" He stopped short, raised his eyes, and said in a decided tone: "Ah, well, yes; I should like to see her."

"If you've quite made up your mind," said Guerchard impatiently, and he went into the anteroom.

Lupin stood very still, frowning thoughtfully. He heard footsteps on the stairs, and then the voice of Guerchard in the anteroom, saying, in a jeering tone, "You're free, mademoiselle; and you can thank the Duke for it. You owe your liberty to him."

"Free! And I owe it to him?" cried the voice of Sonia, ringing and golden with extravagant joy.

"Yes, mademoiselle," said Guerchard. "You owe it to him."

She came through the open door, flushed deliciously and smiling, her eyes brimming with tears of joy. Lupin had never seen her look half so adorable.

"Is it to you I owe it? Then I shall owe everything to you. Oh, thank you—thank you!" she cried, holding out her hands to him.

Lupin half turned away from her to hide his handcuffs.

She misunderstood the movement. Her face fell suddenly like that of a child rebuked: "Oh, I was wrong. I was wrong to come here!" she cried quickly, in changed, dolorous tones. "I thought yesterday ... I made a mistake ... pardon me. I'm going. I'm going."

Lupin was looking at her over his shoulder, standing sideways to hide the handcuffs. He said sadly. "Sonia—"

"No, no, I understand! It was impossible!" she cried quickly, cutting him short. "And yet if you only knew—if you knew how I have changed—with what a changed spirit I came here... Ah,

I swear that now I hate all my past. I loathe it. I swear that now the mere presence of a thief would overwhelm me with disgust."

"Hush!" said Lupin, flushing deeply, and wincing. "Hush!"

"But, after all, you're right," she said, in a gentler voice. "One can't wipe out what one has done. If I were to give back everything I've taken—if I were to spend years in remorse and repentance, it would be no use. In your eyes I should always be Sonia Kritchnoff, the thief!" The great tears welled slowly out of her eyes and rolled down her cheeks; she let them stream unheeded.

"Sonia!" cried Lupin, protesting.

But she would not hear him. She broke out with fresh vehemence, a feverish passion: "And yet, if I'd been a thief, like so many others... but you know why I stole. I'm not trying to defend myself, but, after all, I did it to keep honest; and when I loved you it was not the heart of a thief that thrilled, it was the heart of a poor girl who loved...that's all...who loved."

"You don't know what you're doing! You're torturing me! Be quiet!" cried Lupin hoarsely, beside himself.

"Never mind...I'm going...we shall never see one another any more," she sobbed. "But will you...will you shake hands just for the last time?"

"No!" cried Lupin.

"You won't?" wailed Sonia in a heartrending tone.

"I can't!" cried Lupin.

"You ought not to be like this... Last night ... if you were going to let me go like this ... last night ... it was wrong," she wailed, and turned to go.

"Wait, Sonia! Wait!" cried Lupin hoarsely. "A moment ago you said something... You said that the mere presence of a thief would overwhelm you with disgust. Is that true?"

"Yes, I swear it is," cried Sonia.

Guerchard appeared in the doorway.

"And if I were not the man you believe?" said Lupin sombrely.

"What?" said Sonia; and a faint bewilderment mingled with her grief.

"If I were not the Duke of Charmerace?"

"Not the Duke?"

"If I were not an honest man?" said Lupin.

"You?" cried Sonia.

"If I were a thief? If I were—"

"Arsène Lupin," jeered Guerchard from the door.

Lupin turned and held out his manacled wrists for her to see.

"Arsène Lupin! ... It's ... It's true!" stammered Sonia. "But then, but then ... it must be for my sake that you've given yourself up. And it's for me you're going to prison. Oh, Heavens! How happy I am!"

She sprang to him, threw her arms round his neck, and pressed her lips to his.

"And that's what women call repenting," said Guerchard.

He shrugged his shoulders, went out on to the landing, and called to the policeman in the hall to bid the driver of the prison-van, which was waiting, to bring it up to the door.

"Oh, this is incredible!" cried Lupin, in a trembling voice; and he kissed Sonia's lips and eyes and hair. "To think that you love me enough to go on loving me in spite of this—in spite of the fact that I'm Arsène Lupin. Oh, after this, I'll become an honest man! It's the least I can do. I'll retire."

"You will?" cried Sonia.

"Upon my soul, I will!" cried Lupin; and he kissed her again and again.

Guerchard came back into the room. He looked at them with a cynical grin, and said, "Time's up."

"Oh, Guerchard, after so many others, I owe you the best minute of my life!" cried Lupin.

Bonavent, still in his porter's livery, came hurrying through the anteroom: "Master," he cried, "I've found it."

"Found what?" said Guerchard.

"The secret entrance. It opens into that little side street. We haven't got the door open yet; but we soon shall."

"The last link in the chain," said Guerchard, with warm satisfaction. "Come along, Lupin."

"But he's going to take you away! We're going to be separated!" cried Sonia, in a sudden anguish of realization.

"It's all the same to me now!" cried Lupin, in the voice of a conqueror.

"Yes, but not to me!" cried Sonia, wringing her hands.

"Now you must keep calm and go. I'm not going to prison," said Lupin, in a low voice. "Wait in the hall, if you can. Stop and talk to Victoire; condole with her. If they turn you out of the house, wait close to the front door."

"Come, mademoiselle," said Guerchard. "You must go."

"Go, Sonia, go—good-bye—good-bye," said Lupin; and he kissed her.

She went quietly out of the room, her handkerchief to her eyes. Guerchard held open the door for her, and kept it open, with his hand still on the handle; he said to Lupin: "Come along."

Lupin yawned, stretched himself, and said coolly, "My dear Guerchard, what I want after the last two nights is rest—rest." He walked quickly across the room and stretched himself comfortably at full length on the couch.

"Come, get up," said Guerchard roughly. "The prison-van is waiting for you. That ought to fetch you out of your dream."

"Really, you do say the most unlucky things," said Lupin gaily.

He had resumed his flippant, light-hearted air; his voice rang as lightly and pleasantly as if he had not a care in the world.

"Do you mean that you refuse to come?" cried Guerchard in a rough, threatening tone.

"Oh, no," said Lupin quickly: and he rose.

"Then come along!" said Guerchard.

"No," said Lupin, "after all, it's too early." Once more he stretched himself out on the couch, and added languidly, "I'm lunching at the English Embassy."

"Now, you be careful!" cried Guerchard angrily. "Our parts are changed. If you're snatching at a last straw, it's a waste of time. All your tricks—I know them. Understand, you rogue, I know them."

"You know them?" said Lupin with a smile, rising. "It's fatality!"

He stood before Guerchard, twisting his hands and wrists curiously. Half a dozen swift movements; and he held out his handcuffs in one hand and threw them on the floor.

"Did you know that trick, Guerchard? One of these days I shall teach you to invite me to lunch," he said slowly, in a mocking tone; and he gazed at the detective with menacing, dangerous eyes.

"Come, come, we've had enough of this!" cried Guerchard, in mingled astonishment, anger, and alarm. "Bonavent! Boursin! Dieusy! Here! Help! Help!" he shouted.

"Now listen, Guerchard, and understand that I'm not humbugging," said Lupin quickly, in clear, compelling tones. "If Sonia, just now, had had one word, one gesture of contempt for me, I'd have given way—yielded ... half-yielded, at any rate; for, rather than fall into your triumphant clutches, I'd have blown my brains out. I've now to choose between happiness, life with Sonia, or prison. Well, I've chosen. I will live happy with her, or else, my dear Guerchard, I'll die with you. Now let your men come—I'm ready for them."

Guerchard ran to the door and shouted again.

"I think the fat's in the fire now," said Lupin, laughing.

He sprang to the table, opened the cardboard box, whipped off the top layer of cotton-wool, and took out a shining bomb.

He sprang to the wall, pressed the button, the bookshelf glided slowly to one side, the lift rose to the level of the floor and its doors flew open just as the detectives rushed in.

"Collar him!" yelled Guerchard.

"Stand back—hands up!" cried Lupin, in a terrible voice, raising his right hand high above his head. "You know what this is ... a bomb... Come and collar me now, you swine! ... Hands up, you ... Guerchard!"

"You silly funks!" roared Guerchard. "Do you think he'd dare?"

"Come and see!" cried Lupin.

"I will!" cried Guerchard. And he took a step forward.

As one man his detectives threw themselves upon him. Three of them gripped his arms, a fourth gripped him round the waist; and they all shouted at him together, not to be a madman! ... To look at Lupin's eyes! ... That Lupin was off his head!

"What miserable swine you are!" cried Lupin scornfully. He sprang forward, caught up the kit-bag in his left hand, and tossed it behind him into the lift. "You dirty crew!" he cried again. "Oh, why isn't there a photographer here? And now, Guerchard, you thief, give me back my pocket-book."

"Never!" screamed Guerchard, struggling with his men, purple with fury.

"Oh, Lord, master! Do be careful! Don't rile him!" cried Bonavent in an agony.

"What? Do you want me to smash up the whole lot?" roared Lupin, in a furious, terrible voice. "Do I look as if I were bluffing, you fools?"

"Let him have his way, master!" cried Dieusy.

"Yes, yes!" cried Bonavent.

"Let him have his way!" cried another.

"Give him his pocket-book!" cried a third.

"Never!" howled Guerchard.

"It's in his pocket—his breast-pocket! Be smart!" roared Lupin.

"Come, come, it's got to be given to him," cried Bonavent. "Hold the master tight!" And he thrust his hand into the breast of Guerchard's coat, and tore out the pocket-book.

"Throw it on the table!" cried Lupin.

Bonavent threw it on to the table; and it slid along it right to Lupin. He caught it in his left hand, and slipped it into his pocket. "Good!" he said. And then he yelled ferociously, "Look out for the bomb!" and made a feint of throwing it.

The whole group fell back with an odd, unanimous, sighing groan.

Lupin sprang into the lift, and the doors closed over the opening. There was a great sigh of relief from the frightened detectives, and then the chunking of machinery as the lift sank.

Their grip on Guerchard loosened. He shook himself free, and shouted, "After him! You've got to make up for this! Down into the cellars, some of you! Others go to the secret entrance! Others to the servants' entrance! Get into the street! Be smart! Dieusy, take the lift with me!"

The others ran out of the room and down the stairs, but with no great heartiness, since their minds were still quite full of the bomb, and Lupin still had it with him. Guerchard and Dieusy dashed at the doors of the opening of the lift-well, pulling and wrenching at them. Suddenly there was a click; and they heard the grunting of the machinery. There was a little bump and a jerk, the doors flew open of themselves; and there was the lift, empty, ready for them. They jumped into it; Guerchard's quick eye caught the button, and he pressed it. The doors banged to, and, to his horror, the lift shot upwards about eight feet, and stuck between the floors.

As the lift stuck, a second compartment, exactly like the one Guerchard and Dieusy were in, came up to the level of the floor of the smoking-room; the doors opened, and there was Lupin. But again how changed! The clothes of the Duke of Charmerace littered the floor; the kit-bag was open; and he was wearing the very clothes of Chief-Inspector Guerchard, his seedy top-hat, his cloak. He wore also Guerchard's sparse, lank, black hair, his little, bristling, black moustache. His figure, hidden by the cloak, seemed to have shrunk to the size of Guerchard's.

He sat before a mirror in the wall of the lift, a make-up box on the seat beside him. He darkened his eyebrows, and put a line or two about his eyes. That done he looked at himself earnestly for two or three minutes; and, as he looked, a truly marvellous transformation took place: the features of Arsène Lupin, of the Duke of Charmerace, decomposed, actually decomposed, into the features of Jean Guerchard. He looked at himself and laughed, the gentle, husky laugh of Guerchard.

He rose, transferred the pocket-book to the coat he was wearing, picked up the bomb, came out into the smoking-room, and listened. A muffled roaring thumping came from the well of the lift. It almost sounded as if, in their exasperation, Guerchard and Dieusy were engaged in a struggle to the death. Smiling pleasantly, he stole to the window and looked out. His eyes brightened at the sight of the motor-car, Guerchard's car, waiting just before the front door and in charge of a policeman. He stole to the head of the stairs, and looked down into the hall. Victoire was sitting huddled together on a chair; Sonia stood beside her, talking to her in a low voice; and, keeping guard on Victoire, stood a brown-faced, active, nervous policeman, all alertness, briskness, keenness.

"Hi! Officer! Come up here! Be smart," cried Lupin over the bannisters, in the husky, gentle voice of Chief-Inspector Guerchard.

The policeman looked up, recognized the great detective, and came bounding zealously up the stairs.

Lupin led the way through the anteroom into the sitting-room. Then he said sharply: "You have your revolver?"

"Yes," said the young policeman. And he drew it with a flourish.

"Put it away! Put it away at once!" said Lupin very smartly. "You're not to use it. You're not to use it on any account! You understand?"

"Yes," said the policeman firmly; and with a slightly bewildered air he put the revolver away.

"Here! Stand here!" cried Lupin, raising his voice. And he caught the policeman's arm, and hustled him roughly to the front of the doors of the lift-well. "Do you see these doors? Do you see them?" he snapped.

"Yes, yes," said the policeman, glaring at them.

"They're the doors of a lift," said Lupin. "In that lift are Dieusy and Lupin. You know Dieusy?"

"Yes, yes," said the policeman.

"There are only Dieusy and Lupin in the lift. They are struggling together. You can hear them," shouted Lupin in the policeman's ear. "Lupin is disguised. You understand—Dieusy and a disguised man are in the lift. The disguised man is Lupin. Directly the lift descends and the doors open, throw yourself on him! Hold him! Shout for assistance!" He almost bellowed the last words into the policeman's ear.

"Yes, yes," said the policeman. And he braced himself before the doors of the lift-well, gazing at them with harried eyes, as if he expected them to bite him.

"Be brave! Be ready to die in the discharge of your duty!" bellowed Lupin; and he walked out of the room, shut the door, and turned the key.

The policeman stood listening to the noise of the struggle in the lift, himself strung up to fighting point; he was panting. Lupin's instructions were whirling and dancing in his head.

Lupin went quietly down the stairs. Victoire and Sonia saw him coming. Victoire rose; and as he came to the bottom of the stairs Sonia stepped forward and said in an anxious, pleading voice:

"Oh, M. Guerchard, where is he?"

"He's here," said Lupin, in his natural voice.

Sonia sprang to him with outstretched arms.

"It's you! It IS you!" she cried.

"Just look how like him I am!" said Lupin, laughing triumphantly. "But do I look quite ruffian enough?"

"Oh, NO! You couldn't!" cried Sonia.

"Isn't he a wonder?" said Victoire.

"This time the Duke of Charmerace is dead, for good and all," said Lupin.

"No; it's Lupin that's dead," said Sonia softly.

"Lupin?" he said, surprised.

"Yes," said Sonia firmly.

"It would be a terrible loss, you know—a loss for France," said Lupin gravely.

"Never mind," said Sonia.

"Oh, I must be in love with you!" said Lupin, in a wondering tone; and he put his arm round her and kissed her violently.

"And you won't steal any more?" said Sonia, holding him back with both hands on his shoulders, looking into his eyes.

"I shouldn't dream of such a thing," said Lupin. "You are here. Guerchard is in the lift. What more could I possibly desire?" His voice softened and grew infinitely caressing as he went on: "Yet when you are at my side I shall always have the soul of a lover and the soul of a thief. I long to steal your kisses, your thoughts, the whole of your heart. Ah, Sonia, if you want me to steal nothing else, you have only to stay by my side."

Their lips met in a long kiss.

Sonia drew herself out of his arms and cried, "But we're wasting time! We must make haste! We must fly!"

"Fly?" said Lupin sharply. "No, thank you; never again. I did flying enough last night to last me a lifetime. For the rest of my life I'm going to crawl—crawl like a snail. But come along, you two, I must take you to the police-station."

He opened the front door, and they came out on the steps. The policeman in charge of the car saluted.

Lupin paused and said softly: "Hark! I hear the sound of wedding bells."

They went down the steps.

Even as they were getting into the car some chance blow of Guerchard or Dieusy struck a hidden spring and released the lift. It sank to the level of Lupin's smoking-room and stopped. The doors flew open, Dieusy and Guerchard sprang out of it; and on the instant the brown-faced, nervous policeman sprang actively on Guerchard and pinned him. Taken by surprise, Guerchard yelled loudly, "You stupid idiot!" somehow entangled his legs in those of his captor, and they rolled on the floor. Dieusy surveyed them for a moment with blank astonishment. Then, with swift intelligence, grasped the fact that the policeman was Lupin in disguise. He sprang upon them, tore them asunder, fell heavily on the policeman, and pinned him to the floor with a strangling hand on his throat.

Guerchard dashed to the door, tried it, and found it locked, dashed for the window; threw it open, and thrust out his head. Forty yards down the street a motor-car was rolling smoothly away—rolling to a honeymoon.

"Oh, hang it!" he screamed. "He's doing a bunk in my motor-car!"

Yellowback range available...

1. The Old Man in the Corner by Orczy, Baroness Emma
2. The Complete Max Carrados Vol 1 by Bramah, Ernest
3. The Complete Max Carrados Vol 2 by Bramah, Ernest

THE ARSÈNE LUPIN SERIES BY LEBLANC, MAURICE:

4. Arsène Lupin 1: The Extraordinary Adventures of Arsène Lupin - Gentleman Burglar
5. Arsène Lupin 2: Arsène Lupin vs. Herlock Sholmes
6. Arsène Lupin 3. The Hollow Needle
7. Arsène Lupin 4: 813
8. Arsène Lupin 5: The Crystal Stopper
9. Arsène Lupin 6: The Confessions of Arsène Lupin
10. Arsène Lupin 7: The Teeth of the Tiger
11. Arsène Lupin 8: The Shell Shard (aka The Woman of Mystery)
12. Arsène Lupin 9: The Return of Arsène Lupin (aka The Golden Triangle)
13. Arsène Lupin 10: The secret of Sarek (aka Island of Thirty Coffins)
14. Arsène Lupin 11: The Eight Strokes of the Clock
15. Arsène Lupin 12: The Secret Tomb
16. Arsène Lupin 13: The Countess of Cagliostro (aka Memoirs of Arsène Lupin)
17. Arsène Lupin (bonus book): Arsène Lupin (novelised by Edgar Jepson from LeBlanc's original play)

18. The Complete Raffles by Hornung, E. W.
19. The Mysterious Mickey Finn by Paul, Eliott
20. You Play the Black and the Red Comes Up by Hallas, Richard
21. The Mr. Moto Omnibus Vol 1 by Marquand, John P.
22. The Mr. Moto Omnibus Vol 2 by Marquand, John P.
23. The Complete Father Brown Vol 1 (with original illustrations) by Chesterton, G. K.
24. The Complete Father Brown Vol 2 (with original illustrations) by Chesterton, G. K.
25. A Peter Wimsey omnibus: Murder Must Advertise & The Nine Tailors by Sayers, Dorothy L.
26. Was it Murder? by Hilton, James
27. The Complete Just Men Volume 1 by Wallace, Edgar
28. The Complete Just Men Volume 2 by Wallace, Edgar
29. Carnacki by Hodgson, William Hope
30. Grey Mask by Wentworth, Patricia
31. The Case With Nine Solutions by Connington, J. J.
32. Murder by Matchlight by Lorac, E. C. R.
33. The Crossword Mystery by Punshon, E. R.
34. The Cask by Crofts, Freeman Wills
35. The Bells of Old Bailey by Bowers, Dorothy
36. Crime Unlimited by Hume, David
37. The A. A. Milne Mystery Omnibus (contains: The Red house and Four days' wonder) by Milne, A. A.
38. She Faded into Air by White, Ethel Lina
39. The Wheel Spins by White, Ethel Lina
40. The Spiral Staircase by White, Ethel Lina
41. Murder of a Lady by Wynne, Anthony
42. Thirteen Guests by Farjeon, J. Jefferson
43. The Daughter of Time by Tey, Josephine
44. The Man in the Queue by Tey, Josephine
45. A Shilling for Candles by Tey, Josephine
46. The Franchise Affair by Tey, Josephine
47. Tragedy at Law by Hare, Cyril
48. The Moonstone by Collins, Wilkie
49. The Woman in White by Collins, Wilkie
50. The Circular Staircase by Rinehart, Mary Roberts
51. The Benson Murder Case by Van Dine, S. S.
52. The Philip Marlowe Omnibus by Chandler, Raymond
53. Monsieur Lecoq by Gaboriau, Emile
54. Aurora Floyd by Braddon, Mary Elizabeth
55. The Big Bow Mystery by Zangwill, Israel
56. Dossier 113 (aka The Blackmailers) by Gaboriau, Emile
57. The Mystery of a Hansom Cab by Hume, Fergus
58. The W Plan by Seton, Graham
59. Inspector French's Greatest Case by Crofts, Freeman Wills

60. Mr Bowling Buys a Newspaper by Henderson, Donald
61. A Voice Like Velvet by Henderson, Donald
62. The Deductions of Colonel Gore by Brock, Lynn
63. The Rogue's Syndicate by Froest, Frank
64. The Middle Temple Murder by Fletcher, J. S.
65. The Millionaire Mystery by Hume, Fergus
66. Below the Clock by Turner, J. V.
67. The Rouletabille Omnibus: The Mystery of the Yellow Room and The Perfume of the Lady in Black by Leroux, Gaston
68. The Complete Dupin by Poe, Edgar Allan
69. The Complete Thinking Machine Vol 1 by Futrelle, Jacques
70. The Complete Thinking Machine Vol 2 by Futrelle, Jacques
71. The Complete Thinking Machine Vol 3 by Futrelle, Jacques
72. The Complete Montague Egg by Sayers, Dorothy L.
73. The Complete J. G. Reeder by Wallace, Edgar
74. The Complete Charlie Chan Vol 1 by Biggers, Earl der
75. The Complete Charlie Chan Vol 2 by Biggers, Earl der
76. The Dr Nikola Omnibus Vol 1 by Boothby, Guy
77. The Dr Nikola Omnibus Vol 2 by Boothby, Guy
78. A Prince of Swindlers: The Simon Carne collection by Boothby, Guy
79. The Slim Callaghan Omnibus by Cheyney, Peter
80. The Fu Manchu Omnibus by Rohmer, Sax
81. The Bulldog Drummond Omnibus: The Complete Peterson Rounds by Sapper
82. The Avenging Ray by Seamark
83. The Richard Chandos Omnibus by Yates, Dornford
84. The Alan Quatermain Omnibus: King Solomon's Mines & Allan Quatermain by Haggard, H. Rider
85. The 39 steps by Buchan, John
86. At The Villa Rose by Mason, A.E.W.
87. The Eye of Osiris by Freeman, R. Austin
88. The Weapons of Mystery by Hocking, Joseph
89. The House of Dr. Edwardes by Beeding, Francis
90. The Seven Secrets by Le Queux, William
91. Call Mr Fortune by Bailey, H. C.
92. The Three Taps by Knox, Ronald
93. The Girl at Central by Bonner, Geraldine
94. The Experiences of Loveday Brooke, Lady Detective by Pirkis, Catherine Louisa
95. Mary Louise by Baum, L. Frank
96. That Affair Next Door by Green, Anna Katherine
97. Dead Letter by Regester, Seeley
98. The Tragedy of Pudd'nhead Wilson by Twain, Mark
99. The Big Clock by Fearing, Kenneth
100. The Woman in the Window by Wallis, J. H.
101. The Sexton Blake Collection Vol 1 by Hal Meredeth (or many?)
102. The Complete Simon Iff Stories by Crowley, Aleister
103. The Castle of Otranto by Walpole, Horace
104. The Adventures of the Infallible Godahl by Anderson, Frederick Irving

THE COMPLETE SHERLOCK HOLMES

105. A Study In Scarlet
106. The Sign Of Four
107. The Adventures Of Sherlock Holmes
108. The Memoirs Of Sherlock Holmes
109. The Hound Of The Baskervilles
110. The Return Of Sherlock Holmes
111. His Last Bow
112. The Valley Of Fear
113. The Case-Book Of Sherlock Holmes

114. Graustark: The Story of a Love Behind a Throne by George Barr McCutcheon
115. Beverly of Graustark by George Barr McCutcheon
116. Truxton King: A Story of Graustark by George Barr McCutcheon
117. The Prince of Graustark by George Barr McCutcheon
118. The Complete Zenda Omnibus by Anthony Hope
119. The Mad king by Burroughs, Edgar Rice
120. The Fantomas Omnibus by Souvestre, Pierre

121. The Problemist by Clinton H. Stagg
122. The Dorrington Deed-Box by Morrison, Arthur
123. The Lone Wolf by Vance, L. J.
124. The Complete Martin Hewitt Collection Vol 1: Martin Hewitt, Investigator & Chronicles of Martin Hewitt by Morrison, Arthur
125. The Complete Martin Hewitt Collection Vol 2: Adventures of Martin Hewitt & The Red Triangle: Further Chronicles of Martin Hewitt by Morrison, Arthur
126. Seven Keys to Baldpate by Earl Derr Biggers
127. No Pockets in a Shroud by McCoy, Horace
128. The John Silence Collection by Blackwood, Algernon
129. Lady Molly Of Scotland Yard by Orczy, Baroness Emma
130. Skin O' My Tooth by Orczy, Baroness Emma
131. The Wrong Box by Stevenson, R. L. and Lloyd Osbourne
132. Tutt and Mr Tutt by Train, Arthur C.
133. The Clue by Wells, Carolyn
134. The Complete Trent Case Book by Bentley, E. C.
135. The Luck of the Vails by Benson, E. F.
136. The Rome Express by Griffiths, Arthur
137. The Complete Curious Mr Tarrant by C. Daly King
138. Rope and Gaslight (2-in-1 text) by Hamilton, Patrick
139. Prince Zaleski and Cumming's King Monk by Shiel, M. P.
140. The Assassination Bureau Ltd. by London, Jack
141. Introducing Clubfoot by Williams, Valentine
142. Master of Mysteries: The complete Uncle Abner collection by Post, Melville Davisson
143. The Red Redmaynes by Phillpotts, Eden
144. Thrilling Stories of the Railway by Whitechurch, Victor L.
145. The Grey Wig: Stories and Novelettes by Zangwill, Israel
146. The Lodger by Lowndes, Marie Belloc
147. The Man from Manchester by Donovan, Dick (Joyce Emerson Preston Muddock)
148. Mr. Meeson's Will by H. Rider Haggard by Haggard, H. Rider
149. Devlin the Barber by Farjeon, B. L.
150. Checkmate by Joseph Sheridan Le Fanu
151. Recollections of a Detective Police-Officer by Waters
152. The Widow Lerouge by Gaboriau, Emile
153. The Expressman and the Detective by Pinkerton, Allan
154. Zadig and Vathek by Voltaire
155. The Stillwater Tragedy by Aldrich, Thomas Bailey
156. The Memoirs of Constantine Dix by Pain, Barry
157. Ashes to Ashes by Ostrander, Isabel
158. The Jewel of Seven Stars by Stoker, Bram
159. The Thomas Love Peacock Collection by Peacock, Thomas Love

THE COMPLETE DERLETH SOLAR PONS

160. In Re: Sherlock Holmes - The Adventures of Solar Pons
161. The Memoirs of Solar Pons
162. The Return of Solar Pons
163. The Reminiscences of Solar Pons
164. The Casebook of Solar Pons
165. The Novels of Solar Pons: Terror over London and Mr. Fairlie's Final Journey
166. The Chronicles of Solar Pons
167. The Apocrypha of Solar Pons

168. The Triumphs of Eugene Valmont
169. The Female Detective by Forrester, Andrew
170. Cain's Jawbone by Torquemada
171. The Great Impersonation by Oppenheim, E. Phillips

THE DASHIELL HAMMETT COLLECTION

172. The Complete Sam Spade
173. The Complete Thin Man
174. The Complete Continental Op Vol 1
175. The Complete Continental Op Vol 2